REALM BOOK 2

POSEIDON

BY H.G. AHEDI

Book cover concept by H.G. Ahedi
Book cover designed by Rebecca covers
(fiverr.com)
Edited by Liz

Author's website: harbeerahedi.com

To Find the Realm series by H.G. Ahedi scan

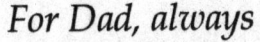
For Dad, always

Dedicated to my nephews
Parampreet & Harshmann

"You cannot buy the revolution. You cannot make the revolution. You can only be the revolution. It is in your spirit, or it is nowhere."

Ursula K. Le Guin

CHAPTERS

CHARACTERS

Emmeline Augury	The young cadet of astrophysics who started it all
Commander Anastasia Waters	Commander of *Titan*, a leader everyone looks up to.
Lieutenant Commander Adrian Olson	*Titan's* pilot, second in command and Evan's best friend.
Lieutenant Evan Weeds	The infamous operations officer on *Titan*
Lieutenant Edward Hawk	*Titan's* tactical officer
Lieutenant Cyr Storm	The calm and collected engineer on *Titan*
Dr. Chris Kent	The ever-curious head of the astrophysics lab on *Titan* (Crystal Lab)
Dr. Aceline Keston	Argon's mother, historian and an archeologist on *Titan*
Selina Keston	Aceline's daughter, who can see what others can't

Dr. Isaac Finch	Exobiologist from Earth, who comes to *Titan* to study the Orias
Dr. Zac Scheben	Medical doctor on *Titan*
Captain Mykel Lockhart	Captain of *Prometheus*
Commander Katia Hart	First officer of the *Prometheus*
Lieutenant Nick Colson	Pilot of the *Prometheus* with a personal vendetta against Evan
Lieutenant Seiko Ishimoto	The nerdy science officer of the *Prometheus* who has clever ideas
Lieutenant Ingrid Elrod	The quirky engineer of *Prometheus*
Ensign Patrick Terra	The anxious communicator officer of *Prometheus*
Lieutenant Lyle Hagg	*Prometheus's* dependable tactical officer.
Ensign Edna Lamer	Junior tactical officer, who takes Lyle's place on the bridge of *Prometheus*
Dr. Peter Hudson	Medical doctor of *Prometheus*
Lady Vermont	Imperial Command's Tribunal, stationed on the *Aurora*
Captain Desmond Allan	Captain of the *Aurora*
Officer Tristan Blake	Operations officer of *Aurora*

Lieutenant Gus Lawson	Science officer of *Aurora*
Officer Oliver Bain	Pilot of *Aurora*
Cadet Argon Keston	Emmeline's love interest and the leader of the *Titan* Squadron
Cadet Byron Thames	Argon's best friend who takes over the leadership of *Titan* Squadron after Argon
Cadet Clio Ranger	Love interest of Byron, and part of the *Titan* Squadron
Cadet Micah Dew	The oddball of the *Titan* Squadron
Delta Dune	Pilot of the private ship *Astra* and Emmeline's best friend
Phoebe Walker	Katia Hart's partner
Admiral Jacob Donovan	Captain of *Freedom* who wants to take over command of *Titan*
Arthur Augury	Emmeline's father, a powerful man who will do anything to save his daughter
Alexander Hendrix	Emmeline's forefather who studied the plaque in 23rd century and led the team that studied Nemesis
Darren Taber	Chef on the *Prometheus*
Admiral Vince	Third Tribunal of Imperial Command who is located on Earth

The queen	The queen of Orias wants the mythical device at any cost
Aithon	Right hand of the Orias queen
The Spector	An ancient being on a forgotten moon that awaits its next victim
Otis	The robot accountable for the safety of the citizen of *Titan* on the outer rim.
Evox	The leader of the robots who stay behind to protect the *Titan* crew

CHAPTER 1: BEFORE THE FALL

TITAN, DECK 5

Captain Mykel Lockhart enjoyed the few minutes of bliss submerged underwater. Swimming brought him immense relief. For a fraction of a second, he forgot about everything happening around him. He swam upward, broke the surface of the water, and relished the silence. Mykel was envious of people living on *Titan*. They had a comfortable life, including a swimming pool. Earth was three hours away, and loved ones were always within reach. After spending four years in deep space, being back on *Titan* had been wonderful. Mykel never thought he would treasure these moments to such an extent. Simple things, like walking in an open space, catching up with old friends, and being around Anastasia. Regardless of the circumstances, he was glad to be home.

Titan's pool was about twenty feet long and ten feet wide, filled with cold, fresh water. The white walls reflected the glow coming from the tiny lights in the corners of the hall. He swam another lap. Breathless, he came to a standstill at the edge of the pool. The large windows at this end revealed a stunning view of the cosmos. Silent, mysterious.

After a few more laps, he left the pool. The water dripped on the smooth floor as he dried himself. The captain of the *Prometheus* was an athletic, aristocratic man with an angular face, a strong jawline, and deep ocean blue eyes. His thick brown hair was turning gray around his temples.

Walking along the edge of the pool, he headed toward the showers. The lights switched on automatically. The white room was divided into several compact stalls. He picked one. Stepping inside, he closed the door behind him.

"Begin," he said.

Water splashed on his body from all directions, helping to soothe and relieve muscle fatigue. Mykel's mind drifted toward the events of today. The inquest had left everyone disappointed and shocked, and Imperial Command had ordered him to return to Earth. A part of him longed to set foot on his planet, eat freshly prepared dishes, enjoy the cool air, and walk on the beach. He had waited a long time to break the constraints of his spaceship and wanted to go home. But Admiral Jacob Donavan would not give up, and he knew it. Mykel had to stick around for Anastasia. She needed him. He felt a bit selfish and reminded himself that his duty was to his crew and his ship. *Prometheus* came first. Nothing else mattered.

The water continued to splash on his body.

Do all captains feel this way? Torn between duty and love?

It was not an openly discussed topic. For him, there was no difference. He felt both *Prometheus* and Anastasia were priorities. He didn't want to lose either of them. Mykel sulked.

There you go again. Just get over it. It was a long time ago.

It wasn't that easy. The news of the Orias lurking around the perimeter had frightened him. All of a sudden, Anastasia's and *Titan's* safety became a priority, and he did everything in his power to return home.

"Stop," he said.

The water halted, and several small holes appeared on the walls. Warm air circulated through the cubicle at high speed. He ran his hand through his almost dry hair. When he was done, he stepped out, got dressed, and left. The door shut behind him, the pool closed, and the lights turned off.

As he strolled toward the elevator, the lights came to life.

It's good to be home.

Mykel had spent most of his life on *Titan* until he took command of *Prometheus*. As he walked down the corridor, he felt the swim, the shower, and the silence had helped him think clearly. Admiral Donavan's actions frustrated him. He was clearly scheming to take over *Titan* and was a powerful element in the political game. Politics didn't matter to Mykel, but many would die if he sat on the sidelines.

There must be a diplomatic way.

Unfortunately, he couldn't think of one. Mykel took the elevator to deck four and then made his way to *Prometheus*. As expected, it was quiet, and he felt like a wandering ghost.

PROMETHEUS, DECK 4

Prometheus's interior differed greatly from *Titan's*. Its corridors were hexagonal, with maroon carpets that covered the frigid floor. Since the ship was in night mode, the lights were dim. The air was sterile, chilly, and devoid of any scents. He walked past several red doors of quarters belonging to his crew. Over a hundred and twenty souls aboard, sleeping peacefully. He hoped.

Mykel's thoughts turned back to the situation at hand. He shook his head. It was not right. For the first time, he was struggling.

Where do I stand? Who do I stand with? I cannot abandon Titan, *and I cannot disobey Imperial Command. How do I resolve this situation?*

Every decision he made could affect his life and redefine the fate of everyone he cared for.

"Deck three," he muttered when the door to the elevator opened.

The circular elevator moved upward so smoothly that it didn't even feel like it was moving. The doors whooshed open, and he walked toward his quarters. He entered the codes on a square panel and unlocked the door. The lights turned on. One of the best parts about being the captain was being entitled to the most luxurious quarters on the ship. It was much cozier compared to the older ships like *Freedom*. The open space was split into three parts: a bedroom, a work area, and a living room. The windows were triangular, pointing upward. He leaned on the window to admire the peaceful night.

His living space was full of books, clothes, pads on the two lounge chairs, and a velvet couch. A small suitcase he had packed for his vacation on Earth sat in a corner. Plants gifted by Anastasia and his first officer, Katia Hart, rested in small pots. To his surprise, the tulips, fern, and sunflowers had survived the journey. Paintings made by his late mother hung over a cabinet with a few artifacts that he had collected during his travels. Mykel didn't want to sleep, but he had a big day tomorrow.

I better get to bed.

Turning away from the window, he entered the small, cozy bedroom. His large unmade bed was in a corner against a wall. The highlight of his sparsely decorated room was a window that gave a spectacular view of Saturn's moon Titan. The moon emitted a soft orangish glow. In the northern hemisphere, a group of gigantic clouds raged in an anticlockwise fashion. He walked to his left and tapped on the wall. The door to his closet opened, revealing a set of uniforms, clothes, shoes, and all his belongings. He changed, got into bed, and dozed off.

PROMETHEUS, MYKEL'S QUARTERS, DECK 3

The strong aroma of coffee dominated Mykel's quarters as he sat on the couch reading reports. He was ready for the day. Not that he had to think about dressing up. The black trousers with a black turtleneck shirt and maroon jacket were his daily uniform. Surprisingly he was very comfortable in it and most of the time didn't bother to change before heading to bed. He read the current reports on his ship's condition. *Prometheus* needed repairs, and the recent ion storm had damaged a few sections of the ship's hull. The four-year journey had been rough, and the ship required complete refurbishment.

He grabbed another cup of coffee and returned to work. The *Prometheus* was due to depart in the next half an hour, and Mykel did not want to leave. No matter what his ship needed, or his orders were, his instincts told him to stay. He studied Emmeline Augury's report. She believed the mythical device could be an invaluable power source to mankind. And that was the problem. Power attracted trouble, and he feared Jacob had his eyes on the prize.

As he sipped his coffee, he thought of recent events. The Orias appeared out of nowhere and began studying the perimeter. Many believed they were looking for weaknesses in their defense system. But when the *Titan* Squadron approached them, they vanished. Then they returned with ten ships and brought chaos and death to his realm. He felt he had made the right decision to cross the ion storm despite the danger to his ship.

After the first battle, he had the situation would get better. He was utterly wrong. He had learned that Emmeline had discovered an ancient plaque about two months before the attack. Soon after the first battle, she unlocked it and found a star map with coordinates beyond the perimeter. Emmeline had sneaked out of the system with her best friend Delta and flew to the coordinates. The plaque opened a portal that led to a hidden planet. On the rogue planet, now called Delta 1, they had found the first piece of the mythical device. From what Mykel understood, no one, including Emmeline, knew how to yield its power.

Intriguing.

He smiled. He would have loved to be a part of such an adventure. But tragedy struck when Delta died, and Emmeline suffered the consequences of her actions. Using Emmeline's ignorance and the fact that she had broken the law, Jacob wanted to discredit Anastasia and take over *Titan*. If Mykel were not mistaken, his next target would be the mythical device.

A bell chimed.

"Come in," he said.

Commander Katia Hart stepped in with her usual stride. Katia's steel-gray eyes regarded his quarters as if scrutinizing every little detail. Her presence made heads turn. It was not only her beauty but the authority and confidence she radiated. She tied her thin blonde hair in a ponytail that highlighted her narrow face. She folded her arms, taking a powerful stance. Making observations was her forte, and Mykel hated it when she did that with him. It worked well professionally, but her demeanor deterred anyone from getting to know her on a personal level. During their four-year journey, she had hardly made any friends.

"Good morning, Captain."

"Morning."

"May I suggest some home cleaning?"

Mykel grinned. "You may suggest, but I am not inclined to listen."

"Right. Captain, the ship is ready to go."

Mykel grumbled and fought his urge to go against his orders. But what would that accomplish?

PROMETHEUS, DECK 1

Several crewmen hurriedly walked past Mykel and Katia as they walked down the passageway. The ship was almost ready to disembark.

"We have a tight schedule on Earth," Katia said, handing over a pad.

"I see," Mykel replied, glancing through the agenda.

"While the *Prometheus* undergoes repairs, the Imperial Command wants to debrief us."

"Really?" Mykel said.

"Yes."

"I see."

"Separately," pointed out Katia.

"That's fine," he replied indifferently.

"I presume they want to debrief us about *Prometheus's* return to the system."

That was routine and as the captain he had done it several times.

"I have submitted a report. We received a distress call from *Freedom*. We responded to the distress call and decided to cross the ion storm because it was the quickest route."

"I agree. If we had gone around it, it could've changed the outcome of the battle," stated Katia.

Mykel nodded.

"That is what I plan to say."

"That's what happened," Mykel replied defensively.

"I am glad we agree."

Mykel felt it. Something was coming. They stepped into the elevator, and the doors closed swiftly behind them.

"Otherwise, it would appear you had an ulterior motive to return to *Titan*," Katia remarked.

Mykel eyed her and smirked.

People never change.

Everyone knew about his romantic attachment to Anastasia, even though the relationship ended a long time ago.

"We pushed the engines beyond its capability. The ship sustained damage," she added.

"Katia, our people needed us."

"Agreed," she responded. "And of course, there was no other reason."

Mykel said no more. He knew she wanted him to admit that he was worried about Anastasia.

PROMETHEUS, BRIDGE, DECK 1

Mykel lowered himself into the captain's chair with some unease. Katia liked to dig deep, especially in his personal matters. Maybe because he was good at hiding his feelings, and she was not. Her life was like an open book. Perhaps having her partner, Phoebe Walker, on this journey made things easier for her. He could only speculate. In his case, as soon as he became Captain, he knew his personal life would be non-existent. It was like he was suddenly unavailable, or perhaps it was because of Anastasia. He never stopped waiting for her, even though she got married, had kids, and became the captain of *Marion*. No longer being with her was devastating for him. Her marriage was proof they were done. At least, that was what he thought. But since the attack, he had sensed something from her. All these years, they had stayed apart, and a war had brought them together. All of a sudden, he felt his Ana was back. The issue was he didn't know what to do about it.

The triangular bridge was broad in front and narrower at the back. The curved viewscreen was opposite a wide arc-shaped console, which was the hub to the helm, operations, and science divisions. The helm was in the middle, while the operation station was to the helm's left side and the science station to its right.

As he looked through his schedule on Earth, his eyes drifted toward the viewer and became fixed on *Titan*. The uneasiness returned. Maybe it wasn't just him. Perhaps everyone felt this way.

"Sir, we are ready to disembark," said Lieutenant Nick Colson, the helmsman of *Prometheus*. He turned to face Mykel. He saw the eagerness to return home in his brown eyes. His ebony features reflected confidence. With a heavy jaw, clean-shaved face, and thick curly hair, Nick looked like a man who took his work seriously.

"Let's go," Mykel said.

He had already said his goodbyes to Anastasia, and he hoped to see her soon.

Katia took her seat at the operations station and said, "All systems ready to go."

As expected, the tactical officer Lyle Hagg spoke up next, "Weapons are working in perfect order, sir."

Mykel casually turned to face Lyle. She was a lean, dark-skinned head of security. Her face was long, alert, and her large black eyes remained steady. Mykel appreciated her calm demeanor, especially in high-risk situations.

"Excellent."

Out of habit, he swayed his chair and found the nervous-looking communication officer.

Mykel asked, "Patrick?"

Ensign Patrick Terra appeared perplexed. Even if he wanted, Patrick couldn't hide his six-foot heavy frame behind the console. Patrick was dashing. Tall, well-built, with a symmetrical face and dark gray eyes. But he lacked conviction.

"Yes, sir. Yes. Everything is in order. We have received no more communication from the Imperial Command."

Mykel said nothing and faced the screen. The engines started, and Patrick alerted *Titan* of their departure. Lieutenant Commander Adrian Olson's solemn face appeared on the viewscreen. Losing Delta had been devastating for everyone, especially for Adrian and Emmeline. Having lost his own love, Mykel understood his pain.

"Good morning, Captain," said Adrian in a low tone.

"Morning. We are ready to disembark."

Adrian looked down at his console. It was a standard procedure to check departures and permits for every ship. "*Prometheus* is all set."

"Thank you. We will try to get back as soon as we can," Mykel replied.

Adrian gave a weak smile. "Have a safe journey home."

The screen went blank.

The *Prometheus* vibrated as it slowly detached itself from the space station, turned, and sped toward Earth.

"Sir, our ETA is two hours, fifteen minutes, and twenty-four seconds," reported Nick from the helm.

"Excellent," he replied and focused on his schedule. Something occurred to him, and he said, "Katia, keep a sensor lock on *Titan*. Patrick, monitor all communications and signals."

Both officers nodded.

The crew could manage without him, but Mykel stayed on the bridge. He got on his feet and walked to the science station. Lieutenant Seiko Ishimoto looked up. The athletic Asian man sat back, twirled on his chair, and crossed his legs. His thick, soft hair was parted to the right, and his thoughtful mahogany brown eyes regarded him.

"Nothing, sir," Seiko said.

Since their arrival, he had been looking for signs of the enemy ships.

"You mean not yet."

"What about the Vipers? Are they ready?"

Titan was preparing long-range torpedoes programmed to target the vulnerable aspects of the Orias ships. Seiko was experimenting with nanotechnology and reprogramming tiny probes that could be used as weapons.

"I think so. I have run several successful stimulations. However, we need to test them in combat."

"Something tells me you will get the chance. Sooner rather than later," Mykel remarked and returned to his chair.

As they traveled away from the danger zone, he felt calmer.

TITAN, BYRON'S QUARTERS, DECK 6

Byron Thames snored with his mouth open. Despite a loud bell ringing, he didn't wake up.

"Wake up!" a voice yelled.

"Oh, for god's sake!" he cried out. He lifted his head to see Micah was on the intercom, trying to reach him. "Go away. I want to sleep!"

The intercom continued buzzing. Byron grudgingly got out of bed and gawked at the watch. It was 0600.

The *Titan* Squadron was scheduled to train at 0800 hours. Since the attack, the squadron originally made up of four ships had grown to twenty. He hated the pilots from Earth. They were older, experienced, and arrogant. The admiral treated them with respect and often complimented them on their hard work. Byron and his friends Argon, Clio, and Micah were constant targets of ridicule and judgment. Byron often wanted to fight back, but Argon tried to smooth things over. He reminded Byron that they needed all the help they could get. But Byron wanted to punch the admiral in the face.

A beep echoed.

"Byron, are you there?"

"What the hell?" he complained, reaching out to the intercom. "Micah, what's your problem?"

"Argon is making his move!"

Byron's sleep vanished. "Oh no. So, what's the plan?"

"I am getting ready...I will meet you and Clio in the passageway on deck four."

"Okay."

The lights turned on in his simple and minimally decorated quarters. Most of his clothes were on the floor, and several pairs of shoes sat in a pile in a corner. Byron ruffled his hand through his silver hair and noticed his tired face in the mirror. There were bags under his gray eyes, and he needed a shave. He felt he looked older. The stress of the last few weeks had taken its toll. His mother had called him several times to return home, but he couldn't. *Titan* Squadron was a part of the fleet. He simply couldn't abandon his friends.

"Byron...I am on my way. See you," said Micah on the intercom.

"Okay," he replied and hastily got dressed and left his quarters.

He knew Argon would do everything to free Emmeline. Last night, Byron had tried his best and wanted to know Argon's plan. But he stayed tight-lipped.

Argon giving up on Emmeline would alter the laws of the universe.

They were concerned about Argon, and Micah decided to check his movements.

Byron met with Clio Ranger in the passageway. Clio's luxurious jet-black hair was tied in a ponytail. Her copper-brown eyes remained fixed ahead, focused. He admired her for her bravery, honesty, and her friendship. Knowing her since childhood had created an unbreakable trust between them.

His eyes traveled down her legs. *Changing a long-term friendship into something more was difficult. I don't know if she feels the same.*

"What are we going to do?" she asked, adjusting her jacket.

"I don't know. I want to make sure he doesn't get into trouble."

"Oh, he is asking for that!" exclaimed Micah as he joined them. "Imagine what would happen if the admiral found out."

Byron sighed and didn't want to think about it.

Micah was heavier and shorter than Byron, with dense, curly red hair and round blue eyes. The foul smell coming from his mouth and clothes told Byron that he had continued to party even after everyone had left Midnight Orchid. He wished Micah had showered.

"I tell you, this will not be easy," Micah remarked.

Byron didn't know what to say.

Everyone was still in bed, and the corridors of *Titan* were silent. Since the Orias attack, Byron didn't believe anyone slept well. They were on edge, feeling as if danger was lurking just around the corner. Then the Imperial Command arresting Emmeline and Delta's death had raised tensions in the space station. For the first time, people were divided. There was a buildup of mistrust. Fear and anger lingered.

The elevator opened, and they walked in silently.

"He is on deck nine," said Micah, studying the pad in his left hand.

"That is where the brig is located. If he plans to free Emmeline, why didn't the alarms go off?" Clio asked.

"Argon must have disabled them," Byron replied, thinking of a strategy.

The elevator doors opened, and they rushed out.

"Wait, they are now heading toward the docking bay," said Micah.

"He's leaving?" Clio asked sadly.

Byron said nothing. He wanted to persuade Argon to let Emmeline go. Perhaps hiding her would give them time to find a better way. Maybe they could speak to Commander Waters and find a solution. The door opened, and he heard voices. It was already too late.

TITAN, DOCKING BAY, DECK 10

The trio armed themselves and saw Jacob with a group of guards, yelling at Argon and Emmeline.

"Argon! You!" Jacob yelled.

Argon turned.

"You'd better let them go," Byron said, pointing his disruptor at Jacob. He had enough. He couldn't watch Jacob demean and insult his friends.

"You shouldn't be here!" Argon said.

"This is unacceptable! Wrong..." Jacob continued shouting like a madman.

Byron was stunned.

When Jacob became silent, his eyes were bulging, and his face was read.

"He has serious impulse control issues," he remarked involuntarily.

Argon eyed him.

Alarms reverberated throughout the halls.

"I thought I disabled it," Argon said to Emmeline.

An enormous figure appeared behind Jacob.

"Watch out, Admiral!" Argon yelled.

They fired at the aliens. The Orias was hit, and with a loud screech, they fell to the ground and disappeared.

"The Orias. How did they get inside?" asked Byron.

"Get to your ships," Jacob ordered.

Titan jolted.

Anastasia's voice echoed in the corridors. "We are under attack. I repeat, we are under attack! All hands to battle stations! All hands to battle stations!"

Three Orias appeared behind Byron and his friends.

"Get down!" Jacob yelled and fired.

Laser beams hit the Orias, and they turned to dust in seconds.

"Oh no. Not now," Argon murmured.

Byron faced Argon and then followed his gaze. His heart sank. The group stared through the window at the enormous purple cloud beyond the perimeter.

Jacob ordered the squad to engage the enemy and rushed to the elevator.

Byron faced Argon. "This is the best chance you'll get. Get out. We'll handle them."

Clio and Micah agreed.

"No! No!" said Emmeline.

"Go! Just go!" Clio said, rushing down the corridor.

"I think she's right," Micah said, following her.

Argon looked at Emmeline.

Byron placed his hand on Argon's shoulder. "You must leave. I am going to miss you. Watch your back, my friend."

Byron felt his heart crush into pieces. Giving Argon a last glance, he followed Micah and Clio.

Uncertainty clouded his mind as he entered the hangar. Fear was spreading. Screams reverberated, and people scrambled, carrying boxes and suitcases. Private ships were launching one after another. Alarms echoed as Byron ran toward his ship. The semicircular spacecraft was ten feet wide and fifteen feet long. Its weapons were positioned at the edges, and the pilot's cockpit was in the elongated section, which emerged from the center.

After unlocking the door, he dashed to the cockpit. As he settled in the pilot's seat, he felt the rush of adrenaline and panic. He stared at the hangar deck. *Titan* was in pandemonium.

Should everyone leave?

He didn't know and knew no one had the correct answers. He watched as the squadron ships powered up and took off one after another.

This is it.

Pushing his fears aside, he pressed the button, and the engines came to life.

Unlike other pilots, Byron preferred U-shaped steering to control his ship. The engines roared, and the craft lifted and sped out of the hangar. Clio's and Micah's ships were right behind him. Byron felt a sense of doom as the fleet glided away from *Titan*. Taking a deep breath in, he looked back at his home. *Titan* remained motionless, and he felt his heart breaking. Something told him this was the last time he would see it.

I am going to miss you, Argon.

Jacob's voice boomed on the communicator, ordering the fleet to prepare for battle and cross the gates. He assessed their situation. Under the fire of the Orias, the perimeter shimmered. It was a sturdy structure with its shields still intact. Fifty Orias ships were attacking the perimeter, and several Orias had boarded *Titan*.

"God save us," he muttered.

Following orders, he and the others fell back as the bigger ships took the lead. Clenching the steering, he thought of all the maneuvers he had learned.

Sweat gathered on his forehead as he waited for their next move. But there was complete radio silence, and the perimeter's gates remained shut.

"What the hell is happening?" he said and tried to contact *Freedom*.

There was no response from the admiral's ship. He tried to raise *Titan*.

Micah's voice echoed in the cockpit, "What's happening? Why aren't we moving?"

"I don't know. No one is responding," Byron replied.

At that moment, the gates opened.

"Okay, I guess we are going in," said Micah sarcastically.

"This is ridiculous," remarked Clio. "There is no way we can win. We should not cross the gates."

Before Byron could respond, Jacob's voice boomed, ordering the fleet to attack. The Imperial Fleet began moving, and the ships slipped through the gates. Byron sulked. He felt he was walking into a death trap. Reluctantly, he pulled the steering, and the ship gradually flew toward the opening.

A loud bell echoed.

"Imperial Fleet, this is Commander Waters. Admiral Jacob Donavan is no longer in command. Do not leave the system!" ordered Anastasia.

Byron instantly reduced speed. The message repeated. Then *Titan* suddenly stopped transmitting.

"That's odd," he muttered, trying to reach *Titan*.

As his craft neared the gates, he searched for the broadcast. He found another transmission. It was from Evan.

"Repeat, do not cross the gates. The admiral is no longer in command. Wait for further orders. Repeat, do not cross the gates!"

"Did you hear that? What do we do?" Micah asked over the intercom.

The message repeated.

Byron watched as the bigger ships crossed the gates, disregarding Anastasia's orders. But he didn't care. Jacob was not in charge anymore, and Anastasia was his commander.

"Turn around!" Byron shouted.

"What?" Micah said.

"You heard the commander. Return to *Titan*!"

Byron swung the steering, and the ship turned away from the gates. The other two crafts followed. Byron was confused and decided to talk to the commander once he reached *Titan*. Suddenly, the stars in front of him vanished.

"What the hell?" he muttered.

Out of nowhere, an immense void appeared and expanded. He maneuvered his craft away from the darkness.

"Proximity alert! Proximity alert!" said the computer.

Alarms boomed, and lights blinked.

"No!" he cried out, changing the ship's course and pushing the engines. The void spread, blocking his path.

"Come on!" he yelled, pulling the handle toward his chest, trying his best to escape. But it was all in vain. Byron screamed as his ship was swallowed into the void.

PROMETHEUS, BRIDGE, DECK 1

An hour passed, and the crew worked silently. Mykel sensed everyone wanted to be left alone with their thoughts. His stomach grumbled. It was time he ate something. He stood up and straightened his uniform. With his hands behind his back, he strolled to the elevator. The doors whooshed opened.

"Captain," called Patrick.

Mykel felt goosebumps line his skin as he faced the communication officer.

"I...I don't understand," Patrick mumbled.

"What is it, Patrick?"

"*Titan*...is..."

Mykel did not let him finish and rushed to the station. The wide, black panel showed colorful graphs on the left side. Various touch buttons dominated the right side of the panel. Mykel knew what Patrick was trying to tell him. Pushing him over, he conducted another search.

"Oh, no," he muttered.

For the first time since its creation, *Titan* had ceased transmitting.

"It's like it was never there at all," Patrick cried out.

"Katia, scan for *Titan*," Mykel ordered.

Katia nodded, and her fingers tapped on the keyboard.

Mykel moved to the side and said, "Patrick, hail *Titan*."

He nodded and began working.

Folding his arms, he tapped his feet.

"Sir, sir! T-*Titan* is not responding," Patrick said with fear in his eyes.

"Hail *Freedom*," Mykel ordered, feeling his anxiety rise.

Patrick's hands were shaking. Mykel looked at the roof, trying to be patient.

"No. No response. Sir. I don't understand."

"Bloody hell. Try the *Freedom*, *Marion*, or the *Jupiter*," Mykel ordered, pacing up and down the bridge.

A series of beeps emitted, and he heard his own heart beating.

"Sir, *Titan* has vanished from standard sensors," Katia said with apprehension.

Their eyes met. He marched to her station to check the readings.

"Captain, there is no reply to our hails," Patrick said in a muffled tone and added, "Maybe *Titan's* communication systems are down."

"Still, it should show up on sensors," Katia replied, "It's gone...as if —"

"It never existed at all," Mykel added, returning to his chair. "Nick, bring us about. Patrick, relay a message to the Imperial Command informing them that *Titan* has vanished from standard sensors. We suspect it's under attack, and the *Prometheus* is returning to investigate."

Patrick nodded.

Engines raved. The *Prometheus* turned, and three bright lights beamed behind the ship, and it sped toward *Titan*.

Mykel was uneasy, and he sensed the tension rise on the bridge. Katia and Patrick were still trying to detect or reach *Titan*. But deep down, he knew.

God knows what will happen. I should not have left. I don't know the size of the enemy fleet, and I do not know what we will be facing.

"Nick, can we get there any faster?" he asked.

"Engines at maximum, sir."

He sensed Katia's eyes on him. Concern and horror clouded her face. He reached for a button on his chair.

"Ladies and gentlemen, this is your captain. We are returning to *Titan*. It has vanished from our sensors and is not responding to our hails. I would have disregarded this if the fleet had responded. We are going to investigate. It is possible the fleet and *Titan* are under attack," he said and paused as his heart leaped to his throat. "Prepare for battle."

Time passed painfully. Mykel hovered over navigation, checking their position. They were getting closer.

"Katia, all system ready?"

"Yes, sir."

"Sir, we are approaching the perimeter," announced Nick.

"Shields up. Fire up the weapons," he ordered, turning away from navigation. Mykel lowered himself into his chair as the viewscreen came to life. He felt as if his chair shook a bit. Every sound around him died. The Orias had breached the perimeter. Debris spread on both sides of the perimeter. Two flashes emerged from *Freedom* and hit the Orias ship, shattering it. Multiple laser beams appeared from the other two Earth ships attacking the Orias targeting the perimeter.

"Status of the fleet!" he yelled.

"Sir, Earth ships have crossed the perimeter and have engaged the enemy. Most of them have been destroyed. The remaining three Earth ships are under heavy attack. I cannot locate the *Titan* Squadron," Lyle reported from the tactical station.

"They shouldn't have crossed the gates," stated Katia.

"*Titan*?" he asked edgily.

The image on the viewscreen changed. Mykel felt a sense of relief. It was still there. Intact. Unharmed. Something caught his eye.

"What's happening?" he asked.

"*Titan* has been boarded," Katia replied. "Sensors show over two dozen Orias. The citizens are being moved to the outer section."

Mykel gulped. His fears were coming true.

"Hail them."

A familiar face appeared on the screen.

"Sorry. It appears I'm always late," he remarked.

"Where have you been? We have been trying to contact you," said Anastasia.

"We have been trying to get in touch with you. When all transmissions from *Titan* stopped and our attempts to contact you failed. It could only mean one thing."

Anastasia nodded.

"I've warned the Imperial Command. More ships should be here," Mykel said.

"Thank you, Captain."

Anastasia vanished from the screen, and the image of the raging battle emerged.

"Sir, there is a dampening field of unknown origin jamming our signals," reported Seiko from the science console. "We cannot send any updates to the Imperial Command."

"It could be the Orias," concluded Katia.

A blast shook the ship. Mykel gulped as he watched two Earth ships crumble into pieces.

Short gasps echoed. The entire bridge crew was shocked. Mykel gripped the arms of his chair, attempting to control his despair and anger.

"Sir, only *Titan*, *Freedom*, and the *Prometheus* are remaining. The rest of the Imperial Fleet has been destroyed!" Patrick cried out.

An Orias ship slipped through the broken perimeter.

Mykel's blood boiled. "Let's make sure as long as we are alive that no Orias ship leaves this section of space. If we go down, they go down with us."

The *Prometheus* surged ahead. Multiple flares left its tubes. Smashing the Orias ship into pieces, it joined the battle.

TITAN, DECK 4

The alarms provoked fear and terror. The battle between the Orias and the robots had left bloodshed everywhere. Selina Keston screamed when a robot ripped the Orias into pieces. The nine-year-old ran to her mother. Aceline Keston grabbed her, and they hurried down the passage. The armed robot followed them.

"Ahhh!" Aceline screamed and came to an abrupt stop. The Orias growled. They ran in the opposite direction. The robot fired, blasting the alien into bits.

The machine was six feet tall, with a bald head and cold gray eyes. It could be mistaken for a human being. But it wasn't. It stood straight, with a gun in its long metallic arm. Its bright blue interior was covered with white, smooth thick armor.

Aceline was never so grateful to the internal security of *Titan*. She wished someone was protecting her son, Argon.

"Mom, I want to go to Argon!" yelled Selina, pulling her hand and shaking her head. Her ponytails flung in the air, and her tiny face was red and wet.

"Dr. Keston, we need to take you to safety," said the machine.

Aceline nodded and walked hurriedly, trying not to look at the mutilated bodies on the floor. Blood splattered the walls.

Oh, God, what has happened to our world?

She tried to keep up with the robot, pulling Selina along with her.

"What will happen to us?" Aceline asked, looking up and down the passageway. Her face and neck were covered with sweat, and she felt as if she was choking. She kept moving. They were not far off from safety.

"I will escort you to *Titan's* outer rim. We have allocated you and your daughter stasis pods 2998 and 2999. A security shield will hold you safely, and you will remain in stasis until the situation comes under control or we receive further orders from the Imperial Command."

"Do we really need to leave?"

"It is for you and your daughter's safety."

"Mom, we shouldn't leave *Titan*," insisted Selina.

She looked at her child and then thought of her son. He was somewhere out there fighting a battle with no chance of winning. A shadow fell over them. She released a piercing cry when a Orias attacked the robot. Aceline grabbed Selina and ran. The Orias roared and ripped the robot into pieces. It growled, throwing its head upward, and chased them.

She screamed, "Help! Help!"

A blast resonated and threw them on the floor. She raised her head and watched the Orias burn alive. From within the fire emerged another robot.

"Are you hurt?" the robot asked as tears gathered in her eyes. "Dr. Keston, we must move."

She nodded numbly. The robot helped her stand, and they hurried behind it.

"No. No. Mom, I don't want to leave!" insisted Selina.

She shook her. "We have no choice! We have to go…"

"No, we have to stay!" Selina yelled.

Aceline didn't listen to her and hurried behind the robot.

Once inside the outer rim, Aceline felt safe. A dozen robots covered the entrance as the colonists were being secured into pods.

Countless white pods about six feet long and eighty inches wide sat along the wall. Each was equipped with glass doors that opened upward. The robot led them to their designated pod and pushed a button. Aceline looked at the interior, resembling a cozy, well-designed coffin.

"Mom, we shouldn't leave."

Aceline was tired of explaining. "Honey, just get in. We will reach safety soon."

"We are not safe anywhere!" cried Selina.

"Dr. Keston, we are running out of time," said the robot.

Getting on one knee, she placed her hands on her shoulders. "Selina, we have no choice. We must leave. Please."

Obediently, Selina stepped inside the pod. With another push of a button, the door closed. Aceline watched as a whitish hue appeared, and Selina shut her eyes and went to sleep. She watched as a steel door formed a shield around the pod.

"She'll be safe. Right?" Aceline asked.

"Yes," the robot replied and stepped forward, leading her to the next pod.

Aceline's heart raced as she got in the pod. To her left was a panel designed to regulate her vitals. To her right was the emergency button.

"Have a safe trip," the robot said.

A white light blinded her momentarily, and then everything went blank.

Aceline screamed and broke out of stasis. She couldn't breathe and felt as if a part of her was dead. Something was wrong.

She heard *Titan's* computer: "Ninety-eight percent separation complete."

But that was not what she had sensed. She felt a catastrophe. Death. Despair. Loss. She gasped for air, her head spinning. Touching the door of the pod, she pushed the emergency button. The door opened, and she fell on her knees, breathless. She lifted her head and saw Selina standing over her.

How did she get out?

Sadness filled Selina's eyes. She extended her hand and said, "Mom, let's go find Argon."

PROMETHEUS, BRIDGE, DECK 1

The ship shook, and Mykel grabbed the arms of his chair.

"Sir, the outer section has separated from *Titan*," reported Seiko.

He watched as the large wheel hovered in space.

"Shields at ninety percent, and holding," said Katia.

The *Prometheus* launched three torpedoes, blowing up the Orias ships, which attempted to sneak into their system.

"Citizens of *Titan* are on their way out of the system," announced Seiko.

Powered by four engines, the large wheel glided ahead.

"Lyle, track them. Seiko, what else can we do except fire at close range? Get me something."

Seiko nodded.

"Nick, show me the status of the Earth ships."

He watched *Titan* and *Freedom* fight a group of Orias ships. At that moment, two Orias ships fired at the *Freedom*. It blew into millions of pieces. A shock wake hit them, and *Prometheus* shuddered, rocking Mykel's chair. But he didn't feel it. Like everyone, he sat with his mouth open.

Patrick said in a low voice, "The *Freedom* is gone."

He banged the arm of his chair with his fist.

"Captain, the perimeter is overloading. Its shields are at twenty percent," Katia said from her station.

"Right! Are you telling me it's going to blow up?"

"Eventually."

"Oh, that's just great!"

Mykel was running out of ideas and the situation was not improving.

"Captain, two Orias ships are following the outer section," Lyle said.

"Nick!" he shouted over the blaring alarms.

The ship turned and chased the Orias ships.

"Thirty thousand kilometers from the enemy ships and closing," said Lyle.

"Get closer."

He heard a beep.

"Captain, *Titan* is transferring more power to the perimeter," said Katia.

"That's good, right?"

"No. Not really. At this rate, it will blow up."

He just looked at her.

What was Anastasia thinking?

"Fifteen thousand kilometers from the enemy ship," Lyle said.

The spikes of the Orias ships turned bright red. They were about to kill the colonists when multiple torpedoes emerged from the *Prometheus* and crushed the ships.

"Good! Nick return—"

A massive blast occurred, almost throwing him out of his chair.

"What the hell was that?"

His jaw fell. The perimeter blew section by section, generating raging inferno on both sides. It burned every Orias ship in its path.

"Move back! Move back!" shouted Mykel.

The engines reversed, and the ship stopped at a safe distance.

"Oh my gosh!" cried Patrick.

"Indeed," Mykel said, astonished. "Was it the Orias or *Titan*?"

"It was *Titan*," replied Katia. "The blast took out most of the enemy ships."

"Sir. Our communications are back online," said Patrick. "I am receiving several messages from the Imperial Command. More ships should reach the perimeter within ten minutes."

He ran his hands through his hair. "Hail *Titan*."

Titan's bridge became visible.

"What was that? Are you okay?" asked Mykel.

"We are good, thanks. We overloaded the generators, creating a blast that took out most of their ships."

"Wow. Good move! We might just win this one," he said, trying to reassure everyone.

Anastasia was about to say something when the transmission was interrupted.

"What happened?"

"We lost the transmission," replied Patrick.

"Get it back."

"I'm trying. I can't get through."

Mykel changed his focus. "What is the status of the remaining Orias ships?"

"They are just sitting there," Nick said, throwing his hands in the air.

"Ah...finally," cried out Patrick.

The transmission came through, and they could see *Titan's* bridge. He was about to speak when Anastasia signaled him to wait. He heard an unknown voice.

"Who is that?" he asked.

Patrick got busy, and the screen split in two. For the first time, they saw the queen. Mykel raised his eyebrows and regarded the lady of Ana's age. Her face was narrow, her skin flawless, and her eyes sparkled with darkness.

"I thought it was an alien," said Patrick.

"She is an alien," replied Seiko, conducting scans.

He listened as the queen threatened Anastasia.

"You are menial, insignificant beings! And I will crush you," shouted the queen.

Everyone exchanged confused glances.

"Menial?" complained Katia.

"Seiko. Where is she?" he asked.

"The transmission is coming from a ship behind the Orias fleet."

On the viewer appeared a substantial craft. It petrified him. It was bigger than *Titan* or anything he had seen. Seventy percent of the gray ship was a circular structure. Two large metallic-looking extensions emerged from the center and curved forward. He wished they had more ships and better weapons.

The queen continued, "You are powerless! Insignificant! You will surrender and serve under me. If you resist, I will destroy you and assimilate your species! This is my realm; I will be your queen. You will either serve me or die!"

"Can we change the channel?" suggested Nick.

"Lyle, can our torpedoes reach the queen's ship?" Mykel asked.

"It's too far away. We'll have to get close to do substantial damage."

At that moment, *Titan* launched multiple long-ranged torpedoes. The balls of fire sped through the debris, destroying six Orias ships and hitting the queen's ship.

"Whoa!" said Nick.

"Captain, the shields of the queen's ship are at seventy percent. I detect fire in one of its sections. If we get closer, we could destroy it."

"Okay, let's—"

"Captain!" shouted Katia.

Three Orias ships fired at the *Prometheus*. The ship shuddered; lights dimmed for a second.

"Return fire!"

Lyle aimed, and the torpedoes hit the hull of two ships.

"Two more ships approaching from the port side!" yelled Katia.

"Sir, we are surrounded!" shouted Nick.

"Evasive maneuvers!" screamed Mykel.

Prometheus tried to sway away when a blaze hit the shields, and a tremor passed through craft.

"Captain! Shields at fifty percent. We cannot take any more hits!" yelled Katia, looking up.

"Lyle, fire!" Mykel shouted.

The next torpedo took out one of the Orias ships. The surviving alien ships converged around the Earth ship.

"Katia, keep the shields up. Take power from wherever you can! Nick, get us out of here!"

The *Prometheus* swayed away, but the aliens blocked its path. The ships fired, and *Prometheus* shook like there was no tomorrow.

"Targ—" Mykel was about to say but paused.

Suddenly, it was quiet. The Orias ships powered down and reversed.

"What happened?" asked Nick.

Mykel noticed Katia smiling. The floor vibrated, and the stars vanished from the top of the viewscreen. *Titan* hovered over *Prometheus*. The Orias ships were retreating when *Titan* fired, obliterating them in seconds.

"Show off," Mykel muttered, smirking.

"*Titan* is hailing," said Patrick.

Mykel nodded.

"How are you holding up?" asked Anastasia, appearing on the screen.

"We are fine. I don't know how long we can keep this up."

"You are right. We have to finish this," she said.

"There is only one way to do that," he said gravely.

She said nothing more.

The channel closed.

"What is the status of the ship?" Mykel asked Katia.

"Damage to two decks, ten injuries reported, shields at eighty percent and holding, weapons and environmental systems operational," Katia replied.

Mykel nodded.

"Nine minutes till the arrival of the Imperial Command fleet," announced Patrick.

He knew it was too late.

"Nick. Take us in position,"

Prometheus glided to stand beside *Titan*. He knew what needed to be done. They had to get the queen. He pushed a button on his chair's arm. "Ready when you are," he said to Anastasia.

"Let's take them down," said Anastasia.

Everyone looked at each other.

"Attack pattern, Lockhart one," he ordered.

As soon as the words slipped out of his mouth, the crew became quiet. The red lights turned blue. The blaring alarm became silent.

The Orias ships moved forward, and the Earth ships didn't back off and crossed the broken perimeter.

"Nick, take cover in *Titan's* wake," Mykel ordered.

Prometheus slowed and allowed the majestic *Titan* to take the lead. Three Orias ships fired at once. *Titan's* torpedoes intercepted them. The explosion ripped through space and destroyed the two Orias ships.

"Hold fire," he told Lyle.

Titan furiously ripped through the inferno. Its beam sliced an Orias ship in half. Two enemy ships fired at once. The blaze hit *Titan* but didn't slow it down.

"Seiko. Ready?"

"Yes."

Mykel opened a channel. "*Prometheus*…prepare for dark mode."

All sensors came online. The computer began duplicating their surroundings, which was a mix of debris of Orias and Earth ships. Remnants of a deadly war.

"Ready to mask all signals of the *Prometheus*," said Katia. "I don't see the point. They know there are two Earth ships."

"Wait for it," he told her. "Nick and Seiko, you know what to do."

"Yes, sir," said both officers in unison.

"Two enemy ships approaching," said Lyle.

"Let's play,"

The Orias ships fired. Torpedoes blasted out of *Prometheus* tubes, matching the Orias firepower. An enormous blast spread through the vicinity.

"Seiko. Now!"

Prometheus sent out a stream of Vipers. They whizzed through the fire unharmed. The tiny bullet-shaped objects attached themselves to the enemy ship's hull.

"Vipers are in position."

"Activate."

Six tentacles emerged from the end of each Viper. The pointed front dug into the ship's hull and waited.

"The ships are getting closer," said Lyle edgily.

He nodded. The spikes of the ships turned red.

"On my mark, one…two…three!"

Two more torpedoes blasted through the tubes and intercepted the blaze.

"Cover fire,"

Lyle punched several buttons. Three torpedoes blasted from the ship's tube and self-destructed, creating an enormous inferno between the ship.

"Initiate dark mode."

Under the cover of the fire, *Prometheus* moved away from the battle. The bridge turned dark. Unwanted equipment automatically turned off. Lights all over the ship faded away. The ship's surface turned black and replicated its surroundings. In seconds, the ship vanished, as if it never existed. On sensors, it was like a ghost, a shadow without form.

"Seiko, now."

The vipers turned red and released an electrical charge disrupting the Orias ship's functions.

The fire died out, and the Orias ships pursuing the *Prometheus* began looking for the Earth ship. But in the vastness of debris and fire, it was undetectable. Their sensors were disrupted, which blinded them to anything beyond a certain point. The Vipers turned red and blew up, rupturing the ship's hull. The crafts whirled out of control and exploded.

"And now they think...there is only one Earth ship," murmured Mykel. "Nick, make it quick. We won't get another chance."

"Yes, sir!" said Nick, entering the coordinates.

Titan fought with valor, with its shield shining brightly under the heavy fire. It shuddered but did not waver from its target. The Orias suffered too. *Titan* wiped out eight ships in minutes. To keep the pressure on, it blasted a series of long-range torpedoes, which hit the queen's ship. Still, fighting with the remaining twelve Orias ships was difficult.

While the Orias were busy dealing with the *Titan*, *Prometheus* took advantage. Since it had vanished from normal sensors, Nick plotted a course around the battle to get to the other end.

Titan was a fantastic distraction.

"On my mark...prepare to fire."

"Ready, Captain," said Lyle.

The *Prometheus* halted twenty-five thousand kilometers from the queen's ship.

"Fire!"

Prometheus appeared.

Realizing the second Earth ship wasn't destroyed, the queen's ship prepared to fire, but it was too late. The *Prometheus* blasted a range of torpedoes that struck several parts of the ship, setting off a massive blaze.

"Fire again! Don't give them the chance to recover!" Mykel shouted.

Another round of torpedoes hit the enemy ship, and fire spread in the central section.

"Sir, their weapons are down, their shields are wavering, and I can detect a fire in the engine room," announced Lyle.

"We have company!" yelled Nick.

Prometheus shuddered, and the lights flickered.

The surprise was gone, but they damaged the enemy ship.

Sweat covered Patrick's face. "Three minutes until the Imperial Command gets here!"

"If they reach here on time...we could win this," said Seiko.

Titan was not far behind and blasted two Orias ships blocking its path. Next, it targeted the queen's ship, destroying a part of the curved wing.

"How many enemy ships remaining?" Mykel asked.

"Eight."

"Still too many. Keep firing...do not..."

A blast hit the *Prometheus*, and it shook, sending a chill down Mykel's spine. The Earth ship returned fire, blowing up one of the enemy ships.

"Sir...I am detecting a massive energy surge!" Katia cried out.

The viewscreen split into two. From the depths of space, a stream of purple light flashed. Mykel watched in amazement as it turned into a massive purple cloud. The queen's ship powered up, moving away from the battle.

"They are opening the doorway!" Nick yelled. "They are retreating…"

Katia narrowed her eyes. "We should withdraw!"

Before Mykel could respond, a group of torpedoes left *Titan*. Two Orias ships intercepted them and exploded.

"They are killing themselves to protect her," said Nick.

"Captain, the doorway is open," Katia said.

It was now or never.

"Do not let her escape. Fire!" Mykel said.

Lyle hit the button, and the torpedoes flew toward the queen's ship. Two massive beams emerged from the queen's ships and blew up the torpedoes. Three Orias ships blocked their path. The *Prometheus* dropped speed. The distance between the queen's ship and Earth vessels increased.

"Damn…keep firing…get around them," he ordered, getting on his feet.

Crushing the three alien ships, the *Prometheus* steered through the debris, pursuing the queen's ship. They were getting dangerously close to the purple cloud.

"Sir, *Titan* is hailing," said Patrick.

"Put it through."

Titan's bridge was dark and misty. The crew was rushing around, and alarms blared in the background. Ana's face was stern, and her eyes cold. "She is escaping."

"We cannot let that happen."

"Captain, we shouldn't enter the rift. There is no telling what will happen!" Katia warned.

"She is not getting away," Anastasia argued.

"Ana, we have to be careful," Mykel said, but his words fell on deaf ears.

Titan had stopped transmitting. A dozen torpedoes left *Titan*, destroying four ships blocking its path. The fire stretched on both sides.

Anastasia was angry, and it showed.

"Four Orias ships remaining," Nick reported.

"Take them out!"

But the last ships fought back, and the damage on both sides was substantial. The *Prometheus* shuddered. Loud blasts resonated on several decks, filling them with gases and fire. The computer and the crew did their best to keep the ship together. But Mykel knew it had its limits. Debris fell from the roof, alarms blared, and a panel blasted on the bridge. Mykel took cover. Seiko jumped to his feet to put out the fire.

"Sir...we can't take this...we should withdraw," Katia said.

"I know. *Titan*! *Titan*!" he shouted, opening a channel. His eyes widened as he saw *Titan* was under heavy fire from the Orias and the queen's ship.

"*Titan*!" he shouted.

"No response...Captain," said Patrick.

Torpedoes fired, blasting two Orias ships.

On the viewscreen, he saw purple waves heading toward them.

"Ana...turn back now!" he shouted on the comm.

The vast cloud of gases appeared like a storm raging through space. The Earth ships were at the brink of the rift.

"Sir...we are entering a minefield. If any of the ships fires inside the rift..." warned Katia.

The tails of the Orias ships brightened, and blaze struck the *Prometheus*. The helm blew, catapulting Nick off his chair. The bridge turned dark. Alarms shrieked.

"Shields at thirty percent and failing. Fire in engineering!" Katia yelled.

"Reroute power from all available sources. Keep her together," Mykel said.

Waves of purple gases shrouded *Prometheus*. On the viewscreen, Mykel saw normal space fade away.

"What is our position?"

"We have entered the cloud," said Seiko.

"No. Give me the exact coordinates."

"I can't! The sensors are not working."

The engine droned, and the craft shuddered.

Titan was still pursuing the queen's ship.

"*Titan*, I repeat, turn back, now!" he shouted.

Katia yelled, "We are going through the doorway, Captain—"

An enormous ball of fire left *Titan*.

"No," Mykel murmured.

An inferno erupted. A wave of fire rippled through the purple gases and threw itself on the ships. The Orias disintegrated in seconds.

"Diverting all power to shields!" shouted Katia.

With immense force, the blaze hit the Earth ships. The bridge darkened as alarms wailed and screams echoed. With massive force, Mykel was thrown off his chair.

CAELESTIS

Fire struck *Caelestis* with a vengeance. The queen's ship shuddered. She stood in disbelief with her hands on the control. The transparent dome above her trembled. Cracks appeared in pillars connecting the dome to the floor. Smoke rose from the vents, and the screens shattered into millions of pieces. The command center became dark.

She saw it all. The ship was part of her, connected to her as if they were one. It was alive. When the fire hit, the inferno rushed through her veins. She sensed a part of her breaking away. A blast in the hull threw the Orias into open space. Focusing, she activated counterattacks. The damaged section was closed. Gases filled the section, extinguishing the fire. Drawing power from several parts of the ship, she directed it to the engines. The *Caelestis* came to life, and its shields were restored. It emerged on the other end of the doorway and came to a standstill in open space. All her energy was gone, and she fell to her knees. Growls echoed around her. Orias in the command center collapsed as well. She felt powerless, life drained out of her and she collapsed.

Chapter 2: Taken

B yron Thames let out a bloodcurdling scream as he got shoved against the stiff seat. The pressure was so immense he feared it would rip him apart. He squinted as bright lights blinded him.

The ship did not respond. Alarms and beeps filled the cockpit. The light vanished, and blackness surrounded him. Byron's head was spinning. In front of him, the stars twirled, and his stomach twisted. Half dazed, he reached for the panel and stabilized the ship. Once it stopped whirling, he turned away and vomited. Breathing hard, he dropped to his knees and waited for the dizziness to stop.

Byron's ship vibrated when another vessel appeared and soared past at extreme speed.

"Clio! Clio!" he called out, turning on the communicator.

There was no response.

"Jeez!"

A burst of light appeared to his left, and he saw Micah's ship appear.

"Micah! Micah! Do you read me?" Panic filled Byron as he watched Micah's ship spin uncontrollably.

"Clio! Micah!" he shouted into the intercom. Byron was about to yell again when the ships stabilized, slowed, and halted.

"Clio, respond," he said, setting a course in her ship's direction. "Micah! Respond!"

"Yeah, I am here. Oh, man...this is..." Micah's voice died out.

Byron heard him vomit.

"Yeah. Man. I just wished..."

Hearing Micah puke again made him nauseous. He shut his eyes trying to keep himself calm.

"Byron, are you there?" asked a disoriented female voice.

"Clio! Are you hurt?"

"I'm all right, I...I."

"Take it easy," he said, firing up the engine.

"I-I am trying. Where are we?" she asked, sounding sick.

His heart raced as he entered the coordinates. His craft steadily neared the other two.

"Just relax. I'll find out," Byron replied. "Micah, how about you?"

"I-I..." he blurted out and gagged again.

Byron let him be and began looking for answers.

"God damn it," he muttered, gaping at the star chart. He checked their location again and widened his eyes in disbelief. Drifting his gaze to his left, he saw millions of asteroids floating.

"Where are we?" Clio asked again.

"We at the boundary of the Oort's belt."

"What?!" shouted Micah.

"That's impossible!" cried Clio.

CHAPTER 3: LOST SOULS

RAVEN

The terrible pain in her head forced Emmeline to open her eyes. She sensed the world spinning as she tried to sit up. Breathless, she stared at the blood on her hands. Nausea took over her, and she felt a powerful urge to throw up.

"Oh, god!" she cried.

She wiped her mouth with her sleeve. Still feeling dizzy, she looked around. Her mind tried to contemplate what had happened. Realization dawned, and her eyes flooded with tears, and she forgot her menacing headache. She sat paralyzed as tears rolled down her face. The memory of the spear ripping through Argon's heart replayed in her mind.

"No, no…it can't be true. No. It cannot be. I don't believe it!"

She stormed to the cockpit and froze. Stripes of orange and white gases dominated the viewscreen.

"I am not on *Titan*?"

Taking a seat, she checked her coordinates. Her heart sank. She was miles away from home. Moving fast, she turned on the engine. She had to go back. Argon must be alive. He was on *Titan*, which had the best medical facilities. If they had found him, they would do their best to treat him. They would keep him alive. Then she recalled blood dripping from the end of the spear and the dark eyes of the queen. No. He was gone. She covered her face with her hands and wailed. Emmeline fell to the floor. The pain was unbearable.

"No. It's not true. You cannot be dead! Argon...you can't leave me..." she cried out, sobbing.

Her father was right. She had been foolish. It was her fault. The Orias attacked *Titan* because she found the plaque and the first piece of the mythical device. If she hadn't, everyone would have been safe. Delta would have been alive. Argon would have been with her.

The fifth planet from the sun was a unique gas giant in the system. Jupiter's windy clouds were full of ammonia and water mixed with hydrogen and helium. Enormous storms of gases dominated the planet. The *Raven* sat on one of the trojan asteroids, far away from prying eyes. For Emmeline, time had stopped. She ran out of tears and lay in the corner in a fetal position. She wondered what had happened to her family. Her father, mother, and her brother. Even if they were alive, she couldn't risk going to them. She was a fugitive, a criminal. Any associations with her would destroy her family's future. She was a curse, a stain. She had already murdered her best friend, and then she had killed the man who loved her. They had paid a high price for her thirst for adventure.

I don't deserve their love. Anyone's love.

Her eyes settled on the disruptor on the frigid floor. It would be easy. Just end it all. She could destroy the *Raven* and the artifacts. If she died, no one would come after her family. Imperial Command would not blame Commander Waters and Dr. Kent. *Titan* would not be in jeopardy. Her death would solve all problems.

Emmeline picked up the weapon and pointed it toward herself. *No one else needs to die because of me.*

Closing her eyes, she prepared herself to press the button. Her heart surged with emotions as Argon's kind face appeared. She felt his presence.

"I'll never give up on you," he whispered in her ear.

She burst into tears, and the disruptor fell onto her lap. Weeping, she collapsed on the chilly floor.

CHAPTER 4: THE FALLEN

TITAN, BRIDGE, DECK 1

Titan stood tilted in an unexplored region of space. Inside, it was dark, silent, and lifeless. Suddenly, red lights blinked, and the computer spoke.

"Backup systems coming online. Backup systems coming online."

The thrusters came to life. The stars moved on the cracked screen and came to a standstill.

"*Titan* stabilized. Assessing damage," said the computer. "Shields offline. Weapons offline. Engines offline. Environmental systems working at ten percent capacity. Sensors offline. Radiation levels increasing. Major coolant leaks in engineering. Isolating engineering from other departments. Hull breaches on decks two, five, and ten. Fires detected on decks seven and ten. Activating countermeasures. Countermeasures unresponsive. Isolating decks seven and ten. Failed. Calculating survival rate of the crew depending on the spread of inferno and damage to *Titan*. Ten percent. Calculating time remaining to activate manual overdrive. Twenty minutes."

Alarms blared.

"Level one emergency! Danger! Activate manual overdrive!"

Boom!

A cloud of smoke emerged, and the viewscreen turned dark.

"Viewscreen offline," the computer added to the list. "Level one emergency! Danger! Activate manual overdrive!"

Anastasia felt a sharp pain and woke up. She squealed. Panting, she looked down. A large piece of wreckage had fallen on her leg. The throbbing pain radiated toward her hip. "Ah!" she cried out as she shoved the debris off her. Blood soaked her pants, and pain ripped through her body.

The alarms were blaring, red lights flashed from the roof, and smoke filled the vicinity. She coughed. Her eyes adjusted to the gloom. She noticed dark figures lying on the floor of the bridge.

The computer's voice boomed: "Level one emergency! Danger! Activate manual overdrive."

Fear took over pain, and Anastasia crawled toward her chair on her elbows.

"Activate manual overdrive."

"Which one!" she shouted.

"Fire control on decks seven and ten," said the computer.

A trail of blood smeared the carpet as she attempted to reach her chair. Panting, she stopped.

Titan shook.

"Update: Fire spread to deck nine. Recalculating survival time. Ten minutes. Activate manual override."

The alarms became louder.

"Damn it!" she shouted, unable to move. Breathing hard, she lifted her head. The manual override button was on the left arm of the commander's chair. She focused. There had to be a way. Her eyes flung open. She moved sideways, and she rolled toward her chair. She stopped at the base of her chair. Her head spun. She waited for a moment. The computer continued the announcement. Using her arms and her uninjured leg, she stood up. Her blood-smeared fingers reached out for the button.

"Manual procedures activated," said the computer.

She hung her head.

A ring sounded.

"Commander, we are at deck seven," said a voice on the intercom.

"Good work. Call for backup!" she yelled back.

She welcomed the momentary silence.

The computer spoke: "Activity detected on decks seven and nine. Fire control measures have been initiated. Reassessing emergency level and survival rate."

She wished it would stop talking.

"Crew survival rate seventy percent." The alarms died out, "Maintenance crew report to engineering."

The bridge became silent.

She reached for a switch. "Medical Bay. This is the bridge. We need help."

The pain was intolerable. She somehow managed to slip into the chair. In the dim light, she noticed Adrian had fallen near his workstation, and Evan lay unconscious close to the viewer.

"Adrian? Evan?"

They did not respond.

"Adrian! Evan!" she shouted.

She stopped to catch her breath. In the dull light, she noticed the blood on Adrian's face and neck.

Anastasia heard a moan. Evan gradually lifted his head and blinked his eyes open.

"Evan, are you okay?"

Evan didn't respond but gently sat up, holding his right arm.

"W-What happened?"

"Are you okay?" she asked.

"Yes, I think."

"Good..."

Evan was still holding his arm, looking puzzled.

"What happened?" he asked again.

"Can you move your arm?"

He tried to extend his hand and yelped. "Ouch! No. I can't..."

"Engineering to bridge. Commander? Anastasia, are you there?" Cyr's voice echoed.

A sense of relief rushed through her body. At least someone had reached out.

"I'm here," she replied, "Can you hear me?"

"Yes... I don't...I," her voice trailed off.

"Cyr, are you hurt?"

"I-I think I am fine. The computer has locked engineering. The doors are not opening."

"Yes. The computer activated safety procedures. Check on your team and we will attempt to unlock the doors from the bridge."

"Okay."

She heard another mourn, and Edward stood up, holding his console. Evan sluggishly got to his feet and walked haphazardly to his chair.

"Edward, can we activate the viewscreen?"

"I shall try," Edward replied in a weary voice.

Light streamed through the screen, and Anastasia looked away. When her eyes adjusted, what she saw amazed her.

"Wow," muttered Evan.

The massive black hole dominated the entire screen. It was shrouded by layers of thick dust and gas, forming extensive rings. Millions of beams of light warped around it.

"What's our position?" she asked, glancing at Edward.

"Commander!" Evan shouted.

She turned, and her jaw dropped. The *Prometheus* was drifting toward the event horizon.

"Hail them!" she yelled.

"Our communication system is offline!" Evan replied, checking using his left hand.

"Edward, zoom in."

Up close, she noted *Prometheus* was shrouded in darkness.

"It's powered down. Why?"

"We have to act fast," Evan cried out.

Anastasia ran her hand on her head. It was then she noticed blood on her fingers.

"You need to go to the medical bay," said Edward, glancing at her head.

"We've to get the *Prometheus* out of there!"

The screen went blank.

"Oh, no!" Evan cried out, banging the console.

"Get the viewscreen back," Anastasia said, ignoring the persistent, intense pain in her leg.

"Rerouting power," responded Edward.

The screen zapped back to life, but it was blurry.

"Adjusting resolution," said Evan.

The emergency lights turned off, and the bridge became bright.

A beep echoed, and the computer said, "Forty percent power restored."

"Cyr to bridge."

"Yes."

"All crew is accounted for."

"That's good. We might need you. Be ready."

"For what?"

The viewer became blurred for a moment.

"Communications are working temporarily," Edward stated.

"It will have to do. Let's hail them."

"No response, Commander," said Edward.

They heard a loud thud, and Dr. Chris Kent stood up, holding his bleeding head.

"Oh, god," he cried out.

"Doctor, glad you are with us."

He didn't answer and clenched his teeth.

"Engineering…can *Titan* move?" Anastasia asked.

"We have limited power," replied Cyr.

"But can *Titan* move?"

Her question was answered when the floor vibrated and the engines came online.

"Engines online, but working on forty percent power," Cyr replied.

"Adrian…" Anastasia paused realizing her first officer was in the Medical Bay.

Evan glanced over his shoulder.

"Sorry. Evan, take us closer to the *Prometheus*," Anastasia ordered.

Evan nodded and took over the helm.

Titan glided forward, and the distance between the two ships decreased.

Anastasia's heart drummed in her chest. "Any response from the *Prometheus*?"

"No," replied Edward.

"Cyr, ideas?"

"Our best option is to use the anchors."

"We do not have enough power," said Edward.

Anastasia looked at him.

"*Prometheus* is a massive ship. Pulling her away from the singularity could put *Titan* in danger,"

"It's dangerous," added Chris.

Anastasia had no choice. "Prepare the anchors." A sharp pain shot up her leg, and she grunted. Sweat beaded on her head. "Try hailing once more," she croaked.

Everyone waited for a response. It never came.

"How much longer?" Anastasia asked.

"A few minutes," Cyr responded.

"Understood."

"How close is the *Prometheus* to the outer rim of the black hole?" she asked.

"One thousand kilometers and closing," replied Chris.

"We should be ready in a few seconds," announced Cyr.

"Evan, bring *Titan* into position," ordered Anastasia.

Using his one arm, Evan pushed one button at a time.

Titan dropped speed, aligning itself with *Prometheus*.

"Ready on your mark," said Cyr.

"Do it," Anastasia ordered.

Powered by small thrusters, six hefty circular objects left *Titan*. Linked with strong tension wires, the anchors darted toward the *Prometheus*. In seconds, they attached themselves to the hull. Back at *Titan*, the massive pulleys rolled back, and the heavy-duty wires straightened.

"Anchors ready," reported Edward.

"Reverse engines!" ordered Anastasia.

Titan shook. The strain on the engines caused a loud droning noise. As it moved backward, it pulled *Prometheus* away from the singularity.

"Commander," Chris said.

"Now what?"

"There is a massive surge in outer rims of the event horizon..."

On the viewscreen, they observed a flare heading in their direction.

"Damn...Increase speed!"

"We can't..." Cyr argued.

"We have no choice...do it. Reroute power to the engines!"

Titan's engines groaned as it dragged the other ship, which shuddered at every pull.

"Faster...faster..."

"*Prometheus* needs to gain momentum," Edward stated.

"Come on, move!" Anastasia balled her hands into fists.

As if it was listening to her, *Prometheus* began moving.

"How long?" Anastasia asked.

"Just a few more minutes," replied Chris.

Titan trembled, and the two ships gained momentum.

With fearful eyes, she watched the massive flare gain on *Prometheus*.

"Without shields, the *Prometheus* will be heavily damaged, and the crew may not survive," Chris said.

"Cyr, can we divert more power?" Anastasia asked.

"We don't have more power!"

Titan's bridge rocked back and forth. She grabbed her chair. The massive wave rushed toward the Earth ships.

"Evan, how long?"

"We are almost there!"

Titan jolted as if an electric shock had surged through its walls. Everyone grabbed the consoles. The lights dimmed, and a deafening blast erupted in their ears.

Evan turned to her.

"We have lost an engine...it's on fire!" Cyr yelled.

The *Prometheus* was pulled away from the event horizon.

"Shut the engine down! Complete stop!" shouted Anastasia.

Silence filled the bridge as if a tornado had just passed. The crew sat with their eyes glued to the screen. Tethered with *Titan, Prometheus* floated away from the singularity.

"Are we at a safe distance?" she asked.

"Yes, but we should move further away," Chris advised.

"Do it," she said, grabbing her numb leg, "Release the anchors."

The anchors detached from *Prometheus's* hull. The thrusters came online, and the six objects returned to *Titan.*

She wanted to sink into the chair. She had hundreds of questions, but her mind was blurred. Evan laid his head on the console. The bridge crew was exhausted.

Her eyes roamed the bridge. "Where are we?"

CHAPTER 5: UTOPIS

RAVEN

Emmeline dreamed about Argon, her childhood, and *Titan*. She saw millions of stars and alien planets. Then the visions vanished when she heard a voice.

"I love you."

She snapped out of her sleep, and she remembered where she was. Sitting up, she looked at the disruptor. Leaving it on the floor, she got on her feet and left the cockpit. Her eyes settled on two bags. She hadn't noticed them.

It must have been Argon.

She opened one of them and froze. It was impossible. The bag contained the plaque, the piece, and the meteoroid she had found in her ancestors' house on Earth. She moved away as if it was cursed. Tears gathered in her eyes.

I should destroy it. The plaque is the reason Argon is dead, and I lost everything.

She stopped at that thought.

Emmeline didn't know what had happened to *Titan*. Was her father alive? Was Anastasia all right? She had to know. There was a chance she could still go home. She rushed back to the cockpit but halted and thought about the consequences.

Argon had paid a heavy price for her freedom. Did his sacrifice mean nothing to her?

She sank into the pilot's chair.

At least I should find out where I am.

Emmeline studied the coordinates on the small screen to her left and smirked. The *Raven* was on one of the Trojan asteroids around Jupiter's orbit. The Imperial Command wouldn't look for her here. She hoped. It was a good place to hide and get a transport ship to leave the system. But Emmeline didn't know if she wanted to run. She didn't know what to do.

At least I should check on Titan.

It only took her a minute to get an answer.

"That can't be right!" she cried out.

She recalibrated *Raven's* sensors and searched again.

"No. I am mistaken!" she yelled.

After several attempts, the truth became evident. Her heart jumped a beat, and she clasped her mouth with her hand. A tear flowed down her cheek. *Titan* was gone. As if it didn't exist.

"No, it's not possible."

Dad is on Titan.

"Oh gosh! This can't be happening."

She had lost enough. Losing *Titan* and her father would be unbearable. Trembling, she tried to search for it. *Titan* had a specific frequency, and it showed up on regular scans. She couldn't find it. Did the queen destroy it? Was her realm invaded by Orias? She searched for any signs of the perimeter. It was gone too. Emmeline could hardly believe it. The perimeter couldn't have just vanished. Unless it was destroyed. She moved away from the keyboard and bit her lips.

What should I do?

Raven's engine came to life, and the ship rose above the asteroid's rough surface, ascending across the cluster of rocks that sprinted in different directions. An asteroid hit the starboard section; the *Raven* shuddered. Emmeline tried her best to navigate through the enormous field of irregular rocks. The *Raven* emerged and vanished into the darkness of space.

Emmeline had always been a copilot and found it tough to fly alone. Handling a spacecraft was an arduous task for her. She double-crossed the coordinates and kept the speed at a minimum to stay in control. What would normally take Argon a few hours took her an entire day.

Utopis remained dead in space, lost, and forgotten. The horseshoe-shaped structure was over ten kilometers long and five kilometers wide. The Imperial Command built it during the creation of the perimeter. For years, Utopis was one of the main communications centers to relay messages between Earth, *Titan*, and other colonies inside and outside the system. But it was abandoned on completion of the perimeter and development of two other advanced centers.

The *Raven* flew closer to the communication center and slowed. Her fingers danced on the console, and the *Raven* adjusted its position to the Utopis docking bay. It took a few adjustments, and the craft vibrated as it attached itself to the station. A clash resonated, and then silence returned. Emmeline left the cockpit. Taking a moment, she looked at the vessel. The ship's wall bore superficial cracks of several sizes that Argon never got the chance to fix. It had limited shields, two engines, one phaser, and was slower than every ship in the fleet. The *Raven* had five small living quarters, a spacious cockpit, a cooking area, a compact storage room, and an exit door that opened outwards and turned into a ramp.

It was not luxurious, but it provided food, water, and shelter. The cooking space was in a corner. On the bench, the beverage and water dispenser stood side by side. The food was stored in two wide cabins below the bench. The two oval machines on curved stands were not much to look at. Argon had done his best and installed old machines. The ship was designed for short trips, not long voyages. Emmeline did not know how she would survive, yet she was glad for a place to live.

She walked behind the cooking area and noted a circular door. She turned the handle and entered. The dark room lit up, and she regarded the five space suits, which sat in sections separated by a thick partition. Emmeline remembered Argon talking about them but didn't realize he had already installed them.

Emmeline put the suit on. Once she was ready, she tapped on the small screen embedded near the wrist of the suit. It began a self-diagnosis. She had used space suits before, but these were lighter and more advanced with backup systems, a camera, headlights, and thrusters. She glanced over her shoulder toward a rectangular box that carried oxygen and regulated the suit's function.

"All systems online," said a mechanical voice inside the helmet.

With a heavy heart, she stepped toward the airlock. It didn't matter how many deep breaths she took; anxiousness clouded her mind. The air inside the helmet was cold. Feared gripped her as she turned the door handle and pulled it. Just beyond her reach was the airlock to Utopis. She gulped and took a step forward. Closing the door behind her, she faced the airlock. She pressed the button on the side, and it unlocked with a whooshing noise. The gravity boots were activated.

Her heart raced, and she wanted to run in the other direction. But she needed to know if it was true.

"It's going to be fine," she told herself as she entered a dark passageway.

It was vacant and gloomy. She turned on the lights on her helmet to guide her path. The metallic floor groaned under her feet as she crossed the compact passageway. While walking ahead, she eyed the narrow open doors that lead to compact quarters with a single bed storage, a narrow table, an overhead light, and a small square window. It was bigger than her closet on *Titan*, and she wondered how someone could live here. But they did. To the best of her knowledge, five crew members lived on this station to keep it running smoothly.

Frightened and sensing her hands turn cold, Emmeline made her way down the windowless passageway. The station was silent like a tomb devoid of radio signals, frequencies, or vibrations. There was no gravity or floating objects. The only source of light was the two headlights on her helmet. Unable to see the stars made her uncomfortable, and it felt as if she was walking into a void.

After a long and tedious walk, she reached the control center and pulled open the hefty door. It was a compact room, and the multiple switchboards appeared ancient with big buttons and levers.

"I hope this thing is still working," she muttered to herself.

Reaching for the left pocket near her thigh, she retrieved a pad and began studying the schematics of Utopis. She checked the panels and discovered most of the equipment was well preserved. But she needed power and studied the station's blueprints to locate the generators.

Leaving the control center, she walked to the generator room at the other end of the station. Four large square boxes stood along the wall. These were connected to multiple solar panels attached to the roof of the space station. She pushed the power button, and the first generator thundered, and for a second, she thought it would break. But the structure was sturdy.

It took an hour, but soon the generators began rolling power. To preserve energy, she only diverted power to the subspace communication array and the control center. She needed nothing else, and if she switched on all the equipment, it might tip off the Imperial Command.

By the time she returned to the control center, she was exhausted. She waited for systems to come online. Sitting alone in a freezing, uncomfortable chair, she thought of Argon. She wanted to go to *Titan* to find him. She knew he was gone, but it seemed like a bad dream. A dim hope lingered in her heart and fought against what she had witnessed. Unable to restrain her sorrow, tears rolled down her face. Emmeline could surrender to the Imperial Command and try to explain. But in their eyes, she was a criminal and a fugitive. She wished she could go back and change everything. Change her fate. Bring Delta back. Save Argon. But there was nothing she could do now.

The panel beeped, and she began working. The first thing she searched for was *Titan*. *Raven's* scanners could be incorrect.

"I don't believe it," she muttered.

After several attempts, she gave up. It was true. *Titan* had vanished.

"Time to try something else."

Reaching for her pocket, she took out the encoder, loaded with algorithms. It was the best way to decode encrypted communications. Placing it on the panel, she began searching. For several minutes, she jumped from one frequency to another and found nothing. Finally, she stumbled upon something and froze.

"Oh, dear."

She felt like a thief, overhearing secret conversations. Her heart skipped a beat as she listened to a transmission between Imperial Command and the *Aurora*.

"It is true then," said a man.

"Yes, Admiral Vince," said a lady in a crisp voice.

Emmeline recognized it.

"*Titan* is nowhere to be found," reported Lady Vermont.

"Are you certain?" asked Admiral Vince.

"Yes. The *Prometheus* has vanished too."

"Vanished?"

"I do not believe they were destroyed," she insisted.

"Why?"

"We found no debris belonging to the *Titan* or *Prometheus*,"

"Then where did they go?"

"The Orias could have captured them..."

Silence fell, and Emmeline wished she had never heard this conversation. Even though she had known about *Titan's* disappearance, hearing the truth was difficult. Her father was on *Titan*. She might have lost him forever. She may not see her friends or people she loved, ever.

"You found nothing?" asked Admiral Vince, sounding desperate.

"Only a vanishing signal..."

Emmeline's eyes widened.

"Is it similar to the one *Titan* reported and investigated two months ago? It was linked with the arrival of the Orias," said Admiral Vince.

"You mean the purple cloud? Maybe. We do not know. The crew of the *Aurora* is doing their best."

The room became silent. Emmeline waiting patiently. She wanted to know what had happened to her friends and family. If they were captured, she knew the Orias would not spare them. But there were other possibilities.

"What about the colonists? Where are they?" asked Admiral Vince.

"We haven't found them."

"Hmm. Commander Waters wouldn't endanger the citizens of *Titan*."

"Maybe she didn't have a choice," replied Lady Vermont.

Emmeline remembered. The Imperial Command did not know that Anastasia had ordered *Titan* to separate. She recalled the computer announcing the beginning of the separation process. It meant that all citizens, including her father, would have been transferred to the outer section. She wanted to jump with joy.

Dad might be alive and well!

Emmeline stood up and paced around the control room. She wondered where Anastasia could have hidden the citizens of *Titan*. Could she find her father before the Imperial Command? She paused.

Should I give them the piece? Maybe I can get them off my back and rescue my father. At least I could save him!

But then another thought invaded her mind.

The queen.

Sadness and regret vanished, and anger rose.

It is my fault!

The queen had attacked Emmeline's home, killed the man she loved, and destroyed her future. She had to pay for everything she had done.

If I give up the piece, I do not stand a chance. The queen will never stop, and I must destroy her!

CHAPTER 6: MYSTERIOUS SIGNALS

OORT'S CLOUD

Byron still felt lightheaded. He massaged his temples as he listened to Clio's and Micah's voices echo on the intercom. His stomach was unsettled and felt slightly dizzy. With precision, requiring no effort or thought, he entered the coordinates to rendezvous with the other ships. Swiftly, the craft charged ahead.

"Are you ready?" said Micah.

"Yes."

Shutting down their engines and firing thrusters, the three crafts aligned.

"Extending connectors," said Clio.

Her ship was in the middle, and two short narrow tunnels appeared from both sides. They joined with the tunnels from Byron's and Micah's ships.

"Connection complete," said Clio.

"Begin decompression," Byron ordered.

The passageways between the ships filled with air. The docking procedure was soon complete.

After half an hour, Byron opened the airlock. He had to bend over and walk a short distance to meet Clio, who stood near the other end. She appeared pale, and as soon as he reached her, she rushed forward and hugged him. She sobbed. Byron felt his heart break.

Why them? Why did this happen to them?

He wiped her tears as they parted. "It will be okay."

"No. No. It won't be."

"Let's not jump to conclusions."

"Byron."

"Clio," he said, placing his hand on her face. "We will find a way. Okay?"

A stream of tears seeped down her face. He held her again. In a minute, the other airlock opened, and Micah stepped in.

A strong, pungent smell flooded the ship. Byron scrunched his nose and turned toward him. "What's that?"

"Uh, just something to get rid of the awful smell."

Byron's stomach churned.

"It's terrible," Clio remarked.

"What do you think happened?" Byron asked.

"Something…grabbed us. That's the best way I can describe it," Micah said, shaking his head.

"The blackness," Byron added, remembering.

"How did we get here? It would take days for a big ship to get to the Oort's belt," Clio said.

They looked at the massive region full of irregular icy objects that moved in different directions.

"This cannot be happening," Clio said, tears filling her eyes.

"I know," said Byron.

"I tried hailing the Imperial Command and *Titan*. I can't get through," Clio said, wiping her tears.

"Me neither," Micah added, "I tell you; this is crazy!"

"What do we do?"

Byron had an idea. "Vega 9 is located ten light-years from these coordinates. It's an unmanned Imperial Command outpost. We can get there in a couple of days."

His friends looked unsure.

"It's run by a computer that monitors this region of space and transmits in reports every month. Perhaps we can send a message to the Imperial Command or *Titan* using its communication array."

"It's too far away," said Clio.

"It's closer than *Titan*!" Byron argued.

"Let's head toward *Titan*," said Micah.

Byron arched his eyebrows. "We do not have the fuel. We'll never get through the Kuiper belt."

"Is there anything on Vega 9?" asked Clio

"I don't know."

"How will we survive?"

"I don't know."

Micah walked up and down. "We only have emergency rations and water and limited fuel, and your strategy is to go to an abandoned station!"

"Look…" He shut his mouth as a buzzing sound interrupted him. The noise was coming from his ship. The trio stepped into Byron's cockpit. A panel to their left beeped.

"What's that?" Micah asked.

Excitement resonated through Byron's, "I programmed the computer to search for signals," replied Byron.

"Looks like it found one," Clio commented.

They peered into the screen.

"What is it?" asked Micah.

"It's an intermittent signal…emerging from a moon."

"Which one?" asked Micah

"Proxima 8."

"What do we know about it?"

Byron accessed the database.

"It's an inhabitable moon. The Imperial Command identified and cataloged it a few decades ago. Both *Freedom* and *Marion* visited it during their first missions."

"Did they detect a signal?"

Byron checked the records. "No."

The trio fell silent. Sitting in his chair, Byron said, "Something brought us here. We need to find why and who."

Micah nodded. "And the signal might have something to do with it."

CHAPTER 7: RUINS

AURORA, BRIDGE, DECK 1

L ady Vermont stood with her head high on the bridge of *Aurora*. Young men and women walked around, looking for the traces of the vessels. The *Aurora* was a medium-size ship, almost the same length as *Freedom*. With six decks, the craft was long, with a pointy front and a round end. Four structures originated at the back, each equipped with an engine. Its smooth white surface was shiny and clustered with small circular windows. The *Aurora* had left the dock six months ago. It had plans to go into deep space, which were interrupted by the unexpected visit of the Orias.

With years of practice, she had learned to control her fears and manage her stress levels during times like these. But then she corrected herself. She was worried. In her long, grueling, and painful life, she hadn't witnessed such a battle.

In between the beeps, and the silent murmurs of the surrounding humans, she felt her heartbeat. It was slow, steady. People thought she was heartless and cared little about others. It was true. She saw only facts. Being less emotional and more practical made her work effortless. She liked to keep it simple. She was efficient at burying emotions, but it had not come easy. Being a product of an experiment that should have failed had its pros and cons.

"Anything?" she asked the operations officer, Tristan Blake. The gloomy young fellow regarded her skeptically. He looked as if he had awakened from a deep sleep. His sloppy hair was cut noticeably short and made his ears pop out. Lady Vermont was glad he was not on the helm, as she felt he might fall asleep anytime.

"Not yet."

"Any sign of the colonist?" she asked, turning toward the science station.

The *Aurora* was not built for scientific purposes, and its crew wasn't experienced.

Officer Gus Lawson looked at her uncomfortably. "We are still looking." Gus was the youngest officer on the bridge, with blond hair, sharp blue eyes, and striking features. She thought that he might be pleasant in different conditions, but his present demeanor was not helpful, and it was evident he wasn't one of her fans.

"Let me know if you find anything," Lady Vermont said to the passive officer. It was unusual for a Tribunal to leave Earth and her presence usually made people uncomfortable. She didn't care. She had to find *Titan*. The mythical device fascinated her, and she did not want the Orias to get their hands on it. When she had boarded the ship, she realized she was making everyone uncomfortable. What choice did she have? She no longer trusted Admiral Vince because he supported Jacob. The result was the destruction of the entire fleet, which forced *Titan* to join the fight. Despite her efforts, they had not reached the perimeter on time, and by then, *Titan* and *Prometheus* had vanished.

Four days passed, and Lady Vermont spent most of it pacing up and down the bridge. She feared she would ruin the fine carpet underneath her feet. She had hardly slept or eaten. Captain Desmond Allan was the same. He never left the bridge, and anxiousness filled his features. They needed to give an update to Imperial Command every twelve hours. Unfortunately, the crew of *Aurora* was not making progress.

Desmond sat extremely straight with his eyes locked on the viewer. His partially gray hair was neatly combed backward. His nose was long and sharp. Lady Vermont had hardly seen him smile. She felt as if someone was holding a gun at his temple.

"The analyzes of the debris," said Gus and handed them over the preliminary reports.

She took a seat beside the captain and read. The entire Imperial Fleet had been destroyed. The perimeter had sustained heavy damage. They had recovered several broken Orias ships, and a few of their parts had been salvaged for study.

This is not good.

Lady Vermont sulked as she read the reports. They had to rebuild the perimeter, and it was going to be a lengthy and tedious repair job. The science team could not explain the disappearance of *Titan* and *Prometheus*. They had nothing except a faint ion trail of the engine heading toward Saturn. It differed from the Orias, and it wasn't the *Titan* or *Prometheus*.

"What do you think of this?" Lady Vermont asked Desmond.

"I do not know, but we can't leave,"

"We have to follow it."

He hesitated. "I think we should stay here. The Orias might return anytime."

Lady Vermont's level of discomfort rose. "Do you think Commander Waters would engage in battle and endanger the colonists?"

"No."

"What if the trail belongs to *Titan's* inner section? What if she sent them away?"

"Lady Ver—"

"We have to investigate."

Reluctantly, Desmond agreed.

The *Aurora* glided toward the rings of Saturn. The bridge was silent, and the tension was high. Fumbling her hands together, Lady Vermont heard her heartbeat again, which was odd. She had never felt like this.

I don't need to worry; why the hell am I worried.

"The trail?" he asked.

"It disappears near the planet's outer rings. Our scanners cannot penetrate. However, a few minutes ago, we detected something that could be a craft. But the reading is scrambled," replied Gus.

"Can we follow?" Desmond asked the pilot.

Oliver Bain, a skinny, tall guy with thin hair and a broad forehead, turned to face them. "No, sir."

Lady Vermont was glad to hear his voice. It appeared he had lost it in the last seventy-two hours.

Desmond nodded. "Gus, continue looking for the craft. Oliver, open a channel."

"Channel opened," said Oliver.

"This is Captain Desmond Allan of the *Aurora*. Unidentified craft, please respond."

The hail was met with silence.

"Sir, I have picked up something," said Gus.

"What?"

"It is a very faint signal. It could be a craft."

"Put it on the viewer…"

Between the clouds, they saw a tiny black object.

"What is that?"

Lady Vermont asked, "Could something survive there?"

"It can't. They would be destroyed," replied Desmond.

Like a ghost, the craft vanished into the dense atmosphere. Alarms went off on the bridge, and the *Aurora* glided toward the unknown craft.

CHAPTER 8: REPERCUSSIONS

TITAN, BRIDGE, DECK 1

Anastasia waited for answers.

"The sensors are offline. We have limited power, and I will need to do a long-range scan to find our current position," said Chris.

Edward remained silent.

Anastasia recalled the last torpedo, the purple cloud, and the rift in space. She shut her eyes. In her anger and eagerness to kill the queen, she had ignored Mykel's warnings.

The doors opened, and the medical team rushed to aid the bridge crew. Dr. Zac Scheben came next to her and placed his medical bag on the floor. The oldest crew member refused to retire. His hair was white as snow, and wrinkles creased his narrow face.

"Commander," he said in his soft voice.

"How is the crew?" she asked, wheezing. The floor dimmed in front of her eyes. Her breathing was labored, and her throat was dry. Ignoring her, he began his examination.

"My crew," she mumbled, feeling as if her muscles were on fire.

Zac stopped at her right leg. "You have sustained a fracture," he said.

"I'm fine…"

"No, you are not."

"Doctor! The crew!"

Before answering her, he drew out a pen-like object and pushed it into her left arm. In a moment, the pain became bearable, and with it, her breathing became normal.

"Better?" he asked. "We are still assessing the situation and got here as fast as we could."

Anastasia nodded.

The bridge brightened, and she noted the broken lights above her head.

"Commander, how are you?" asked Edward, coming to her side.

The tactical officer had scratches on his bruised face. His uniform was torn at the arm.

"I am fine. Are you hurt?"

"No. I will check on the crew."

"Thank you."

Zac worked wordlessly. Her eyes set on Adrian. A nurse was attending to him. A sense of relief rushed through her when he opened his eyes.

"Doctor, he might have a concussion," said the nurse.

"Take him to the medical bay."

Her pain reduced, and Anastasia got the chance to weigh the damage to the bridge. There was debris everywhere. Two of the consoles were scorched. The viewscreen was cracked, and pieces of glass and rubble covered the floor. The roof bore several cracks. Anastasia cursed under her breath. It was her fault. She should not have followed the queen. In her quest to end this war, she had forgotten about the rift. Emmeline's words echoed in her mind.

Do not enter the rift. It's a gateway.

Tears welled up in her eyes.

It is my fault. This one is on me.

"Commander, you have a broken ankle, and the wounds on your forehead and shoulder need treatment. We should head to the medical bay," Zac said.

She had no energy to argue with him. With Zac's support, Anastasia got on her feet. Sadness engulfed her as she saw Dr. Isaac Flynn on the stretcher. Blood flowed out of his left ear. The medics carried the unconscious exobiologist to the elevator. Anastasia felt dizzy, and her pain returned. Her eyes began eyes shut. She heard the doctor's voice but couldn't reply. Suddenly, she blacked out.

TITAN, MEDICAL BAY 1, DECK 3

Anastasia went in and out of consciousness, barely aware of her surroundings. She saw shadows moving at a fast pace and heard voices and beeping. Her mouth was dry, and she couldn't sense her leg. She had the urge to rush to the bridge, but she had no energy. Soon it was quiet again, and she fell into a void.

The next time Anastasia opened her eyes, she was fully alert within minutes. She no longer felt pain. The medical bay was bright, busy with doctors and nurses attending the crew. Six crew members occupied patient beds, and the beds to her left were empty.

"Ah…Commander!" Zac said happily. "You are awake."

She managed a smile. "What happened?"

"You fell unconscious. The injuries to your ankle, shoulder, and head are healing."

She moved her feet and wiggled her toes.

"How is the crew?"

"Recovering."

"I am glad." She let out a deep breath. "How long was I out for?"

Zac moistened his lips. "Two days."

"Two days!" she replied, startled.

"Your injuries were extensive."

She gradually got off the bed and stood. Except for a slight ache in her right ankle, Anastasia felt nothing.

"Take it easy," said Zac.

PROMETHEUS, INFIRMARY, DECK 7

Mykel felt a sharp pain. Gasping for air, he opened his eyes.

"Ah!" he screamed in agony, and the bright light over his head increased his agitation.

"Captain, please stay calm," said the nurse, appearing in his vision.

He wasn't listening and tried to sit up. The medical bay spun in front of his eyes. He felt a stabbing pain in the back of his head. The ear-deafening alarm wasn't helping.

"What's happening?" he asked the nurse.

"Sir...you have got—"

"Don't sir me!" he yelled.

A sturdy pair of hands eased him down onto the bed. The doctor regarded him. The seven-foot, tough-looking man with sharp green eyes was Peter Hudson. In another life, he could have been a boxer.

"Captain...you have a severe concussion. You need to lie down and take it easy," Peter said gently and eyed the nurse.

"What's wrong with the ship..." he asked but passed out before the doctor could reply.

Mykel was calmer when he reopened his eyes. The alarm had stopped blaring, and the pain was gone. Katia stood at his bedside. The skin on her neck was blue and bore several scratches.

"Hello, Captain," said Katia.

"Hi. Did the doctor have a look at your injuries?"

"Yes. I am fine. I was the lucky one."

"How is the crew?"

"Struggling."

He held his head, "The ship?"

"You do not have to worry. It's under control."

the robot lift the head of the Orias and walk in the other direction.

Chapter 9: The Girl Who Doesn't Cry

Titan, Anastasia's Quarters, Deck 4

The pain in Anastasia's ankle had settled, and Zac was sitting beside her doing a follow-up scan. She was reading recent updates from each department on the pad.

"You need to take a break," he said.

It was not the first time she had heard that. How could she rest? They were at the edge of an event horizon, lost. She didn't even know their location, and they couldn't reach Imperial Command. Their sensors, long-range scanners, and communications were offline, and power was still at fifty percent capacity. The crew was working round the clock to finish the repairs.

How can I relax?

Zac was doing his job, and she decided not to argue with the doctor.

Zac left, and she spent the better half of her day going through reports. They were making progress. The crew was busy doing damage control. After the incident, ninety percent of the crew had reported to the medical bay. Most of them endured minor injuries. However, a few had suffered major injuries, including severe burns. They were still recovering. The doctor told her the crew was frightened.

That's expected.

As their commander, Anastasia needed to be their rock. But she felt embarrassed, guilty, and angry. She wanted to weep and tried to stifle her tears. The ache in her chest was growing. It was her mistake. She should have never followed the queen's ship. *Titan* should have never fired.

There's no point in thinking about it now.

Sleep-deprived, she pushed herself to work. But she was exhausted and couldn't focus. Guilt, pain, and tiredness took over. She lay back on her bed and watched the stars as she fell asleep.

TITAN, BRIDGE, DECK 1

The next day, Anastasia returned to the bridge. Chris was at his post, Edward was checking the status of the weapons, and Evan was busy on his console. Adrian was at the helm. He looked better and had reported to duty yesterday.

"Report," she said, looking at Chris.

"I have done multiple long-range scans and assessed all incident logs and data. Here is what happened. We know the cloud is a doorway that takes the Orias from one point to another. When *Titan* entered the rift and fired, there was a breach. The Orias ships were thrown to the opposite side, while the explosion opened a new fissure, and *Titan* and *Prometheus* were pushed through it.

"We are not in enemy space?"

"No. Thank God! I have not detected any Orias ships or the purple cloud. I think if *Titan* hadn't fired, we would have definitely reached enemy territory."

"Are you telling us we were lucky?" remarked Adrian.

"We were lucky," Chris replied, glancing at Poseidon.

Anastasia didn't know how to respond.

"Where are we?" she asked, feeling her heart drumming in her chest.

"If the sensors are working correctly, we have traveled through the rift and a distance of..." His voice faded away.

"Chris?"

"Twenty thousand light-years," he mumbled.

Every sound on the bridge died except for the beeping of the science workstation.

"Are you sure?"

"I am sure."

She shut her eyes. "Bring the viewer online."

On the edge of a black hole, thousands of miles from home. There was no help. No calling for backup. The *Prometheus* was damaged. How would they get back home? She did not know and shivered at the realization.

TITAN, DECK 1

Anastasia went through Chris's report over and over. She accessed Crystal Lab scans to make sure he was not mistaken. She hated what she found. They were lost, millions of miles away from home. Anastasia covered her face with her hands.

What the hell did I do?

Abruptly, she stood up and marched to the window. With most of its lights off, *Prometheus* stood silently. Their attempts to reach the ship had failed. The ship had sustained heavy damage. *Titan's* sensors showed life on the *Prometheus*. Its core was damaged, and she speculated the communication system was down. She would have to wait.

The monitor beeped.

She returned to her desk.

"Yes."

The face of a robot appeared.

"Commander, Evox reporting."

Evox was the contact point for the remaining robots on *Titan*. She assigned tasks to Evox, who handed them out to the other robots. As soon as she had awakened, she ordered Evox to seal the decks that had become a part of a war zone. There were Orias and human corpses with blood and gore everywhere. She felt the need to protect her crew from horror.

"Update."

"The cleanup is complete. The quarantine on decks ten, four, and five has been lifted."

"Excellent."

"The casualties of war have been taken to the medical bay. As instructed, I took ten intact Orias corpses to the morgue for study."

That should keep Dr. Isaac Finch busy for a while.

"Thank you," she spoke numbly.

She left her office and walked toward the bridge.

"Commander," called a familiar voice.

Adrian caught up with her.

"Yes, Adrian."

Adrian gulped and looked uncertain.

"What is it?"

"I think you need to come with me to the hangar deck."

Her heart skipped a beat. She had forgotten. How could she? "Argon."

Adrian's eyes dropped. "I know. But it's worse than you think."

TITAN, DOCKING BAY, DECK 10

With Adrian on her side, Anastasia sensed her pulse rise as she almost ran toward the end of the corridor. The doors hissed open, and she saw Aceline.

"Dr. Keston! She should be in the outer section. She shouldn't be on *Titan*."

"I know," answered Adrian, "Her daughter is here too…"

Anastasia's eyes widened when she noticed Selina was standing a little away from her sobbing mother.

"How? How?"

"The robots found them on deck three. They were trapped in an elevator because of a system breakdown. Fortunately, Selina wasn't hurt, but Aceline suffered a head injury. She was in the medical bay and has just gained consciousness."

"Why didn't we find Argon before?"

"The docking bay was quarantined, and the crew has been doing their best," Adrian replied.

We should have done better.

Anastasia rushed toward the crying mother but froze. Argon's body lay where she had left him. His lips were blue, skin gray, eyes dull with exploded pupils. She looked away. She wanted to ask Aceline what she was doing onboard *Titan*, but she controlled herself. A mother was grieving. Aceline fell on her knees and held Argon's hand. Anastasia's heart was crushed, and she wondered how she would react if she lost her daughters. She heard a sniff and saw Adrian wiping tears off his face.

"Sorry, Commander."

"It's all right," she whispered.

Sorrow filled the hangar as men and women mourned the loss with Aceline. Her eyes then settled on Selina. She stood near her mother, silent and still as stone. Her eyes were fixed on her brother's dead body. Anastasia waited for a reaction, but there wasn't any. Her face remained blank and expressionless. Her brown eyes turned toward Anastasia, regarded her for a second, but then turned back to her mother. She took a step forward and held her weeping mother. Aceline's wailings resonated throughout the hangar deck, and everyone, including Anastasia, felt her pain. Tears filled the commander's eyes, but she noticed Selina did not shed a single tear.

CHAPTER 10: HIDDEN SORROWS

UTOPIS

Emmeline considered her options. She was a fugitive, hunted by her own people. Her next move could be her last. For the last four days, she had continued to listen to transmissions, only returning to *Raven* for a couple of hours to sleep and eat. She had downloaded several transmissions between the Imperial Command, Discovery, and Challenger colonies. Heaps of information were at her disposal. But right now, she craved hearing about her family and friends. She changed the frequency and waited.

Nothing.

She kept searching until she heard the word *Titan*. She read with great interest. Imperial Command had not yet found *Titan* or the *Prometheus*. The Imperial Command fleet, under the command of Admiral Donavan, had been destroyed. Her chin dropped to her chest.

Where is Titan? *What happened to the commander? Did the Orias kill them all?*

No one could give her an answer. Feeling dejected, she decided to leave. She programmed the communication center to continue downloading messages from specific frequencies and relaying them to the *Raven*. As she stepped out of the door, something occurred to her. Thrusting her hands into her pocket, she removed a small transparent box with a hexagonal object. It was called the trojan. A device specifically designed to receive messages only from her. She placed the trojan underneath the dashboard, glanced around for a moment, and walked away.

RAVEN

The airlock closed with a loud thud. She immediately removed the uncomfortable suit. Despite the stale, chilly air, she felt better. Spending most of the last four days in the suit was rough and confining. At least on the *Raven*, she could walk around and breathe freely. As she stretched her legs, a thought came to mind, and she sighed. On *Titan*, there were many people around her, and she wanted to be alone. Now she was alone, without a soul in sight.

She stifled her tears and walked to the cockpit. *Raven* was still docked with Utopis. Sitting quietly on the chair, she glared at the stars. Watching the cosmos always comforted her. It was fascinating, yet dead and bare. A bleep resonated. She gulped. Sensors had detected an Imperial Command patrol ship. Her first instinct was to run. But that would attract attention. Emmeline quickly switched off the equipment, and the ship became dead silent. She folded her arms and waited.

Time passed sluggishly. The patrol ship had left a long time ago, but Emmeline did not have the heart to turn on the engines. Fear gripped her. Various scenarios ran through her mind, and she pictured spending her life behind jail or on the run.

What kind of life would that be?

After twelve hours of struggle, she had no choice. With a heavy heart, she flicked the switch. The console beeped, and the short-range scanners came to life. Taking a sharp breath, she began searching. Emmeline sat back and put her hands behind her head. The patrol ship was long gone. But she had to be careful. She needed to disappear.

Miles away from where *Titan* had once stood, *Raven* flew along the remains of the perimeter. Sadness engulfed her as she observed the wreckage. Putting her sentiments aside, she tapped on the console. *Raven* glided at the inner edge of the perimeter. The complex network of pillars stood in silence. Far away from the remnants of the battlefield, the *Raven* came to a stop. She studied the maps on the pad downloaded by Argon. Just like Delta knew of the perimeter's vulnerabilities, so did others. Argon had uncovered coordinates of another gap in the perimeter.

The *Raven* reached the coordinates, and Emmeline saw the gap. The last time she had crossed the perimeter, it had resulted in her best friend's death. Still unsure what to do, she wanted to vanish and clear her head.

She paced the ship through the large pillars. The vessel inched toward two pillars that were broken in the middle. Fortunately for her, this was less tricky than last time. It looked easy, but Emmeline struggled with changing the coordinates and managing the speed. The *Raven* bumped into a pillar.

"Shit!" she muttered.

She reversed engines. After adjusting the coordinates, she gradually increased speed. The ship emerged on the other side.

Delta would have done this better.

She wanted to cry. She missed her friend, but she controlled herself.

A thin rim of asteroids formed the rings of Uranus. They rotated around the planet in a reformed motion. Most of *Raven's* systems were not automated. She constantly struggled between scanning the vicinity and flying the ship at a regular pace. It had taken her two days to get here. She had no trouble finding it. A year ago, she had tracked and detected a new asteroid that had arrived from another system. It was caught in the planet's gravitational pull, becoming a part of the asteroid family that circled the planet. She slowed and picked a location on a forty-mile-long interstellar object. She calculated and recalculated her approach. Then, matching its speed and rotation, she made a successful landing. Once the *Raven* landed, she sat back and closed her eyes.

I am safe for now.

No one would look for her here. They thought she was on *Titan* or following her father's escape plan. Only two people knew of this asteroid: herself and Dr. Chris Kent. Of course, it was cataloged in the Discovery Colony's database, but she did not expect the Imperial Command to go through the list of all the interstellar objects Crystal Lab had detected, cataloged, and monitored.

Shutting down all systems, she walked to the corner and sat on the icy floor. After a while, she got bored.

I should check out the piece. I never got a chance to study it.

She zipped open Argon's bag, pulled out the plaque, and froze. Another figure had appeared on it.

CHAPTER 11: REMNANTS

AURORA, BRIDGE, DECK 3

The *Aurora* gradually entered the sea of small rocks floating freely in space. A massive asteroid threatened the majestic ship. It targeted and destroyed the asteroid in seconds. The bridge shook as the small pieces collided against the shields. The craft glided ahead, looking for any trace of the citizens of *Titan*. They had picked up a faint ion trail, but the sensors could not identify its origin. It could be a hoax, or it might be the survivors. They had to find out.

The dead silence bothered Lady Vermont. She wished one of the crew would speak. Her eyes searched the area, but all she saw was dust and rocks of all sizes. Lady Vermont huffed, and frustration filled her. She was grateful she felt little or nothing at all. She had to train herself to control her emotions to survive. It had worked well so far. But today, they were getting the best of her. There were too many questions, and she was getting tired of waiting for answers.

Titan *can't just vanish*.

It was just not her. The bridge was engulfed with a sense of dread, sadness, and loss.

"Can we still detect it?" asked Desmond.

"Yes, but it keeps disappearing from our sensors," replied Gus.

"Don't lose it," ordered Desmond.

"Are you sure they are here?" Lady Vermont asked, "How could the outer rim survive in the middle of this?"

Desmond eyed her. "Good point. It could be a ruse."

"Sir, I detect the object...now at our port side. I don't understand. A minute ago, it was right in front of us."

Desmond and Lady Vermont exchanged worried glances.

"It's a ruse," she concluded.

"Helm, get us out of here," said Desmond

The engines revved, and the ship turned. Soon, the *Aurora* emerged out of the rings.

"Helm, put the ship in lower orbit and start searching."

Many hours later, Oliver reported from the helm, "Sir, I have something. An object. It's within the gases of the planet."

"Are you sure?"

"Yes. It's in the troposphere. The dense cluster of gases makes it harder to trace."

"It's the perfect hiding place," commented Desmond.

"What is it?" asked Lady Vermont.

The image on the screen changed, and they saw the object. It was round, wheel-like.

Before the words left Lady Vermont's lips, Desmond said, "It's the outer section of *Titan*. Scan for life signs."

Gus got busy on the science panel. "Sensors show ninety-five percent of the colonists are alive and in status."

"Ninety-five?" she said. "What happened to the five percent?"

Gus shrugged his shoulders.

"Open a channel," said Desmond, "Citizens of *Titan*. This is the *Aurora*. Please respond."

Silence engulfed the bridge.

"This is Captain Allan of the *Aurora*. Please respond."

They saw a white beam emerge from the object.

"We are being scanned," Gus said.

"We are here to help. Respond," stated Desmond.

The round object remained motionless.

"They have activated their weapons," Gus reported.

"What?" Lady Vermont said.

"There is no cause for concern. The Orias have left the system, and the fleet is guarding the perimeter."

Suddenly, the light vanished.

"They are lowering their weapons," said Gus.

"Sir, we are receiving a transmission," said Tristan.

"Put it through."

A robot appeared on the viewscreen. Multiple lights shined above it. Its white armor protected its blue humanoid body. Millions of circuits came together to give it vision, hearing, smell, but no sensation or taste. Its dead gray eyes gawked at *Aurora's* bridge crew. Its identification was printed in the left corner of his chest.

"Captain Desmond Allan," said the robot. "I am Otis. Apologies. I had to be certain. I am under strict instructions by Commander Waters to protect the citizens of *Titan*."

"Understood. Is everyone safe?"

"Nineteen thousand, eight hundred and nineteen citizens are in stasis."

"What happened to the rest of them?" asked Lady Vermont.

"Presumed dead."

Sadness filled the bridge.

"Are you sure?" asked Desmond.

"They are not in the inner section. Either they are dead or on *Titan*," it replied.

"Where is the inner section?" asked Lady Vermont.

"I do not know. To protect the citizens, Commander Waters separated the outer section and instructed us to leave and hide for four days. Once a safe passageway was assured, the Commander instructed me to head for the Discovery Colony."

"Good work, Otis."

"Thank you, Captain,"

"Do you know what happened to *Titan*?" asked Desmond.

"No."

AURORA, DESMOND'S OFFICE, DECK 1

Lady Vermont fumbled with her fingers as she paced around in the captain's office.

"Stop it. You are making me anxious," Desmond said.

"Sorry," she replied.

They had awakened a few citizens of *Titan* and were hoping to gain more information.

"I am going through the logs. *Titan* was boarded, and over fifty Orias ships attacked the perimeter."

Lady Vermont took a seat opposite him.

"There was a disagreement between Commander Anastasia Waters and Admiral Jacob Donovan. Anastasia believed Jacob was unstable. Against Anastasia's suggestions, the Earth vessels followed Jacob, crossed the gates, and engaged the enemy."

"That was stupid," muttered Lady Vermont.

"Agreed. Before joining the battle, Anastasia separated the outer section and sent her people to safety," Desmond read.

"After that?"

"Nothing."

She hung her head. "Who is unaccounted for?"

"Well, it's a lengthy list," Desmond responded, reading the names. "Oh…Emmeline Augury."

Lady Vermont froze. "What about her? She isn't aboard?"

"No. She was supposed to be in the brig. Technically, during the attack, they should have transferred her to the outer section with the others."

"So, she is on *Titan*," concluded Lady Vermont.

"I can't say," he said. "Dr. Chris Kent. He is not amongst the citizens."

"He is on *Titan*. He will go down with the Crystal Lab," said Lady Vermont without hesitation.

"This doesn't give us much." He put the pad aside. "I have asked my crew to look for more trails."

"Is that possible?"

"We have to try. There is one person we need to speak to."

The doors opened, and Arthur, Emmeline's father, stepped in, followed by two officers.

"Leave us," said Desmond.

The guards stepped out.

Lady Vermont approached him. "Mr. Augury."

"Lady Vermont."

"I am sorry for what happened to your daughter."

He gaped at her. "Are you?"

She smirked. "Taking it out on me will not help. We need to know what happened to *Titan*."

"I thought you knew."

"We would like to hear your side of the story," stated Desmond.

"Really. How about the Imperial Command fucked up!"

Lady Vermont tried to control her amusement. In her perspective, it had. Politics was a game, and not everyone knew how to play it. Jacob wanted unlimited power, which led to nothing but his own demise. Unfortunately, because of him, many innocent people died.

"Mr. Augury," said Desmond.

"You have nothing on me," Arthur said.

"We are not accusing you of anything," said Desmond. "I want to know what happened."

Arthur's face turned grim, and he sank into the chair. In the next ten minutes, he recited the events in great detail. Lady Vermont was disappointed. They had discovered nothing new.

"Thank you," said Desmond.

"Am I free to go?" Arthur asked sarcastically.

"You are not a prisoner, but your daughter is a fugitive. We might like to talk to you soon. And you should alert the Imperial Command if Emmeline contacts you."

Arthur folded his arms and regarded the captain. "Are you done?"

"Yes. Thank you."

Arthur simply got up, turned, and left without another word.

"He is not going to help us, is he?"

"What do you think?" remarked Lady Vermont.

The intercom buzzed.

"Yes?"

"Captain, we found another trail in this area. It doesn't belong to the Orias or any Imperial Command ships."

"Are you sure?"

"Yes."

"Can you identify it?"

"Yes. It belongs to the *Raven*, registered to Cadet Argon Keston."

Their eyes met.

"Begin a search for the *Raven*," ordered Desmond.

Lady Vermont sat thoughtfully. "Emmeline escaped with Argon."

"We don't know that."

"Who else would rescue her?"

"We shouldn't make any assumptions."

She disagreed. "But it is possible. Who else is missing?"

Desmond checked the list. "Dr. Aceline Keston and Ms. Selina Keston," he read as his face turned stern. "Argon's family is on *Titan*."

CHAPTER 12: THE FORGOTTEN PROTOTYPE

TITAN, ADRIAN'S QUARTERS, DECK 6

Adrian felt dizzy from time to time, but he ignored it. After completing his shift, he returned to his quarters. He recalled little, except darkness, after *Titan* fired the last torpedo. He raised his head and looked up at the heavens. The open space around them was unnerving. It felt like anything could appear and snatch them.

Adrian reached out to the small box and picked up the transparent, soft, oval-shaped pill. He swallowed it and walked into his bedroom.

After changing, he slid under the blankets. According to the commander, everyone was supposed to get at least six hours of sleep. Adrian grumbled. For the last two nights, he had nightmares. On the first night, he watched Delta dying. No matter how much he tried to save her, it was in vain. Yesterday he saw Argon's dead face in his dream. He wanted to scream, sob, and let it all out. But for his comrades, he had to be strong. He was the second in command. He was glad that they hadn't lost any of the commanders. The idea of taking over command of *Titan* daunted him.

I am not ready for that.

RAVEN

Emmeline sat staring at the plaque. She bit her lip. A new puzzle had appeared.

Seven pieces. Seven puzzles.

She had discovered one piece, which had brought chaos and death. Just two months ago, her life was simple, peaceful, blissful. She had everything. And now she was alone, drifting among the stars, not knowing where to go. She placed the plaque on the cold floor and glared out of the window. What was she to do? She had no passion, no need or desire to continue her quest. In the last forty-eight hours, she wondered if it was best to leave this to fate. Just drift into space and die. Vanish from history. Who would care? Why would they?

The two bags and a backpack left by Argon caught her attention. Getting on her knees, she emptied one of them. She regarded the piece, the meteoroid, and the plaque. In the other bag, she found a small rectangular box. It looked like a jewelry box. She flipped it open and saw the mesh of thin wires and tiny round sensors.

"A mask," she muttered.

A perfect tool to fool prying eyes.

She smirked placed it back in the bag. In a corner underneath a T-shirt, she noticed another plastic box. It was lightweight. She opened it to find hundreds of thin rectangular chips.

"Credits…" she muttered.

Of course, to vanish, they needed credits, and Argon had made arrangements. She was sure these were untraceable and placed the box back in the bag.

I don't know what I want to do.

She picked up the two decoders and observed them. They were designed to run algorithms at immense speed and extract access codes from any panel.

"Well, I know what it feels like to be a thief."

The communicator buzzed, and it automatically transferred recent messages on the pad.

One by one, she went through the messages. Most of them were irrelevant to her. She wasn't interested. But then she stumbled upon communication between Imperial Command and *Aurora*. At first, she was excited. They had found the citizens of *Titan* alive and well. Her heart broke into pieces as she continued to read. They had her father.

"No."

She thought the entire universe was scheming against her. Lady Vermont sent him over to Earth to be interviewed further.

"No. No. Not Dad. I should go back. Say sorry and beg for forgiveness," she mumbled. "This will be over. I should just give myself up."

Then she thought, *will it be over?* She clenched her jaw. It wouldn't solve anything. Her family name would still be tainted. She started this, but she did not know if she could finish it.

Confused, Emmeline stood up and grabbed Argon's backpack. Something fell near her feet. Her breath shook, and she gradually picked up a small square-shaped device. It was light as paper, around three inches wide. She rotated it in her hands and observed the hexagonal green striations with a red circle in the middle. It was a message. She placed it on the floor, pushed the red button, and took a seat. She almost jumped, and her heart pounded against her chest. A 3D image of Argon appeared. She blinked her eyes in disbelief. Seeing him was surreal.

"Hello, my darling," Argon said in his soft dreamy voice. "If you have found this recording, that means you will have to go on this journey alone. And I am sorry I'm not there with you."

Tears flooded her eyes.

"You are a fugitive. Your father or I—even *Titan*—may not be able to help you."

She wrapped her arms around herself.

"As daunting as it may be, I want you to continue on your journey. It is the only way to clear your name. To set things right."

"I can't. I-I don't know how," stammered Emmeline.

"Since I have known you, you have always found answers. You always did what was right." Argon paused, and his eyes dropped. "Promise me one thing. Tell me you will never give up. You will find your way home. You will finish what you started and return home. Even if you have to do it without me."

Grief shattered her, and her eyes remained fixed on Argon's face.

"All your life, you have chased mysteries to indulge your curiosity. I've supported you and never asked for anything. Today I will. Find the pieces, complete the mythical device, and clear your name. Finish what you started. Promise me you will never give up." He paused, then said, "I'm always with you, always."

With those words, the message ended, and darkness fell.

She sat there. Argon's words repeated in her mind.

Finish what you started. I'm always with you.

Emmeline remained frozen. A section of the vast blue planet was visible. The asteroids that formed the thin rim around the planet danced to the unheard tunes of the gravitational force and clashed with one another.

She wiped her tears with her sleeve.

"Okay," she muttered and forced herself to get up. She grabbed the plaque and tapped it. The borders of the plaque shimmered. She felt like she was peeping through a window with a frame made up of millions of stars and nebula of different colors. A figure of the sun appeared. She watched as dots emerged one after another, forming an elliptical shape. When the two points met, a tiny glow emerged. Then the plaque turned dark. From another corner, a dotted line appeared and formed an oval shape. It was shorter than the first one, and a small glow appeared when the dots met.

"What does this mean?" she muttered.

She returned to the cockpit and made herself comfortable on the chair in front of the computer. As she was about to start, she realized *Raven* was not *Titan*. The capacity of *Raven's* computer was limited, nor did it have access to databanks like *Titan*. She huffed and slammed her fist on the console.

Emmeline left the cockpit and walked in circles, thinking of her options. To solve the second puzzle on the plaque, she needed an enormous database and a powerful computer.

Where can I get one?

An idea popped into her head. Rushing to the pilot's chair, she began scanning her surroundings. At first, she checked for patrol ships. There weren't any. Then she extended the search parameters and stopped when she found the coordinates.

"I hope you are still there," she muttered, starting up the engines.

The *Raven's* engines groaned as it reduced its speed. Emmeline was grateful for the two-day uneventful flight. Tall towers that form the boundaries of the salvage yard stood with red lights on top of them. The *Raven* came to a halt, and Emmeline ran multiple algorithms and found the access codes. She transmitted them, and the lights on two towers turned green. The craft entered the salvage yard, and Emmeline looked with overwhelming grief at multiple, lifeless ships.

The salvage yard was an unorganized space. Several bulky debris, once part of the ships, were mixed with long-forgotten crafts floating in awkward positions in dead space. There was no catalog or systematic way of tracking a specific vessel. After their long voyage, the fate of several Imperial Command and private ships was decided here.

Emmeline's fingers danced on the keyboard, and the *Raven* slightly tilted to avoid a large piece of debris in its path. She reduced speed and saw a massive machine. The automated disintegrators were enormous, ugly structures resembling a large container that swallowed ships and debris, tore them apart, and recycled the parts. A cargo ship arrived and transported the recycled bits back to Earth monthly. She wished there were more of these machines because humans generated more waste than they recycled.

She maintained a sharp eye, which was the only way to find the derelict. Wreckage of all sizes surrounded the craft, and the *Raven* flew past two small ships drifting in space. She observed the cold, disfigured vessels and felt as if they were calling to her.

Emmeline was becoming restless; this was taking too much time. She had combed through at least half of the salvage yard and found nothing. Among a cluster of pieces floating in space stood a bulky gray craft. Her heart jumped with joy. The *Intrepid* was dark and appeared intimidating. Its middle part was seven decks tall, and its wings bent downward from the middle, almost giving it a look of a gigantic bird.

Emmeline pushed several buttons, and the craft adjusted its position alongside the lifeless ship. One thruster came online, and the *Raven* drifted closer. Emmeline made a few adjustments, and the *Raven's* airlock attached to the protruding docking area.

A loud thud echoed. Leaving only the essential systems online, Emmeline got ready. Once more, she stood in front of the airlock.

"I guess I should get used to this," she told herself.

Cautiously, she opened *Raven's* airlock and walked through. She glared at the hefty white circular door with a panel on one side. Ready with her scanner, she approached the panel. She ran several algorithms and found the access codes. Quickly, she punched them in, and the door opened with ease.

Emmeline peered into the bleak, void, dark interior. The door closed behind her. Usually, the lights would turn on, and the deck would be flooded with air, but this ship had been abandoned a long time ago. Emmeline's heart pounded in her chest. She constantly checked the scanner. There was no one else on board. However, she couldn't shake the notion that she was being watched. She cautiously took one step after another.

As she walked down the narrow corridor, she couldn't comprehend how people lived in such confined places. *Titan's* corridors were wide and roomy. *Intrepid* was a different story. It was made for a small crew, had narrow corridors, and only twenty living quarters. Unlike *Titan* or *Prometheus*, it did not have any recreation areas for people to come together. Overall, they did not design it for luxury.

Over one year ago, a private company, Zex, collaborated with Imperial Command to build two prototypes with advanced computers and Artificial Intelligence (AI). The first ship, *Endeavor*, was tested and worked efficiently for a while, but it suddenly self-destructed. The investigators first believed that the AI had malfunctioned but soon discovered a design flaw in the engine and decided not to launch the second ship, *Intrepid*.

Zex's representatives got into legal wars with the Imperial Command to take it back and fix it. But the contract was tight. The *Intrepid* was Imperial Command's property, and two months ago, they had scheduled to destroy it with no further testing. Emmeline knew about *Intrepid* because AIs fascinated her. She wanted to work with them and wished that *Titan* would get involved. That never happened. She was glad she got the chance to see it before it was destroyed. Today she wasn't interested in AI. She wanted an advanced computer, and *Intrepid* had one of the best ones.

The walk down three decks was exhausting, and she was weary. Finally, when she arrived at the science lab, Emmeline pushed the button, but the door did not open. Noticing it was ajar, she tugged her fingers in the gap and used her energy to shove it open. Out of breath, she glanced around the dark square room.

Under the bright stream of the lights on her helmet, she noted a long workstation sitting in silence. The room looked smaller than she expected. Taking a deep breath in, she began scanning part by part. Soon she discovered that the heart of the computer was integrated into the wall. It made it hard for her to get the central processor.

"Oh, this is going to be tough," she muttered.

With utmost patience, she studied and chose a section of the wall. Adjusting her disruptor, she aimed and began cutting. She didn't wish to damage the ship and had hoped to pick up the processor and leave, but there was no other alternative.

Cutting through the wall took her around three hours. She pressed her right arm, trying to relieve the pain. Cautiously, she removed the section of the wall and gaped. Several colorful cords intervened with each other and attached themselves to a hefty silver-colored oval structure inside a five-foot frame.

"This is not good," she said and slouched.

Fatigue took over, and she could not work any longer. Emmeline returned to *Raven* and got undressed. After ensuring no other ship was in the region, she came to stand in front of a door. It was Argon's quarters. Emmeline had been sleeping on the floor or the chair in the cockpit. She stepped inside the small room. It had a few pictures of Argon with his mother and sister. A narrow gray desk with a lamp hung from the roof. The desolate room appeared like a prison cell, dark and cold, with a small window opening into the cosmos. He had tried to decorate, but it was not home, and nothing compared to what she had on *Titan*. She got into the bed and snuggled the blanket. Her mind jumped from one pleasant memory to another. She felt better. Unknowingly, she smiled, and before she knew it, she fell asleep.

The next morning, she found one of Argon's T-shirts and wore it. She didn't bother to change her shorts and left the quarters. Emmeline barely ate and walked into the cockpit. The salvage yard looked the same. The automated disintegrators continued to break down the ships. Sitting on the pilot's seat, she turned on the scanner. Her scans were negative. The *Raven's* exterior was gray, dull, and matched the appearance of the debris around it. To an outsider, it almost looked like a part of the junkyard. But she had a bad feeling. She watched as a few pieces of rubble collided with each other and flew in different directions.

The faster I get this done, the quicker I can get out of here.

RAVEN

Toiling alone in the dark and cold was hard. By the third day, Emmeline had enough. She wanted to blast this thing, but she told herself it was worth it. There was no other sound except her breathing. She felt a strain on her neck, back, and hands, but she kept working. She had almost given up hope when the last connection severed.

"Thank god," she muttered.

Once disconnected, the massive frame with the processor lifted from the floor and began floating. She grabbed it immediately.

Once the airlock was secured, she removed her helmet and gave a sigh of relief. Getting the processor onboard had taken everything she had. She left it near the airlock and walked away.

Emmeline was in no shape to work, so she changed and ate. After leaving *Raven* in surveillance mode, she went to bed.

Emmeline tried to sleep but opened her eyes when she thought she heard something. Stretching her arms, she slept a bit more. A beep resounded. It was the scanner. She ran to the cockpit. Her heart leaped. A patrol ship was within scanning range. She bit her lips and peeped through the data. Gnawing her nails, she wondered what she should do. *Raven* was between a cluster of broken ships and still out of visual range. Maybe staying here longer would be best.

RAVEN

The patrol ship had not left the vicinity, and for now, the salvage yard was the perfect hiding place. Emmeline glanced at the food, and she knew she had enough. The rations looked like soup, full of processed potatoes, vegetables, and meat. It tasted fine, but she wanted to eat something else. Argon had not planned to stay on the ship for long and better rations would have been the least of his concern. But at least she wasn't starving.

She had limited time, so she began thinking of a way to integrate the *Intrepid's* computer. The *Raven* was more or less made up of secondhand parts, and its computer was no different. She looked at the schematics and found *Raven's* processor under the workstation.

Compared to *Intrepid's*, disconnecting *Raven's* computer was simple. She had considered leaving it intact, but that made little sense. Given the size of the new processor, she wondered if *Raven* had the extra power supply. She realized she might need a better workstation.

"This is irritating!" she screamed and turned away.

Emmeline cried and kicked the bed. She sat in the corner thinking about the past and cursing herself. After dealing with her frustration, she sat with her elbows on her knees and began thinking of solutions. The processor needed bigger space and more power, and for efficiency, she needed access to it from the cockpit.

"Time for more stealing," she muttered.

Her trip to *Intrepid* was shorter this time, and when she finished, she looked at the multiple screens and two large white boxes. She stepped into the unoccupied quarters that were next to the cockpit. She walked into the storage room, grabbed the toolkit, and returned.

Ready to begin, she said, "Sorry, Argon."

The smell of smoke spread in the compartment as she disconnected the bed from the wall and dragged it out of the room. Then, one by one, she installed the monitors on the wall. Once that was complete, she carefully set the processor in a corner. She drilled the frame with the processor into the wall of *Raven* and made sure it was secure. She pushed the two large power packs under the workstation in the left corner.

As time passed, Emmeline enjoyed the process and worked through the night. She forgot about the patrol ships. Crumbs of metal fell to the floor as she cut through the wall. When she was done, she removed the section of the wall and peered at the cockpit. Picking up the last screen, she walked into the cockpit and attached it to the wall.

One by one, she switched on the monitors. They functioned perfectly. Then she tested the power packs and linked them to the computer. It was ready. Fear grabbed her for a moment.

What if this didn't work? What if I did something wrong?

"Oh well, I have nothing to lose," she said and pushed the button. On the screens, three stars orbited around each other. She waited as the computer took time to reboot. Her legs felt tired, and she began to sit but stumbled backward.

"Oh, shucks!" she cried out, sitting on the frigid floor.

She hadn't thought of getting a chair.

Not wanting to disconnect the limited chairs on *Raven*, Emmeline paid a last visit to the dead ship. By the time she returned, the computer was still rebooting. After setting the chair, she returned to the cockpit and glared at the lifeless debris. It had been days since she had seen anyone. She missed her family, friends, and *Titan*. Dismissing her thoughts, she turned her attention to the new computer.

It took her more time than she thought to complete the configuration and get the computer ready for use.

"Good afternoon. This processor is equipped with an AI. Do you want to grant the AI access to the ship's mainframe?" said the computer.

Emmeline's heart jumped to her throat. "No."

"Thank you," responded the computer and began a diagnostic.

"Can you do this any faster?" she complained.

The computer did not respond.

To pass the time, she looked for other ships in the vicinity. There were none. When she returned, the computer was ready.

"At last!" she grumbled and searched for databases. To her horror, there was nothing.

"What?" she shouted. "How is this possible? Computer, what happened to your multiple databases?"

"The databases were removed when the Imperial Command took control of the *Intrepid*."

Emmeline smacked her forehead with her hand. "Ah! I hate them!"

Stomping her feet, she cursed the Imperial Command. "Stupid idiots! What am I going to do now?!"

Emmeline bent forward and took a deep breath. Closing her eyes and pushing her anger aside, she tried to look for a solution. *Titan's* computers were updated regularly, and it received its data from the relay centers on the Discovery Colony.

Her eyes flung open, and she straightened her shoulders. "Oh shit."

Chapter 13: Lost Causes

Titan, Deck 8

T he crew of *Titan* stood at attention. Silence dominated the enormous hall. On the wall in front of them were large circular compartments that held the lifeless bodies of their comrades.

Twenty-seven people lost. The ones we could find. She didn't know if the rest of the citizens were alive. Did the Imperial Command find them? Only time would tell.

Anastasia's heart crumbled. Each commander had to bear the loss of his or her crew, but her situation was different. She was responsible for her crew and the citizens of *Titan*. Twenty-seven killed by Orias would haunt her forever.

Dr. Aceline Keston stood by the capsule that held her son's body. She kissed her son's hand and stepped away from Argon's capsule to come to stand with Adrian and Evan. Selina stood on her toes and looked at her brother for the last time. With her head bowed, she turned and came to stand near her mother. A whistle sounded. The capsules closed and rose above the ground, entering the holes in the wall one by one. The circular doors shut, and blue lights flashed. Everyone quietly mourned the loss of their people. The hall cleared, and Aceline left with her daughter. Standing alone, Anastasia gaped at the blue circular lights and hoped to return the bodies to their families on Earth.

She couldn't help but wonder, *how many more would end up in a wall like this?*

TITAN, ACELINE'S QUARTERS, DECK 4

Staring out of the window into the unknown space, Aceline sensed peace for the first time after several days. Her son was gone, and there was nothing she could do. The pity and constant condolences were becoming painful and unnecessary. *Titan's* crew was kind, and she understood. They wanted to support her, be there for her, and make sure she was all right.

How can I be all right?

She felt as if there was an invisible hole in her chest. No one could bring her son back. Even the most powerful men or women could not help her.

Aceline couldn't shed any more tears, as if she had used them all. Her home felt vacant and full of memories of a life that no longer existed. Will she be able to live? Survive? The stars looked so foreign, but a part of her was happy that they were no longer in their system. She couldn't face her husband, not now. What would he say? How would she explain? How would he react? He would blame her for leaving him behind.

But he chose it. He was a part of the Imperial Fleet.

Argon had been fighting a formidable enemy, and he died. Was he prepared? She did not know. But she knew he was on the hangar deck trying to help Emmeline. A few of her colleagues expressed their concerns and suggested that Argon had made a grave mistake. Aceline was not interested in gossip, although she blamed Emmeline. She was the reason Argon was there. If she had not left the system, perhaps both Delta and Argon would have been alive today.

For several days, she had debated over this matter. She wanted to scream. She wanted to give up and walk away. Who was to blame? What could she do? Disheartened, she stepped into her room and remembered the last time she had seen her son. He was here, holding her hand. He said goodbye. She would have preferred it if he had escaped with Emmeline. At least he would have been alive.

Sadness took over her, and she gazed at Poseidon for a long time. She wished it had swallowed *Titan*. She would have died in her sleep and never found out the truth. It would have been good. But she remembered it all too well. The pod's door opened. She felt panicked, claustrophobic, and collapsed on the floor. Selina was waiting for her. They had left the outer rim while the robots were busy fighting the Orias. She didn't know what she was doing, but she wanted to find her son. The computer informed her he was on the hangar deck. They rushed into the elevator. She heard a loud blast. The elevator shook and tumbled. A loud bang echoed, and everything went dark. She woke up several days later in the medical bay, and today she had buried her son.

Nothing is worth living anymore.

That thought sent a shiver down her spine, and then she realized. She had to live for Selina.

Aceline sat in the dark. She could hear the commotion outside her door. *Titan* was under repair. All the decks were being cleaned. Soon all the evidence of the war and massacre would be gone. But she could never forget. Never. A stream of light brightened the room. With sore eyes, she saw Selina.

"Lights," said Selina softly.

The living room brightened.

Selina came to her, holding her purple blanket.

"Mom, I can't sleep."

Aceline took her in her arms and stroked her hand on her back. For several minutes, they sat in silence.

"Selina…can I ask you a question?"

"Anything, Mom."

"Did you pull the emergency button?"

Selina lifted her head, and their eyes met.

"What is that?" she asked.

"The button that opens the door to the stasis chamber."

Selina shook her head from side to side.

"How did your door open?"

"I wanted to get out."

Aceline didn't understand. "What do you mean?"

"I told it I wanted to leave."

Aceline head ached, and she didn't want to think.

"Did you open the door to my pod?"

She nodded.

"Why? Why did you want to leave?"

Selina's face turned solemn. "Because I heard Argon. He was calling me."

Blood drained from Aceline's face.

CHAPTER 14: PROXIMA 8

PROXIMA 8

The ships turned and headed toward the spot where they had exited the dark portal. It had taken them over two days to reach the moon where the mysterious signal had originated. The signal had long vanished, and no matter how many times Byron scanned, he didn't find it. He didn't know what they would discover and hoped to find a way home. If they found nothing, they could always head to Vega 9.

The moon dominated his view screen. The ships entered the atmosphere which was light bluish and full of deadly gases like methane. His spacecraft vibrated, and Byron adjusted his heading. The ship became stable, and they flew toward the northern hemisphere, following the signal's origin. Once the ships neared the surface, it was a different view. The moon's surface was red, unwelcoming, and marked with remnants of several dead volcanoes. Byron saw mountain ranges and dunes covered with red dust.

"How much further?" asked Micah over the intercom.

"We should have a visual soon."

The ship reduced speed, and Byron sat with his eyes wide open.

"This cannot be happening," he muttered.

Triangular structures stood on a spacious, rough plateau.

"What the heck?" yelled Micah.

"Are you sure they did not report these structures?" asked Clio.

"Absolutely sure," replied Byron.

"I tell you, next, we will find an atmosphere that supports human life," mocked Micah.

Byron wasn't paying attention. The terrain around the structure was uneven, full of cracks and rocks of all sizes.

"We cannot land here," said Byron.

The ships moved north and found a plateau surrounded by hills.

"Okay. Let's land here and then walk," Byron said.

"Wow. That is going to be a long walk," Micah said.

Dust particles flew into the atmosphere as landing gears of the three crafts emerged. The vessels landed with a thud on uneven ground full of pebbles and sand. The engines became silent.

"Has the signal returned?" Byron asked, rising to his feet.

"Not yet," Clio replied. "Are you sure it came from here?"

"Definitely, let's check it out," he said.

They suited up. Byron felt strange. The *Titan* Squadron had been trained for space exploration. Their extensive training involved spacewalks, piloting several crafts, tactical and weightlessness training. He had spent over six weeks on the moon. But being on Proxima 8 felt more real and terrifying. There was no trainer, no help, or backup. They were on their own. His life had taken a sudden turn. After finishing his qualification and training, he was meant to go home. Spend time with his family. Instead, he was in an alien world, trying to find answers.

Excited and terrified, he pushed the button, and the door to his ship gradually opened. As he took his first step, his heart drummed in his chest. The moon was red, barren, and unwelcoming. Multiple times, he checked the display in his right hand. It measured his heart rate, blood pressure, body temperature, and respiratory rate. He then scanned the surrounding environment. His suit calculated methane, water, carbon dioxide, nitrogen, dust, and radiation levels. The environment was unsuitable for life. Setting his fears aside, he walked toward Clio and Micah.

The trio began their walk on the alien surface. The wind was silent, the ground covered with layers of fine sand. Soon they reached the base of a small hill. Gradually, they climbed over the rocks. Byron stood at the top and saw the structure.

"Wow, I tell you, that thing should not be there," said Micah.

"Come on, keep moving," Byron ordered.

It took them five hours to reach their destination. He felt exhausted, wishing there was fresh air to breathe. As they neared the triangular structures, Byron's curiosity grew.

"What are they made up of?" Clio asked.

"Unknown material," replied Byron.

"Maybe that is why they weren't detected," Micah said.

Byron was worried. "Or it didn't want to be detected."

Clio and Micah looked at him.

It terrified Byron. He inhaled a sharp breath, sensing the danger. But what was he to do? Turn back? He was not ready to do that yet. They might get some answers from this alien structure. The trio gradually moved toward it. Clio inspected the structure using her device. Byron's eyes were glued to the massive formations. Their pointy tips appeared to be reaching for the stars, and their broad bases vanished under the surface of the moon.

What secrets did they hold? Were they created in the last decade?

"How old are these?" he asked.

"As old as the moon itself," reported Clio.

"That's unbelievable," he commented.

"I tell you, anything is possible," remarked Micah.

"The structure could have easily escaped standard scans because it's built from an unknown material," Clio said.

"And Imperial Command ships have been focusing on habitable planets. This doesn't even come close," Micah remarked.

"True," Byron added.

Byron couldn't take his eyes off the flat surfaces of the structure. The surface was refined and reflected the red mist that dominated the sky. Byron tapped on the screen planted near the wrist of his suit. Once more, he checked his vitals.

With every step, they got closer to the alien structure. Byron halted when he noticed Clio was not on his side. She stood staring at something. He followed her gaze and watched in astonishment. From within the wild colors of the red moon, he admired the thin line of the asteroid field. The universe was indeed full of surprises. Despite their situation, he smiled.

"Come on," he said to her.

They stopped in front of the wall. Their scanners showed that this was the signal's origin. Byron turned to his left and started walking. The others followed. The trio wandered around the massive complex. Byron's eyes moved from the structure to his device, but then he stopped dead in his tracks.

"What is that?" asked Clio, staring ahead.

Byron didn't answer.

The moon had swallowed the nose of the craft. Split in half, the rest of it lay in silence at a distance. Its wings had long vanished, and its cracked and punched hull was proof of its suffering.

CHAPTER 15: REALITY

PROMETHEUS, MYKEL'S OFFICE, DECK 1

Mykel's headache returned with a vengeance. The doctor wanted him to take things easy, but that felt wrong. His ship was immobile until the core was repaired. He read Lieutenant Ingrid Elrod's report. *Prometheus's* engineer had done an outstanding job. When the ship was struck, and they lost gravity, the engineering team had restored it and brought the fire under control. His crew had been working overtime, and he appreciated it. He felt annoyed that he was unconscious when his crewmen fought for their lives.

I should have been there!

When he was incapacitated, Katia was available to the crew and efficiently managed the crises. The explosion had hurled them through the rift and shoved them closer to the event horizon. The core and engine were offline. Even if she wanted, Katia could have done little to save the ship. By sheer dumb luck *Titan* had detected them and pulled them out. If they had entered the inner orbit, *Prometheus* would have been lost forever.

Mykel, count your blessings.

The door opened unannounced. Katia and Ingrid stepped inside amid an argument.

"Oh no, not again," mumbled Mykel.

"I think it's dangerous, and we should wait and assess the situation," said Katia

"We have to send someone, or the repairs will never be done!" replied Ingrid, with her hands on her waist.

"Captain, we have detected a radiation leak in the core. We have quarantined the deck."

"How did that happen?"

Ingrid groaned. "It's the damn energy surge, Chief!"

There it was again. Except for Ingrid, no one else called him Chief. Katia had corrected her several times, but it had little effect. Ingrid's face was long, with short ash brown hair and sharp hazel eyes. Physically, the chief engineer was a sturdy woman with a high-pitched voice who never hesitated to express herself.

The first officer was about to argue when Ingrid cut her off.

"The surge hit the hull and then transferred to the circuitry, burning everything in its way, including half of the core. Then it hit the tanks, and…"

"There was a leak," said Mykel, running his hands through his hair.

"Chief, we should be able to seal it. I know it is dangerous, but it will contain the damage if we do it now. If we wait, it could spread to other parts of the ship," argued Ingrid.

"The level of danger?"

"Medium. But I can handle it."

"Do it. How long?"

"A week at least." Ingrid nodded and walked out.

Mykel was not surprised. Ingrid hardly stuck to social norms. People thought she was friendlier with the engines than with her team. He knew she cared but never showed it.

Katia stood with his arms crossed.

"Condition of the crew?"

"We have had two casualties. Several crew members sustained minor injuries. Three had severe injuries and are in a coma."

Mykel frowned.

PROMETHEUS, MYKEL'S QUARTERS DECK 3

Mykel had taken the last dose of the medicine and felt dizzy. It was too strong but mentioning it to the doctor was not an option. He would ask him to rest, and Mykel couldn't. How could he? He had already lost time. He was unconscious for forty hours, and it had left a blank in his memory. This was not the time to rest. His ship and crew needed him. He drank a couple of glasses of water and turned to his monitor, reading one report after another. Patrick was trying to reach the Imperial Command and had no success until now. Phasers were damaged, and senior tactical officer Lyle York was in a coma. The junior officers were doing repairs. The fire burned half of the air filters, and the crew was replacing them.

A bell chimed. It was *Titan*.

Anastasia's face appeared, and he was grateful that she was well and *Titan* had come to *Prometheus's* rescue. One day, he hoped to repay the debt.

Never mention that to her. She will kill you.

"You look well," she said.

"I have been better. How's your ankle?"

"It's better. What did the doctor say about your head injury?"

"He gave me a clean bill of health."

Anastasia looked skeptical. "Okay. If you say so."

"Thanks for getting us out of there," Mykel said.

"Don't mention it. Like ever!"

He plastered a smile on his face. Mykel couldn't help it. Keeping scores was his forte, not hers. When they were together, this was one of his habits that made her furious.

"You don't have to thank me. It's because of me we are stuck here," she stated sadly.

It was true. Anastasia's impatience and drive to destroy the queen had almost killed them.

"You should've listened to me. Why didn't you? All you had to do was back off. Turn away!"

Anastasia touched her forehead. "I thought we could do it."

"You wanted to kill the queen."

She looked him in the eye. "I wanted to end it. End the war."

Mykel's mouth curved into a smile. "I can understand."

"Sorry, I wasn't thinking."

He calmed down a bit.

She changed the subject. "How is the crew? Any losses?"

Mykel felt as if someone had pushed a dagger into his chest. "I have lost two crew members, and three are in a coma."

Sadness filled her eyes. "I am sorry."

"What about *Titan's* crew?"

She eyed him. "Twenty-seven, including Argon."

Mykel's heart sank. "Oh, god. I'm *really* sorry. How did he die?"

"The queen killed him."

"Why?"

"She was after the piece. Argon must have given it to Emmeline."

Mykel rubbed his face with his hands.

Anastasia remained speechless.

"What is our plan?" he asked.

"As soon as repairs are done, we head home."

"I agree. It's a long way back."

"Let's think about one thing at a time."

The commanders became silent until Mykel said, "If you want to talk, I am here. Okay?"

She forced a smile. "I'll talk to you later."

The screen turned blank, and Mykel stared at it for a long time.

CHAPTER 16: STRAY OBJECTS

TITAN, BRIDGE, DECK 1

Anastasia stepped onto the bridge, and for the first time in the last week, it looked cleaner, and her crew appeared less anxious. Repairs continued, and two men stood on chairs fixing the roof. They had sealed all the cracks in the walls, and it seemed as if they were never there at all.

"Evan is the viewscreen fixed?" she asked.

"It's ready, Commander."

Never was she so glad to see the viewer fully functional. The massive black hole was a beautiful sight and took up most of the screen. The stars were hardly visible due to their proximity to the event horizon.

"*Prometheus* is hailing," said Edward.

"Put it through."

The viewer split and they could see the bridge of *Prometheus*.

"Nice to see everyone," remarked Mykel.

"Likewise," said Chris.

"So, what have we found?" asked Mykel.

"Can we have an update, Dr. Kent?" she asked Chris.

"Yes. This one is interesting. I have to say I have never been so close to an event horizon. Nicknamed Poseidon by

Captain Lockhart, the singularity is double the size of the last black hole we have in *Titan's* database. Its photon sphere spreads over several kilometers."

Anastasia eyed the glowing disk. A strong gravitational field drove the multiple streams of photons at the edges of the singularity. It felt as if supersonic winds were pushing them.

"I have detected no relativistic jets means it has not recently swallowed any stars or gases," Chris continued as the image zoomed out. "It's innermost orbit is stable and can be a good place to start."

Anastasia glanced over her shoulder. "Start?"

"We should study it."

Keeping her eyes on the viewer, she said, "We need to get back home, and I'll not send the crew of *Titan* or *Prometheus* back into the mouth of Poseidon. Send a probe if you must. Use it to gather all the information you need."

"But we..."

She looked Chris in the eye. "Your scientific curiosity can wait. We have more pressing matters at hand."

Chris rolled his eyes. "We are here, might as well explore this region of space."

"Doctor, our ships are heavily damaged, and our realm is in danger. As soon as repairs are complete, we are heading back."

"It will take us ages to fly back," argued Chris.

"Eight years, if I am not mistaken."

"By that time, God knows what will happen," Chris said.

Anastasia felt the tension rise on the bridge. "We'll find a faster route. Can you trace our entry point into this region of space?" she said, eager to discuss important topics.

"Yes. I've found it."

The image changed and showed their current location on a star map. A bold yellow dot represented their entry point.

"Can we open the rift?" she asked.

"No. We do not have the power or the equipment to open the rift. Only the Orias can do that."

Anastasia huffed. Mykel looked thoughtful.

"Anything else?" Anastasia asked.

"The Crystal Lab is back online, and I have finished long and short scans. There is a cluster of asteroids half a light-year away from our position. There are three systems within our scanning range with multiple planets."

A beep resonated. Anastasia looked at Evan. Then another beeping was heard. She realized it was the science station.

"What is it?" she asked.

"A wave..." mumbled Chris.

"Wave?"

Chris turned and observed the data on the screen behind him. "A gravitational wave originated about twenty light-years from here."

"Origin?"

"Unknown."

Beep. Beep. Beep.

"Now what?" demanded Anastasia.

"*Titan's* scanners detected something," Evan responded.

"Another wave?" Anastasia concluded.

"No. An interstellar object," answered Evan.

"I detect it too. It wasn't there a minute ago!" Chris added.

Anastasia raised her eyebrows. "Is it a comet?"

"No. Too slow for a comet. It could be an asteroid," replied Chris.

"Surely, we would have detected it earlier," Anastasia stated.

"I've scanned that sector before and found nothing," responded Evan.

"Perhaps due to our proximity to the black hole, our sensors didn't detect it," Anastasia offered.

Evan looked frustrated. "Commander, I have been scanning this region for the last twenty-four hours. It wasn't there."

She nodded. "That's fine. It's here now."

"The asteroid is in visual range," announced Chris.

The image of an enormous irregular asteroid replaced the black hole. On one side of the screen, she could see Mykel standing beside Seiko, peering into the panel.

"What do we know about it?" Anastasia inquired.

"Scanning," said Chris.

Everyone waited eagerly.

"Unknown origin. It is about thirty kilometers long. It is dominantly made up of silica and nickel. My scans show it has six major craters spanning over one to three kilometers, and its surface is heavily fractured. Its surface is covered with one-meter-thick unconsolidated loose superficial deposits. I have calculated its trajectory and believe it's headed toward the next system," said Chris.

Anastasia smiled.

"That's curious," muttered Chris.

"What?"

"I can't scan its interior," replied Chris. "Can we get closer?"

All eyes turned toward him.

"Is that wise?" asked Mykel.

"It's just a harmless asteroid on its way to another system. I'm sure it's no threat," explained Chris.

Adrian eyed Anastasia. Her eyes drifted toward Mykel, who nodded.

"Go," she said.

Titan's engines came online. Leaving the *Prometheus* behind, it glided to intercept the asteroid.

Chris left the bridge and rushed to Crystal Lab.

Mykel looked thoughtful. "What is special about this asteroid? Why can't we scan it?"

"It came out of nowhere," muttered Evan.

"Just accept it. You made a mistake and missed it," said Adrian.

Evan's face turned red. "I didn't!"

"Gentlemen," interrupted Anastasia.

Everyone waited in anticipation.

She watched the harmless-looking interstellar object. Surely it appeared like any other asteroid, but then she remembered Nemesis. It came out of nowhere and hit Earth.

"This is odd," Chris muttered on the intercom.

"What is?"

"There is a compartment inside the asteroid."

"Shields up! Battle stations!"

Alarms sounded.

"There is no need for concern. I do not detect an engine or weapons," Chris suggested.

"What about this compartment?" she asked, not listening to him.

"It's not clear. The outer shell of the asteroid is making it hard for scanners to penetrate."

"How big is this compartment?" asked Mykel.

"Twice the size of *Titan's* bridge," replied Chris. "There are several layers of rock with heavy metal deposits surrounding it. Its density is five-point-six, which is a bit higher than other asteroids in our database. The gamma-ray spectrometer or infrared spectrograph reveals nothing because they cannot penetrate beyond thirty meters. Radiation levels are above normal but not life-threatening, and temperature on the surface is around negative seventy degrees."

The alarms continued to blare.

The asteroid kept moving at its pace, ignoring *Titan*.

"Can we send in a probe to find more about the compartment?" asked Anastasia.

"Well, it wouldn't work. The compartment is at the center of the asteroid. The probe would never reach it," said Chris.

"Could this be a natural phenomenon?" asked Anastasia.

"Unlikely. The compartment was built into the asteroid."

Anastasia tapped her fingers on the arms of her chair. "Are there any life forms in the system it is headed for?"

Evan referred to his console. "The *Marion* visited the Crux system six years ago. It reported no living organisms on the five planets."

Anastasia's eyes remained glued to the screen. She secretly wondered if she had the time to explore the asteroid. But the *Prometheus* was under repair, and crews of both ships were recovering from a catastrophe. She had no time for this. She needed to find a way back. "Repairing both ships is our priority. Keep a sensor lock on that asteroid. Adrian, turn back," she ordered.

"Acknowledged,"

Titan left the asteroid alone and sped toward *Prometheus*.

PROMETHEUS, INFIRMARY, DECK 7

As he did his rounds, Mykel thought about Poseidon. A few weeks ago, he submitted a project to the Imperial Command to study the gravitational waves detected far beyond Poseidon. Their studies had been inconclusive, and he wanted to know more. Despite his curiosity, he had half-heartedly written the project, not knowing if he actually wanted to be a part of another deep-space mission. He would never know if the Imperial Command would approve it. They had accidentally landed in the vicinity of the singularity, and Seiko wanted to pursue the origin of the waves. Mykel was weary. He was worried. The ship and the crew were still recovering, and he wanted to return home.

Mykel's first stop was the infirmary. It was a compact space divided into several sections: the medical lab, doctors' office, and nurses' station. The patient beds were lined against the wall and were separated from the other areas by a glass door. The doctor, Peter, was in his office.

Disturbing no one, Mykel walked straight to the patient area. The nurses were attending two injured crewmen. The three crew members, including his tactical officer Lyle, were still in a coma. He stood beside her bed and wished she would wake up.

"How's she?" he asked when Peter approached him.

"No improvement."

"Can *Titan* help?"

"No, I've spoken with Zac. We have done all we can. We have to wait and see."

With a heavy heart, Mykel faced him.

"Captain, are you here for your next checkup?"

"No. Report."

The doctor rolled his eyes. "Yes, I know. Katia came and informed me to prepare an inventory. When I asked her why she needed it, she pointed toward the window."

Mykel leered.

"What the hell are we doing here?" Peter demanded.

"It looks like we have taken an unplanned trip."

"I know. Why not a resort? Why does it have to be a black hole?"

"Well, only if I could control the rift," Mykel remarked. He felt it too. The loss, the anger, and the edginess. He had not slept properly since he had gained consciousness. After four years in deep space, Mykel had just returned home. He wanted to spend time on Earth, visit a beach, eat fresh food, and relax. But now they were stuck here, millions of miles away. He wished to scream, break down, and cry. He wasn't lucky; captains did not have that luxury.

"Why the hell did we enter the rift in the first place?" demanded Peter.

Mykel shrugged.

"Yes. I know. I know. The bloody Orias!"

Raged bottled up inside him.

"Sorry, Captain. How are you feeling?"

"I'm fine."

"That means you are not."

Mykel ignored him. "The medical inventory?"

"Medical supplies for two years were transferred to the *Prometheus* docked with *Titan*. So, for now, we are good."

"Good. Any damage to the inventory?" he asked.

"No. All good."

Leaving the infirmary, Mykel walked down to the environmental systems. The last time he had checked, they needed filters. He had gone through Katia's report. As soon as they were on their feet, his crew had replaced the filter in a timely manner. For now, they can breathe easily.

PROMETHEUS, ENGINEERING, DECK 5

Mykel's next stop was engineering, and he found Katia waiting for him. She looked better today. The engineering was a mess two days ago, and Ingrid expressed her unhappiness without hesitation. She marched around the enormous hall barking orders. He felt for the crew. They had been through a lot, and she was pushing them.

Today it was in better condition, but the engines were quiet. The core was offline, and that meant *Prometheus* was stuck. According to Ingrid's report, the engines had sustained no damage, but the surge had taken out the core and destroyed multiple power packs. In addition, they had uncovered multiple coolant leaks all over the ship. The radiation leak reported by the computer had been resolved.

"How is she today?" he asked.

Katia rolled her eyes upward. "Let's find out."

He followed her gaze to look at the roof. The core was above their heads. Mykel once again felt uneasy as he got into the tube-like elevator. The glass door closed behind him. The elevator moved upward. Katia took the next one. When he stepped out, he felt a lump in his throat. His head began aching again, and his neck was sore. Exhaustion was taking over him, and he wanted to doze off.

The core was a large area. Its roof and floor curved in the middle into two sturdy white spheres. Usually, the core was lit up like a Christmas tree. Today, it was dimly illuminated. Ingrid and two junior engineers were working in a corner with flashlights.

As if sensing someone was here, Ingrid got to her feet.

"Chief," she said.

"Hello. Any progress?" Mykel said, getting straight to the point.

"Still a lot to do."

"Do you have everything you need?" Mykel asked.

"For now, yes. But if the core is hit again...we might run out of stuff to fix it with."

"What about getting spare parts from *Titan*?"

"Well, we could borrow a few from them. But Chief, we must be mindful, or we might have to beg or steal spare parts to keep the ship running."

It's always enlightening talking to her.

"I'll keep that in mind," Mykel replied, preparing to leave.

"And, Chief..."

He pivoted.

"Just get us back home, please."

Mykel smiled and casually walked away.

PROMETHEUS, ARMORY, DECK 8

Keeping Ingrid's words in mind, Mykel headed toward the armory. Katia walked along with him. He didn't mind. It was good to have company. Wordlessly, they entered the Armory.

"Captain," said Edna Lamer.

The petite woman with short hair and blue stripes stood at attention. Her ebony skin shined under the dim light, and her black eyes remained fixed ahead.

"At ease, officer. How are you?"

"I am well, thank you, Captain."

"And your team?"

She stiffened. "Everyone except Lyle is on duty."

"And they are fine?"

"That's what I gather, sir."

Mykel didn't believe her and looked around. The tactical team appeared engrossed in work. If they had any concerns or worries, they knew how to mask them well. So far, there were no complaints from any of the crew.

That could change anytime.

"Status of the weapons?"

"The torpedoes bay sustained no damage. Two of the phasers burned out. We are fixing them. Once the phasers are fixed, all weapons will be online."

"How long?"

"I need a minimum of three days."

"Can we go into dark mode?"

"We do not know. There is no damage to the equipment, and it was offline during the attack. We can test it once the core is online."

"Okay," Mykel replied unhappily.

Mykel spoke with the entire tactical team. It was mostly small talk, but he wanted to ensure they were all right. The team was rattled but repairing the ship had kept them focused. So far, he was somewhat satisfied. They had power, weapons, air, and the ship would be fully functional, possibly in a week. Now, there was another thing he had to check.

PROMETHEUS, DECK 6, DINER

Mykel and Katia entered the diner, which looked nothing like *Titan*. A simple hall with three large windows, long tables, and chairs on both sides. It was painted white, with bright lights placed in the corners. He never liked it and hardly ate his meals here. He wished the designers had thought about creating a more homely space for eating. One crew member was sitting in the corner, staring at his coffee cup.

"Crewmen," he said, approaching him.

"Captain," the man stood up, looking confused.

"At ease, Jake. How are you doing?" Mykel said.

Jake seemed surprised that he remembered his name.

"I am good, sir."

Katia stepped forward and asked, "How are things in engineering?"

"All good. All good."

"What's on your mind?" asked Mykel.

Jake glanced at Poseidon.

"Do not worry. We'll find a way home," said Katia.

"Let's focus on work and take it slow," added Mykel.

"Yes, sir."

"Enjoy your break," Mykel said.

Jake tried to smile.

Mykel left him and found Darren Taber, the chef. He was a short, hefty man with small eyes, soft black hair, and a thick graying beard.

"I was wondering when you would show up, Captain," said the chef.

Mykel knitted his brows.

"We are in trouble."

So, it begins.

"Why?" asked Katia.

"It's the inventory."

"How short?" Mykel asked, fearing the worst.

"We will be fine for two years. After that, I will have to get creative," said Darren.

"Two years?" Mykel said. *That was not enough.*

"Yes. We were not expecting to leave the system. I contacted the bridge, and they told me it might take us around eight years to get back. Unless we can find a bucket load of food hidden on *Titan*, we are in trouble."

Mykel and Katia shook their heads and, without another word, left the diner.

Reality hit him hard as he dragged his feet. He stopped and leaned on a window to observe the stars. The throbbing pain in his temples was becoming unbearable. Katia stayed with him as if sensing his pain. He did not know whether to laugh or cry. A few days ago, he was worried about saving his world and Anastasia. Now he wondered how they would survive the trip back home.

TITAN, DECK 1

At the end of the day, when he thought everything was under control, Adrian looked forward to a nice little break. As he walked toward the elevator, Evan joined him.

"Hiya."

"Hi," Adrian replied.

"Are you heading toward the Midnight Orchid?"

"Yep."

"I'll come with you. Let's grab a drink."

Adrian's shoulders slumped.

Nick and Patrick from *Prometheus* appeared around the corner and headed in the elevator's direction. The doors opened, and the men stepped in. Adrian and Evan were a few steps away from the elevator when Adrian noticed Nick's face turn tense. Nick pressed a button and the elevator doors shut at once.

"What the hell?" Adrian muttered.

"Don't mind him," said Evan.

Adrian pushed the button and regarded him. "What's the story between you two?"

"Ah…nothing. He hates my guts."

Adrian scowled. "What did you do?"

"Nothing. Nothing!"

The elevator doors opened, and they stepped in.

"You slept with his sister, didn't you?" Adrian concluded.

"You think I would do such a thing!" replied Evan defensively.

The elevator moved toward deck three.

"Of course, you would!" argued Adrian and then raised his hand. "You know what! Never mind. Never mind. Don't tell me. Please don't!"

"It would have been simpler if it had been his sister," responded Evan

A dread overshadowed Adrian, and his imagination ran in every direction.

What could be so bad? Why does Nick hate him so much? Why am I surprised?

He kept his mouth shut. It's best not to ask any more questions.

TITAN, MIDNIGHT ORCHID, DECK 3

They entered Midnight Orchid. The majestic Poseidon sat at a distance, dominating most of the view. It was pleasant, and Adrian almost forgot it nearly swallowed them alive. The atmosphere was lively, and they weren't the only ones who were celebrating. Adrian spotted Ingrid and Katia having a drink with a couple of their crewmates. Cyr sat alone, enjoying her drink on a corner table. Nick and Patrick sat near the window, chatting animatedly.

Adrian walked to the panel behind the long, shiny bench. He keyed in his order and waited. Evan did the same. Since they had left the system, they were short of staff. The one chef they had was still recovering from his injuries. For now, they had to depend on rations. A moment later, a bell rang. Like a vending machine, a part of the wall opened, and their food and drinks appeared. They grabbed their trays, chose a table, and relaxed.

As time went by, the crew of both ships came and left. After a few drinks, Adrian felt his head spin.

I think I should return to my quarters.

Evan was drunk and was babbling. Ignoring him, Adrian noticed a familiar face. It had been years. A friend he remembered playing within the fields on Earth. That was before his parents separated. Before *Titan* or Delta.

Their eyes met, and her eyes glinted.

Evan followed his gaze. "Who's that?'

"That's Lydia Lennon. A-A friend. I didn't know she served on the *Prometheus*."

Evan's face brightened. "A friend? I didn't know you have a friend that was a girl."

"Stop."

Evan gave him a puppy-dog look. "Oh geez, would I ever do anything to embarrass you?"

Adrian regretted bringing him along, "Evan..."

Evan stood up.

"No...no," warned Adrian.

Evan walked toward the adjoining table. "Hey, Lydia, how are you doing?" he said.

Adrian simmered with anger.

Lydia's face flushed. "Hi...do I know you?"

"I am Adrian's best friend," Evan said, pointing toward him.

"This is bad. This is very bad," muttered Adrian as he waved and faked a smile.

Adrian watched Lydia blush as she spoke with Evan. Before he knew it, she joined them. Adrian tried his best to remain calm. This was unexpected, and he preferred to be in control. Unfortunately, with Evan, life was like a roller coaster.

As they chatted, he found out that Lydia had left Earth two years after him and was a medical lab assistant on *Prometheus*.

"It's not the most exciting job," she said, playing with her food, "but I get to explore."

"It's a fantastic job," countered Evan. "Isn't it, Adrian?"

"All members of a crew are important," replied Adrian.

Evan tilted his head and gaped at him.

Lydia beamed. "I thought you had forgotten me."

"No, I didn't."

"Really? I have been on *Titan* several times."

Adrian's face fell. "Oh, you should have told me."

"You appeared preoccupied."

Adrian didn't answer. From the corner of his eye, he noticed Ingrid finished her last drink and banged the glass on the table. She stood up and brushed her hands against empty glasses, which tumbled on the floor, leaving shards of broken glass. She approached Cyr, and they began talking.

"You know what, I think I should head off," said Evan.

"No. No. Stay," begged Adrian.

Evan scowled at him. "I could. But I have something *really* important I need to do," he said, getting on his feet.

Loud voices distracted them.

"Oh really? You think we should have done better. How about *Titan*?" yelled Ingrid.

Cyr stood with her hands on her waist. "Last time I checked, we saved the *Prometheus* from the singularity."

"If I have got my facts right, *Prometheus* wouldn't be in danger if *Titan* hadn't fired the last torpedo!" shouted Ingrid.

"We were trying to destroy the queen's ship. Your captain should have backed off!" Cyr argued.

"Your commander should've had common sense! It was the chief's idea that gave *Titan* the chance to bring down the queen's ship. Without us, you are nothing!" Ingrid shouted.

Adrian got on his feet. He watched Katia approach the two women. He was the senior officer on *Titan*, but he was unsure if he should intervene. But Evan never learned to hold back.

"Ladies…ladies…there is no need for this. I am sure it's no one's fault," said Evan, walking calmly toward the women.

"Evan, stay out of this!" yelled Cyr. "It's none of your business. This woman thinks she is better than us!"

Cyr was drunk, and the stress of the situation was taking its toll.

"Of course, I am better. I would have handled the situation better!" said Ingrid proudly.

Cyr took a step forward. "Oh, really?"

Evan came to stand in between the two women. "No. This is not the way. These things happen."

Their eyes darkened, and the women glowered at him.

"This is a bad idea," Adrian murmured, taking a step forward.

"And there is enough of me for both of you," Evan mocked.

Adrian froze.

Ingrid's face reddened. Her fist swung, and she punched Evan in the face.

"Ow!" Evan cried out.

Cries echoed.

Before Ingrid could hit him again, Katia stopped her.

TITAN, MEDICAL BAY, DECK 3

Evan sat on the examination table, holding his bleeding nose. The nurse appeared with a tray of instruments. She could hardly hide her amusement.

"How could she punch me?" complained Evan.

"How could you say something like that!?" Adrian countered.

"That's my pickup line."

"There is a time and a place for everything."

Evan laid back, closed his eyes, and mourned.

Leaning forward, Adrian said, "I hope you learned your lesson."

"Ha. Ha. Hilarious!"

PROMETHEUS, MYKEL'S OFFICE DECK 1

Ingrid smirked as she stood in front of Mykel, who couldn't stop laughing when he found out about the fight. Even now, he had trouble maintaining a straight face.

"Look, Chief, he's a jerk."

"He is. But let's talk about your behavior," he responded, folding his arms.

"It was his fault!"

"You shouldn't have started an argument with Cyr. You are a senior officer."

She crossed her arms and leaned on her left leg. "I do not care. If *Titan*..."

"Violence is not the answer, and getting on each other's nerves or blaming *Titan* will not get us home earlier," he said in an authoritative voice. Getting on his feet, he looked her in the eye. "Ingrid, I will not tolerate this kind of behavior. You must find a way to work with them. I don't care how you feel."

"But they are morons!"

Mykel frowned. "Morons with the best technology known to man and without whom you are unlikely to survive."

TITAN, BRIDGE, DECK 1

It was the night shift, and there was no one on the bridge except Adrian and Evan. Adrian couldn't sleep, so he relieved one of the crew members, who he knew was exhausted. The computer was running diagnostics on the power packs. He wanted to make sure everything was working at optimal levels before giving his final report to Anastasia. On the edge of the screen was the asteroid, traveling at its own free will, ignoring the world around it. Adrian adjusted the sensors, and *Titan's* cameras moved to capture the asteroid before it drifted out of its field of view.

A whooshing echoed, and Adrian rolled his eyes upward. He wished Ingrid had broken more than just Evan's nose. He claimed he couldn't sleep either and found a new toy. The problem was that he thought playing with it on the bridge was a good idea.

Oh, this sucks! What did I do to deserve this?

Adrian tapped his feet, and the chair swirled. While he savored reading mythological books, Evan enjoyed playing classic games. He had heaps of them in his quarters, but this was his favorite. With his legs parted, Evan handled the club like a pro. Opposite to him were two towers extending to the roof. He hit the ball, and it vanished between the towers.

"Excellent shot," said the game.

"Yes!" Evan cheered.

"Just stop it!" Adrian yelled.

"No."

Another ball appeared, and he continued playing.

"This is annoying," said Adrian.

"No, you are annoying."

"You are not supposed to be here,"

"Neither are you!" argued Evan.

It was true. It wasn't his shift. "Why are you doing this?"

"Don't you see I am doing this to entertain you?"

Adrian threw his head back and laughed.

"No. This is revenge. You are annoying me because I didn't support you in front of the Commander. I cannot. I will not! You are wrong, and you should apologize to Ingrid and Cyr."

"Why should I apologize?"

"What you said was inappropriate!"

"But I've said it to many women."

"Well, I am surprised no one punched you before," Adrian remarked sarcastically and turned to his workstation.

Evan continued playing.

The diagnostics would finish soon. Except for the fourth engine, which was still under repair, *Titan* would be totally functional within twelve hours. On the screen was a stray asteroid. He folded his hands and observed. It cruised at the speed of twenty kilometers per hour and had not changed trajectory. It was about twenty thousand kilometers away from them.

"Stop watching that stupid asteroid. I can overtake it on a bicycle," Evan boosted.

Adrian turned. "Seriously?"

A beep interrupted them. Adrian caught the horror on Evan's face. Adrian twirled and winced as a bright light blinded him momentarily. In a flash, the asteroid vanished.

"What the hell?!" he shouted.

"Where did it go?" Evan asked, rushing to his workstation.

"It...it just...vanished!" Adrian replied.

"I know! I saw it, but I don't believe it!" Evan yelled.

CHAPTER 17: UNSOLVED MYSTERIES

AURORA, LADY VERMONT'S OFFICE, DECK 2

L ady Vermont never thought she would be involved so much. She longed to return home, but the Imperial Command wanted her to stay on the *Aurora*. As the days passed, she dealt with several aspects. Being a liaison wasn't easy, and she was in a tricky situation. Should Earth prepare for worse? How would they fight the Orias if they returned with a bigger fleet? She gulped.

Sitting in her temporary, dull office, she wondered about the past several days. Multiple round ceiling lights cast a glow on the white carpet. Two chairs with a table stood against the wall with a triangular window. She leaned on the semicircular desk and peered into the sleek screen.

Fear was spreading through the system, and they had received several recommendations to vacate all outposts and bring everyone home.

Yes, Orias was a formidable enemy, but shouldn't they fight? Should they hide just because they were afraid, and the Orias were stronger? Should they surrender?

She gritted her teeth. "Never."

Humanity hadn't been kind to her, but it was all she had. They doubted her, experimented on her, trying to understand why she had survived while the rest of her brothers and sisters died. There were no answers. When she turned twenty, she met Peter Lathom. With his help, she gained control of her life. He became her mentor, her protector, and someone she trusted. She spent the first ten years enjoying life, traveling, and studying law. Soon she wanted to know why she had survived and turned every stone. It was all in vain, and for years she waited for answers.

She glanced at the monitor, examining the latest report on her health. Although she was over a hundred years old, her test results were perfect. No muscle degeneration was noted. Her bones were as healthy as a twenty-year-old, and her eyesight was as sharp as before. Immortality was still a dream for humanity, and she was an example that it was possible. But what was the secret of her long life? No one knew.

She tried to focus. The whereabouts of the *Raven* remained unknown. Emmeline and Argon were good at hiding. They didn't find any traces of the ship except a faint trail that led nowhere. Six ships, including *Aurora*, were guarding the perimeter. At the moment, they couldn't spare ships to look for the *Raven*.

Her fingers danced on the fine keyboard embedded in the desk. An image of the plaque and the piece appeared. She studied it for a long time.

What was it? What can it do?

Never had she seen or heard of anything like it. The artifact was left in the care of Argon, and now both Emmeline and Argon had vanished. Private ships were hard to track, and unlike the Imperial Command ships, they did not need to report in. She read the notes made by Emmeline and was astounded at her abilities. Delta's death was an unfortunate event that changed everything. She wanted to study the piece and the plaque. It was why she had arranged the artifacts to be sent to her. She felt someone so young shouldn't handle them. She stopped and considered everything Emmeline had achieved. She might be young, naïve, but she was smart.

I should have handled it better.

Lady Vermont thought about the whole scenario. All she had was a remnant of a battle, a puzzle with several missing parts. Where was *Raven*? Could they be wrong? Might Emmeline and Argon still be on *Titan*? Where were *Titan* and *Prometheus*? Destroyed? Captured by the Orias? She hoped not. But from what they knew, Orias were destroyers and invaders. Taking prisoners wasn't their style. But they might have taken the Earth ships to extract information. *Titan* carried a lot of sensitive information on their realm, and its capture could have devastating impacts.

The sudden shaking of *Aurora* snapped her thoughts away. She stood up and watched as the gigantic wheel full of people headed toward Earth.

"So, it's done," she said.

After several discussions, it was decided that the citizens of the *Titan* would return to Earth.

That was sensible. What would they do out here? They were civilians, and for now, Earth was the safest place. She hoped.

Returning to her desk, she read further. *Titan's* Squadron had vanished without a trace. Three ships, gone. Reports confirmed they had not been destroyed; the *Aurora* or other ships had found no debris. Amongst other things, this was another mystery.

How could they just disappear?

She looked over *Freedom's* Space Flight Recorder (SFR) data and watched the video. An anomaly appeared out of nowhere and swallowed the ships.

What a loss?

She bit her bottom lip and looked at the images of cadets Byron Thames, Micah Dew, and Clio Ranger.

Why these ships? Perhaps because the other ships were bigger. Maybe it was attracted toward smaller masses. But where did it come from?

"Computer, merge all the scans from the battle, and display on the screen," she said

"Affirmative," replied the computer.

"Mark the anomaly near the gate, as point A."

"Done."

"Search and detect any other such anomalies in the sector during the battle and compare them with the Orias ship's energy signatures."

"Working," said the computer.

Lady Vermont looked away from the screen and sat in wonder. She got to her feet and peered at the broken perimeter. All her life, she felt peculiar and knew people disliked her. She treasured safety more than anything. With the perimeter gone, a sense of discomfort loomed over her. As if an intruder had knocked down the door to her house.

"Search complete," announced the computer.

She returned to her desk.

"Intriguing," she mumbled.

During the battle, this anomaly appeared several times. Its energy pattern differed from the Orias, and it only targeted the squadron. She gazed at the monitor. *Why?*

CHAPTER 18: DISCOVERY COLONY

VEGA 1

I t was reckless, and she knew it. Emmeline felt she had left her safe place and was heading into trouble. Space was crawling with Imperial Command ships. But they were not just after her. They were also hunting for Orias ships. The *Raven* approached the moon. Vega 1 was a busy colony on the outskirts of the system. It was also a good place to get transport. She charted a course toward the northern hemisphere, and *Raven* passed through the atmosphere with no difficulty. Emmeline gulped as she neared the vast black mountain ranges. Memories flooded her mind. This was where Delta had learned how to fly and would often practice her piloting skills. It was fun. She remembered sitting in the back seats, watching as Delta's father taught her new maneuvers.

Dread loomed over her when she recalled Delta vanishing in the clouds. Wiping her tears, she focused on flying. The *Raven* dipped closer to the surface. The ship wobbled.

"Damn! Why is this so hard?" she muttered, trying to control the craft. Sweat gathered on her forehead.

The ship glided through rugged mountains. Turning, it entered a tunnel before reducing its speed. With a thump, it landed on a solid surface. She shut down all the systems and deliberated what she would do.

I have no choice. I must do this for Argon.

Making sure the *Raven* was secured, and out of sensor range, she emerged out of the ship in a spacesuit. Preparing herself, she melted into the dark tunnels of Vega 1.

The walk was rough because of the daunting pitch-black tunnels. They snaked through the heart of the mountain. The lights on her helmet were the only source of illumination. The rocky ground was full of potholes and large cracks. She had to be on her guard, and her gravity boots made a slight squeaking noise.

Three hours later, she emerged out of the tunnels and took a breath in.

Thank God.

She believed she was lost several times but kept reminding herself that she had done this before. Although the suit protected her from the heat and radiation and kept her alive, she wanted to take it off. It was confining and unbearable. But she needed the spacesuit. The methane and the carbon monoxide in the atmosphere would finish her in seconds. She kept walking.

Vega 1 differed from other stations. The moon had gigantic mountains created by tectonic plates rich in metals and iron. Powered by geothermal energy, it was one of the most prosperous places in dead black space. The second attraction was an underground liquid methane river in the southern hemisphere. Over twenty years ago, an enormous processing plant was built to extract natural gas, creating a flourishing energy resource.

The colony itself appeared like a giant octopus that sat in the middle of the plain and extended its six tentacles over five miles in every direction. It housed over ten thousand humans and was a business hub with transport ships heading to Earth and other colonies. Under the surface were several caves and tunnels. Some naturally made, others man-made and abandoned after metal extraction.

As she neared the structure, she mixed with the crowd arriving at the colony through a massive door. Most miners working at the plant preferred to suit up and return home on foot. Men and women wearing suits resembled overweight robots walking awkwardly. It gave her a unique opportunity to blend in. It was perfect. Everyone was dressed like her.

The door closed behind the crowd, and the lights turned red. A horn blared, and a heavy flow of gases filled the hall. No one moved. Not if they valued their life. Gravity was restored. Emmeline felt lighter when her gravity boots were deactivated. The air became breathable, and the light turned green. The massive wall in front of them opened, and a computerized voice said: "Welcome to Vega 1."

Emmeline tried not to bump into anyone and found her way to the exclusive cubicles. Picking one, she used her credits to pay for the next twenty-four hours. The circular eight-foot-tall and ten-foot-wide area fitted her needs. Inside, she instantly removed her suit, showered, and selected a pair of old pants with a loose white top. Afterward, she picked up a small box and opened it to observe a mesh of sensors bound with thin metallic chains.

I hope this works.

She placed the mesh over her head, covering her from the neck up. She turned to her pad and activated it. For a moment, it glowed. She adjusted the settings, and it glued itself to her skin. She pushed the execute button, and it glowed again. She was no longer Emmeline. The face she wore was of a young girl, of her age, with red hair and deep black eyes. She wore lipstick, and makeup highlighted her cheekbones with a pinkish hue. Her eyes looked larger due to the thick eyeliner. Other girls would have been happy with this look, but Emmeline disliked it. She felt like a phony. But the fact was, she could have anyone's face except hers.

Sweat beaded on her forehead, and her chest stuttered. She glared at strange faces and felt relieved that no one appeared interested in her. The mask was working. Emmeline walked casually with her hands in her pockets, eyeing the displays on the walls to her left. The crowd was heading toward the dome. She easily blended in and headed in the same direction. When she entered the dome, she glanced upward and saw several people on the five levels of the colony. She turned, entered the square hall, and browsed various displays. Three transport ships were heading for the Discovery Colony, and one of them was fast, but it was going to cost her more credit. She did not mind.

Quietly, she got in the queue. Transport ships within the realm did not have checkpoints, which worked in her favor. Every human had a free pass to travel to the colonies, including the Discovery Colony. The ticket dispenser was a white panel embedded in the wall. She fumbled with her hands, her eyes roaming, making sure no one noticed her. She had half expected her picture to be displayed on every screen. Till now, she hadn't seen it but had noticed a note on the corner of the screen. The Imperial Command considered shutting down all colonies and might request all humans to return to Earth. *That's understandable.*

The man in front of her grabbed his ticket and disappeared into the crowd. She took a step forward.

"How may I serve you?" said the machine.

"Um...complete loop to Discovery Colony, Transport Three."

"Affirmative."

She paid for the trip. A few lights blinked, and then there was a loud beep. She jumped, but it was not the ticket dispenser but a child playing with a toy next to her. The mother rushed toward him, grabbed his hand, and scolded him for wandering off. Emmeline's heart sank. Would she ever see her mother again?

"Transition complete," said the machine. A section of the wall opened, and a shiny, rectangular pass slid out.

"Proceed toward hangar three. The ship leaves in thirty minutes."

Emmeline stared at her ticket.

"Next!" said the machine.

She glanced over her shoulder and saw other people were waiting in the queue.

On level one, Emmeline hurried down the aisle, trying to recall the last time she had come here with Delta. She had noticed something that she thought would be useful. Emmeline scratched her neck; the mask had begun to irritate her skin. She hurriedly walked through the busy market, flooded with people. Maybe it was a good thing. She wouldn't be easy to spot. Between the screams of the salesmen and the crowd, she found what she was looking for. The shop was still there. Infinity Tech. She gazed at the young man behind the counter. The last time they had been here, it was an older gentleman with a beard.

"What can I do for you?" asked the young shopkeeper.

"I want a powerful databox."

The young man eyed her.

"I want the one with the fastest downloading capability and the largest storage."

His hand reached under the counter, producing a round black object.

She glared at him. "I want the actual stuff."

"Little girl, this is the best I have got."

Emmeline's blood boiled. She despised when people lied to her and wasted her time.

"Sixty-five days ago, I visited this very market. I want the SS89...now!"

"Out of your league."

Emmeline presented two white rectangular weightless chips and placed them on the counter. "Try me."

Clearly disbelieving her, he placed the chips into the machine. His eyes widened, regarding her from top to bottom.

"I believe that is the right price?"

"It is."

"Good, then we have an understanding."

Without question, he turned to open a cabinet and pulled out a small box. She opened it, examined its contents, and left.

Transport three was a small old passenger ship built to carry around twenty people. Emmeline took a seat in the far corner, away from everyone's prying eyes. She surveyed the compartment and did not see any cameras. Nervously, she waited for the ship to move. There were a couple of people on the transport, but they minded their own business. She turned her head and saw a reflection in the window glass. She gasped at the stranger looking back at her. Then she remembered she was wearing the mask. She tried to divert herself by watching various displays on the hangar deck. Most of the news was about the Orias attack and the destruction of the perimeter.

The craft jolted as it lifted from the ground and flew out of the hangar. Emmeline felt she could relax for now. But another daunting task was ahead of her. The Discovery Colony would not be so easy to penetrate.

The half-hour journey seemed like an eternity, and Emmeline kept checking her mask just to be sure. She couldn't change her entire physique but changing her face should keep her safe from security monitoring the interior and exterior of the Discovery Colony. A sound whipped her out of her thoughts. It was an old, stout passenger snoring. She disregarded him, and her thoughts turned to her ship. The *Raven* was not a small craft, and she hoped no one had noticed it heading toward the mountain on Vega 1.

The transport ship glided toward the massive colony floating in space. Emmeline's heart drummed against her chest, and she took a slow breath in and out. She wanted to turn back, hide away, and forget the last two weeks. The truth was, there was no turning back.

The Discovery Colony was a massive structure with a radius of about seventeen hundred kilometers. It was located between Mars and Jupiter. It looked like a big atom surrounded by six rings with multiple globes. The light blue colony stood in the middle and looked like Earth. But it had no water, continents, or clouds. Instead, it glittered with artificial lights that spread across twenty-five levels. The six glass-made rings provided the perfect transport for the colonists.

As if flying through the air, a space train passed through a small tube inside the rings and vanished within seconds. Then another one appeared and dashed in the other direction. One of the globes blinked, and a space train stopped. A large group of colonists, along with several robots, left the train and headed for the colony through a narrow passageway.

On the colony, Emmeline noticed several men and women working on their stations. Except for a glorified library, the Discovery Colony was the hub of scientists responsible for developing new and faster ships, weapons, and technology for the Imperial Command. Several of its sections were restricted to the public.

The transport ship slowed its pace as it dove under the glass ring at the equator and gradually made its way to the hangar deck. Her lips curved into a big smile as she watched the crowd, full of children, men, women, and robots. A fleet of guard ships flew out of the hangar deck. The egg-shaped crafts formed a circle around the colony.

I guess that is necessary. The Orias could attack anytime.

The transport ship glided into the hangar deck and set down between two lines.

As she stepped out, she felt every eye on her. She didn't see any Imperial Command ships or crews and guessed most were stationed around the perimeter. Regardless, she felt unsafe. Gathering her courage, she sauntered through the crowd and looked at the displays from the corner of her eye. She almost expected the words "most wanted" to appear, and her name displayed in bold letters. Still no sign. She had to work fast.

The passengers who disembarked had to check maps to find the routes. Emmeline knew them by heart. During the last year, she had visited the Discovery Colony several times on behalf of Dr. Chris Kent. But today, she didn't use her usual route because she didn't want the curator to notice her.

Discovery Colony held the biggest collection of database libraries outside Earth. The archive was extensive and took the entire second floor. She usually took the elevator to the first floor and used the main entrance. But today, she took the stairs to the first floor. The floor was packed with colonists working in cubicles. She kept her head low, and without looking at anyone, she walked toward the door to the maintenance shaft. She retrieved the decoder from her bag and placed it on the door. Circular red lights glowed, and she glanced behind.

"Come on…faster," she muttered.

The lights turned green, and the door opened. She expected the alarms to go off. Luckily, they did not. Closing the door behind her, she rushed down the narrow gray passageway with multiple ladders that led to the upper floor. Before anyone appeared, she checked the pad and found maintenance shaft twenty-three.

She took one step after another. After ten minutes, she was breathless and looked overhead. She wanted to give up and leave immediately. But she didn't have time to second-guess. The transport would leave in an hour, and she had to get back to Vega 1 before anyone suspected anything.

By the time she reached the second floor, she was sweaty and exhausted. Emmeline paused and listened as a low humming echoed through the narrow tunnel. It was the ventilation system. Ignoring it, she pushed herself to keep going. At one point, she stopped and accessed the pad to check her location. She was in the right spot. The iron door to her left was locked, and she used the decoder again. The door opened with a soft click. Stepping into the bright passageway, she quickly closed the door behind her.

Never thought I would have to use the maintenance shaft.

Glad that no one was in sight, Emmeline adjusted her attire. She touched her face to ensure the mask was still working.

Peeping out, she noticed the curator was at the desk, busy serving others. She calmly walked past the aisle with multiple shelves on both sides. These held microchips loaded with information that was available to the public. But she was not interested in them.

The partially painted doors opened noiselessly. Cool air hit her face. The archives were vast, round pillars that touched the ceiling. The chilly air turned her hands cold. Beyond the hall of pillars, she walked to an arched door. Taking a deep breath, she punched in Dr. Chris Kent's codes. They worked perfectly. The room was a colossal, dimly lit dome with small lights lining the floor. People stood in front of panels that appeared to be hanging from an unseen thread. Moving away from them, she walked to a far corner. Sensing her presence, a face appeared. It was not human but looked like one. The hairless face with big eyes, thick eyebrows, and a sharp chin stared at her.

"Greetings, how can I help?"

"I need access to all the databases stored at the colony."

The face dematerialized, and a panel appeared out of thin air and solidified. She pushed multiple keys and placed the databox on the panel. A blue light blinked, and the download began. Although it took only a few minutes, it felt like an eternity. Every minute she spent at the station brought her dangerously close to getting caught.

The face reappeared. "Download complete."

"Thanks."

"You're welcome. Please come again and have a nice day."

Emmeline hurried out of the dome and walked past several people to return to the maintenance shaft. The climb down the shaft was easier and faster. Feeling happy, she walked through the crowd. She had done it. She had what she wanted. But her happiness was short-lived. She spotted a group of Imperial Command officers heading in her direction. Men, women, robots, and children surrounded her. She couldn't make a sudden turn or change directions since it would look suspicious. Making up her mind, she took a deep breath and kept walking. The men were dressed in black uniforms, armed to the teeth. They were tall, stern-looking, with short hair. To Emmeline, the robots looked less intimidating. They walked past her without a word, and she increased her pace toward the hangar deck.

Once inside the transport ship, Emmeline wiped the sweat off her forehead and exhaled a long breath. Taking a seat near the window, she looked at the neighboring passengers. She glanced at the pilot, who stood leaning at the door of the cockpit. He looked in his forties, with a heavy jaw and curious eyes. She turned away, trying to conceal her face. When all the passengers were on board, he vanished into the cockpit, and the ship started.

The ship departed the colony. Her eyes widened as it flew past an Imperial Command ship. She looked away; her heart almost stopped. It was impossible for them to spot her through the small window. Still, she felt the need to hide. Several minutes passed before she had the guts to peer outside. The glass of the window reflected her face. The dark eyes and red hair bothered her. The disguise was perfect, and she hated it. Tears built in her eyes; she couldn't believe this was happening. She was hiding from her own people.

VEGA 1

In an hour, transport three returned to the colony. Emmeline left the ship with the other passengers and mingled with the colonists. It was noisy, smelled of oil and gases, and was nothing like Discovery Colony. She returned to her cubicle, did not bother to change, and grabbed her suit.

Ready to head back to *Raven*, she stepped out and joined the colonists leaving the colony. Her heart was beating fast, and she wanted to return to safety as soon as possible. The hair on the back of her neck stood. Glancing behind, she spotted the pilot of the transport ship. He craned his neck from side to side as if looking for someone. Did he know who she was? She touched her face. The mask was active. His eyes set on her, his jaw dropped, and he spoke into the communicator. Emmeline turned and ran.

CHAPTER 19: HIDDEN PATHWAYS

TITAN, BRIDGE, DECK 1

With her arms folded, Anastasia glared at the viewer. The entire ordeal fascinated her. An asteroid that could just vanish.

"Replay the recording," she said.

They all watched. There was a flash of light, and the asteroid disappeared.

"Commander, there was an energy surge, and the asteroid vanished," replied Evan.

"It wasn't destroyed?"

"No."

"How far away were we from the asteroid?"

"About twenty thousand kilometers," replied Adrian.

She walked to the science station, "Do you have anything more?"

"The source of the energy surge was a portal. Before the asteroid vanished, it emitted a signal and opened the portal."

"What?"

"Yes."

"Any similarities to the portal that Emmeline and Delta found?"

"No. This one is different," replied Chris.

She lifted her head and gawked at the stars. "Can we open it?"

Her question was met with silence. She turned to Chris. "Can we open the portal?"

"I don't know."

"Maybe we can duplicate the signal and attempt to open the portal," suggested Anastasia.

Chris looked thoughtful.

"Hold on…hold on…we do not know where it leads!" said Adrian, getting on his feet.

"Well…we might get closer to home," said Chris.

"Or away from it," argued Evan.

"Adrian is right. We first need to find out where it leads," Chris said.

"How?" she asked.

"Well. I don't know," Chris retorted.

TITAN, ENGINEERING, DECK 5

The doors slid open, and Anastasia stepped into engineering. Cyr was occupied working on the panel but noticed her immediately.

"Commander."

"Hey…how is everything?"

"Well…what can I say? One engine caught fire. Fortunately, it didn't completely burn down. We need to change a lot of parts, but we can save it. Also, six of the coolants and fuel injectors still need repair. Commander, we better not push our luck. I need more time."

Anastasia merely smiled. They were stuck here and had all the time in the world. The Orias were far away, probably destroying their world. Without the perimeter, their realm was defenseless.

"Keep me posted," she said.

She left engineering in silence. As she walked down the corridor, she thought about their situation. She had assigned two junior science officers to study the event horizon. The rest of them, including Dr. Aceline Keston and Dr. Isaac Finch, were assigned to help Chris.

After losing Argon, Anastasia thought she should not assign any tasks to Aceline. But she had helped Emmeline decipher the plaque, and Anastasia hoped she could do the same for Chris. They could work together to solve the mystery of the asteroid. If Emmeline was here, she had a feeling Chris wouldn't need anyone else.

It was cruel to burden Aceline with work. With utmost hesitation, she knocked.

"Come in."

Anastasia stepped in. The quarters were gloomy, and Aceline stood peering at the stars as if searching for answers. She wasn't the only one. Anastasia had noticed several crew members watching the cosmos. Even from a distance, she sensed their sorrow, their loss. No one knew what had happened to their families, friends, and she hoped they didn't suffer Aceline's fate.

Anastasia felt unsettled. There was a startling difference in Aceline's appearance. She had cut her hair short. The shades of purple were still visible, but the glow on her face had vanished. Anastasia felt terrible.

"Commander, how can I help?" she asked.

"Has Chris contacted you?"

"Yes. You want me to work on the phantom asteroid," she said.

Phantom asteroid. Nice.

"It would be good if you could help."

"I'll try."

"Thank you. How are you?" she asked. She had waited long enough to ask. Anastasia might never see her children again, but at least she knew they were with their father. Safe. No matter what happened between them, he would protect them.

"I'm fine."

Aceline sounded very formal. Why wouldn't she be? She was speaking to the commander of *Titan*.

"How is Selina?" she asked.

"She is doing well."

Anastasia wanted to ask if Selina cried after the funeral. But it felt like a stupid question.

"That is good to know. She seemed unsettled."

"Of course, her brother is dead," replied Aceline.

Anastasia gulped. "Of course. I just wanted to see how she is doing."

"Thank you for asking. She is... coping. At the moment, she is in her room."

"Let me know if I can help," she said.

"Sure."

Anastasia thanked Aceline and left. She felt she had been too formal and could have offered moral support. But did she know Aceline? Anastasia bobbed her head. She didn't know her at all. All this time, especially in the last two years, Anastasia had been only thinking about herself. Her divorce, her children, and her career. It was selfish of her. She was so worried about *Titan*, but it was nothing without its crew and people like Aceline.

TITAN, MEDICAL BAY 1, DECK 3

Anastasia visited the exobiologist. She didn't know if Isaac could help Chris and found him in the medical bay observing the corpses of the Orias. When she stepped in, he looked up from the magnifier.

"Ah, Commander?"

"Doctor. How are you?" she asked. She had hardly seen him, and Adrian had told her he refused to leave his quarters for a week. She was happy to see him here.

"Did you find anything new?"

He shook his head. The wound on his left cheek and ear was still healing.

"I'm keeping myself busy," he stated.

"Good idea," she said and explained the reason for her visit.

He looked uncertain. "I do not know how much I can help. I am an exobiologist, not a guy who chases asteroids."

Anastasia tried to control her smile. "I would like you to talk with Chris."

"Sure, I'll try, but do not expect me to dissect it."

"I respect your limitations," she joked.

He glared at her.

"Have a nice day, Doctor. Tell me if the dead Orias start talking."

He blinked several times.

"Oh, God knows I try," she muttered. "Bye, Doc!"

Anastasia strolled down the corridor with her head low. She paused and gazed at Poseidon through the window. For several minutes, she watched it. It was beautiful, and its glow extended several kilometers on both sides. It was glorious and daunting at the same time. She wished they had arrived under different circumstances.

She felt a twist in her gut as she recalled her actions. Only if she had listened to Mykel and not gone after the queen. Anastasia was enraged. She gritted her teeth and cursed herself for failing. Even if *Titan* had been destroyed, killing the queen would have ended the war. It would have been worth it.

HAIDES CASTLE

A small fleet of the Orias ship flew over the dark forest. The large flying beasts screeched as they hovered over the castle. Fires were burning in a few sections of the fortress. With no wind or water, a barren land full of awkwardly bent trees surrounded the castle. The entrance to the fortress was open, leading to the hall with the throne. In the hall, figures embedded in walls stood silent, staring into the void. The rectangular pools were filled with boiling purple liquids. Steam emerged from them and rushed toward the ceiling. On a stone-made platform sat a gray throne. The wall behind it was adorned with a circular rim full of glittering figures.

Suddenly, the dark figures emitted a dull green light. It was absorbed by the walls and transferred miles below the surface to a massive chamber. Two-headed creatures with sharp fangs slithered on the cracked floor. The hissing died out when the stream of green light emerged through the wall and glided toward a large crypt. It absorbed the green light and glittered. A red mist appeared and hovered over the crypt. The slithering creatures disappeared into the darkness.

The mist took shape, and Aithon appeared. A dull light shined over his bald head. The ageless man stood patiently with his hands clamped together. Aithon wondered about his existence. He didn't recall when he was born or created. It was a long time ago. He felt his memory was undependable. All he knew was to serve the queen. Serve his species. After the attack, the queen had used most of her life force to save her ship and the Orias. He had brought her here to regenerate. With a loud thud, the top of the crypt split open. Green smoke rose, and the queen opened her eyes. She was still in humanoid form.

"My queen."

She looked confused. "I am at the castle. What happened? How did I get here?"

"You were in danger...so..."

Her eyes widened as she realized what he had done. "You opened the doorway! Why?"

"They were too close to your ship."

"Who told you to interfere!?"

"I am sworn to protect you."

Her face reddened. "You have no right!"

Aithon lowered his head and repeated, "My queen, I have vowed to protect you."

"I could have won!" she shouted, stepping out of the crypt.

Aithon lifted his head. "If you die, what is the point?"

"It is unacceptable," she hissed.

"Our strategy failed. We have to look for other opportunities."

Her annoyance flared. "Failure is unacceptable!"

"Staying alive opens doors to turn failure into a victory," he replied calmly.

The queen's eyes turned red, and the floor of the castle shuddered. "What happened to our fleet?"

"We have returned with only two ships. Ten thousand Orias are dead. Six Orias ships were destroyed protecting their queen."

The wind turned silent, and the tremors stopped.

"*Titan* has to be destroyed," she said, remembering the blast that had burned down her fleet.

" Yes, before that, we need to find the piece."

"Emmeline...Augury," she muttered.

"Who is that?" he asked.

She turned into a white mist without another word and left the chamber. Passing through the rock, she moved upward. Once it emerged on the terrace, the mist came together. The queen stood at the edge of the fortress, looking over her realm. Her long black gown touched her feet, and her crown glittered in the faint light from the red moon that shined at a distance.

Aithon appeared a few paces behind her. "I've not told you everything."

She faced him.

"I opened the gateway, and *Titan* followed along with another Earth ship," he said.

A wicked smile appeared on her face.

"*Titan* fired, generating an explosion that hit both Earth ships."

She eyed him, not knowing if this information brought her any pleasure. But one thing did. "So, *Titan* is no longer protecting its realm."

"No."

"Was it destroyed?"

"I do not think so."

"So, where are they?" she asked.

"I do not know yet. The piece might be on *Titan*."

"It's with the girl, and she is not on *Titan*," the queen replied.

Aithon raised his eyebrows. "We need to find her and retrieve the piece."

"Yes, we do. Then I shall burn her alive and kill everyone on *Titan*."

CHAPTER 20: SHADOWY GETAWAYS

VEGA 1

Emmeline ran fast. Stopping even for a second could mean her capture or death. Uncertain of what was coming for her, she pushed herself. The suit didn't make it easier, and the gravity boots were heavy. The uneven terrain was punishing and full of rocks. Breathing hard, she sprinted straight ahead, not once glancing over her shoulder. She feared if she looked, she would lose the courage to keep going. The *Raven* was in the caves, and she hoped that the heavy metal terrain had kept it hidden.

A loud whirring echoed. Breathless, she stopped and saw a gigantic cloud of dust. They were coming. She had little time.

When she was halfway through, Emmeline hid behind a rock. One-manned, oval-shaped dark green ships flew in different directions. Catching her breath, she watched in anticipation. The oxygen supply inside her helmet didn't feel like enough. Perhaps she made a mistake, and the pilot was looking for someone else. The ships vanished from her view, and calmness returned to the vicinity. Emmeline relaxed her tense shoulders. Maybe she wasn't the target. A sudden roar of an engine echoed at a distance.

Two large vehicles with enormous wheels and caterpillar tracks drove over the rough terrain. They looked like big tanks with a hefty circular cutter attached to the front. The Imperial Command used the Therans to cut through the mountains to extract metals in their mining operations.

"Damn!" she muttered.

Staying low, she sprinted toward her ship. The sky was turning crimson, and the temperature was dropping. Emmeline kept walking, trying to stay in the shadows. The suit made it exceedingly difficult, and the gravity boots were not helping. She wished Vega 1 was a different place. The roaring vehicles were right behind her. Feeling exhausted, Emmeline had no choice. She took refuge behind a cluster of rocks. Thirst and exhaustion took over, and she sat on the ground with a thud.

Two Therans were not far behind, and the ships were still hovering over the area. Emmeline wondered why they hadn't detected her yet. Grabbing her scanner, she studied the readings. They were scrambled, and the device failed to scan more than a meter. It was the heavy metallic deposits on the moon's surface. She looked at the small hill a few miles ahead. She remembered playing with Delta in those caves.

The laughter and joy remunerated in her mind. Her father would often come to Vega 1, and she would insist on bringing Delta along. While he conducted business, they would explore the caves. Her father had told her to stay away from them, but Delta and Emmeline never listened. The friendship that she had for so long was lost.

If only she could return to that time.

The patrol ships circled like vultures in the sky, and Emmeline had no choice but to wait. The two Therans continued searching. Emmeline kept her head low and closed her eyes.

The noise stopped. Emmeline opened her eyes and thought she had fallen asleep. She peeked out through the holes between the rocks. Two Imperial Command guards stepped out of the enormous machine. Grabbing her device, she searched for the most common frequencies used by the Imperial Command. Once she had access, she listened with interest. It was wrong, but she did not care.

"Are you sure she left?" demanded a guard.

"She was just another passenger! I got a message from the Discovery Colony that a lady fitting her description had boarded my ship. I responded to the message. Next thing I know, you guys showed up. I do not want to cause trouble. Why are you after the young lady?" the pilot of the passenger ship demanded.

"That is of no concern of yours," replied the guard. "Do you know her next destination?"

"Hey! I do not harass my passengers. I just did my duty as a citizen. I need to go back to my ship…you have wasted my entire day!"

"We'll keep looking," the guard said acidly.

Emmeline sulked.

They got back in the vehicle and drove off. Emmeline took her chance and ran. It was agonizing, but she pushed herself. Having rested a bit had worked in her favor. The gravity boots, the suit, and the rocky terrain were a strain on her energy. She had to take breaks frequently. The Therans were ahead of her, and once they reached the foot of the mountain, they would turn left, putting them on her path. She had to make it.

She dashed at full speed like she used to race with Delta. Emmeline almost skidded and was about to fall but regained her balance. Heading toward a cluster of rocks, she sneaked between the stones and vanished into a narrow passage. Before she knew it, she was in one of the tunnels underground. Emmeline relaxed. Turning on her helmet's lights, she looked at the long, dark tunnel.

The walk was hard and long, and she wished she had eaten and drank some water. It was quiet, but she was deep underground and did not know if they were still looking for her. At a point, she paused. She couldn't walk anymore. Bending forward, she put her hands on her knees and thought about her next move. Her greatest fear was getting lost. The scanner didn't work, but from memory, she knew she was on the right track. She stretched. A rumbling noise resonated, followed by steady thumps.

"Oh, damn." She turned and ran.

Emmeline's mind became foggy, and she sensed she would faint at any given moment. The suit was keeping her alive, but her feet and legs were killing her. Her back was stiff, and taking each step was becoming tiresome. She didn't know if she would get to the ship. It was all too much. But she couldn't give up. At a point, she stopped, looked up, and froze. Her jaw dropped, and her heart sank. The tunnel ended in a dark wall.

"Shit!" she muttered. She had taken a different route back because she knew that most of these tunnels were interconnected.

Maybe I took the wrong turn.

Then she remembered.

"Oh, how foolish of me!"

She bent forward. Under the yellow glow of the helmet lights, she saw an opening.

Oh, it's still there.

Grabbing her disruptor, she adjusted the setting and fired. A small ball of dust rose. Getting on the ground, she crawled through the narrow hole. It was difficult; she wasn't thirteen anymore. Rolling down, her leg bumped against a rock.

"Ouch!" she cried out, cradling her ankle.

Aware she had little time, she looked to her left. Her mouth curved into a smile when she saw the *Raven*. She was home. Limping, thirsty, and wishing she were dead, she hurried to the ship.

The door closed behind her with a clang. Emmeline ripped off the helmet and took a deep breath. A sense of relief rushed through her. She was alive and home. She grabbed a water bottle and took a few sips. With the bottle still in her hands, she entered the cockpit, turned on the scanners, and sat in the pilot's chair. The *Raven's* sensors showed that the Therans were in the tunnels. One was to her north about ten miles, and the other to her west about five miles. The screen flickered. The computer automatically repeated the scans and reported slightly different locations of the vehicles. It didn't matter. They were coming, and she had to get out.

She typed on the keyboard, and a map of the moon and the tunnels flashed on the screen. She studied them. After calculating her options, she turned on the engines. Flying was not her forte, but she hoped her idea would work. The lights switched on, illuminating the tunnels. *Raven* lifted above the ground and turned. Punching in the coordinates, she navigated away from the opening.

The tunnels shuddered as the ship passed through, leaving a trail of dirt and rock.

She looked at the screen. The tunnels ahead were wide enough. Trying to stay in control, she pushed a button. The phaser blew through the solid rock, slashing the walls of an older tunnel. *Raven* slipped through the opening and glided ahead. The loud humming of the engines spread through the tunnels. Darkness surrounded the craft, and like a beacon, it moved through the rock and rubble. Debris fell from above, and the ship shook.

An alarm went off as the *Raven* approached a dark wall. She fired, and the phasers blasted an opening in the mountains. The ship emerged in a vast valley, hundreds of miles away from the patrol crafts and the Therans. She pushed the engine, and the ship crossed through the reddish hue. Quickly, she scanned for other vessels. She was alone. The *Raven* broke through the planet's atmosphere and vanished into space at full speed.

AURORA, BRIDGE, DECK 3

Standing on the bridge, Lady Vermont was amused. However, the man on the screen did not share it.

"How did that happen? How did Emmeline Augury have access to the archives?" asked Desmond.

"She used Dr. Chris Kent's codes. The Imperial Command had flagged them. The system detected it during a regular sweep."

"And your men tracked her down to Vega 1," said Desmond.

"Yes, but she escaped, and she had a different face," said the curator.

Lady Vermont exchanged curious glances with the captain.

"Different face?" she asked.

"She used a device to change her appearance."

"Was there a man with her?" asked Desmond.

"No. She was alone as far as we know."

"She took a great risk," remarked Lady Vermont.

"I know. Why?" asked Desmond.

"She needed information," she replied. "Did she take anything else?" she asked the curator.

"No."

Lady Vermont's mood plummeted.

"What do you want us to do?" asked the curator.

"Call your men off. You will need them to defend Discovery Colony. Let us handle her," said Desmond.

The curator bowed, and the image of the broken perimeter cropped up on the screen.

Lady Vermont examined the curator's report. Emmeline had downloaded all databases, including historical, astronomical, scientific, and biological.

Why did she need them?

"Do we send out another patrol?" asked Desmond.

"What would it achieve? The perimeter is offline, and we have limited ships. I think we should focus on the Orias. What if they come back?"

"I agree. We can't be worried about one girl. But we must track her. A direct confrontation may not work."

"Agreed, and she has the piece," replied Lady Vermont. "And we are not the only ones looking for it, so we have to be prepared."

Desmond nodded.

CHAPTER 21: A DIFFERENT LIFE

RAVEN

In the blackness of space, Emmeline finally found some peace. It had been forty-eight hours since she had left Vega 1. She felt safe for now. Flying past Neptune, the ship headed for one of the remotest moons, Proteus. The moon, which passed close to the planet's equator, was not spherical but looked more or less like a box. Its surface was scarred with multiple craters of all sizes, and it spent most of its time in darkness, hidden from the sun.

Emmeline turned to the monitor and located a crater big and stable enough for *Raven* to hide.

"Got it," she muttered.

Entering the coordinates, she increased speed. The *Raven* hovered over the lifeless surface and then set down with a thud. Powering down the ship, she felt relieved.

Emmeline settled on a small table against the window to eat. She gazed out. As far as she could see, it appeared God had accurately placed varied sizes of pearls on a black blanket. The tiny apple juice can was the first one she'd had since she left *Titan*. She enjoyed every sip. Her eyes drifted to the enormous eighth planet in the solar system. It was cold, dark, and supersonic winds dominated its surface. Millions of kilometers away from the sun, Neptune took over six thousand days to complete one rotation.

She ripped the cover off the ration pack and regarded the food. They were not exotic. The meal was bland and had begun tasting like raw cotton. But it was all she had. Until she figured out what to do, she had to stay in the shadows.

She watched the faint vertical rings of the planet made up of debris and clumps of dust. As she swallowed the food, she calculated she had rations for the next three weeks. Soon she would have to think of alternatives. Emmeline remembered her childhood. Her parents were loving, caring and kept her brother close, no matter how busy they were. Emmeline had never felt lonely. Her father gave her everything without asking. And how had she repaid him? She shook her head and balled her fist. Even if she went to prison after destroying the queen, it would be worth it. All her life, she did everything to fulfill her own curiosity. Now, she would do this for Argon. For her father.

She stepped into the science room. The databases were being transferred to the computer.

In a while, the computer said, "Data download complete."

She began calibrating the databases. The screen to her left flickered. Emmeline was puzzled. A small section of *Intrepid's* processor opened, and a hologram appeared. Emmeline cried out, moving away.

The figure appeared unsurprised. "Greetings."

"What—what are you?" said Emmeline.

"I am the *Raven*."

She glared at it in disbelief.

TITAN, ANASTASIA'S OFFICE, DECK 1

Anastasia didn't believe it, but they were taking an inventory of food, water, and other supplies on *Titan*. It was also an effective way of keeping the crew busy. Another thing to do, besides finishing repairs and investigating the disappearing asteroid. The door to her office opened, and Adrian stepped in.

"Here is what we have in the storage," he said.

She went through the list. "It looks good."

"We should be good for the next two years. We also have two drills aboard, plenty of medical supplies, power packs, generators, spare parts, and sixty-two personal and ten cargo containers. We never got the chance to send them to Earth."

"What's in the personal lockers?"

"We don't know. They belong to the citizens of *Titan*, and according to our laws, we cannot open them without permission."

"Agreed. Leave them as they are. But when the time comes…we might have to open them," Anastasia said.

"Agreed. Anything we can salvage to support the crew."

"What about the cargo containers?"

"They are owned by three private companies on Earth. Again, we are not supposed to open them without permission or a plausible reason."

"Right. Any more information about the asteroid?" she asked.

"Nothing yet."

"Have we found any habitable planets?"

He eyed her. "Not in this system. There are two in the next system about thirty light-years away."

"Fuel?"

"We are good for now."

She looked out of the window at the vast singularity.

"I know what you are thinking. *Titan* has the capability and can use its collectors to get the fuel, but the gravitational force around the singularity is too strong. It might rip *Titan* apart."

She smirked. He knew her too well.

"What about the *Prometheus*?"

"It's still under repair."

"I see. How is the crew?"

"They are getting better. I have arranged crew roasters for the entire week. Some of the crewmen are insisting on doing double shifts. I've ignored their request."

"Excellent."

Adrian clamped his hands together. "I've also noticed the commander of *Titan* is doing too many shifts…"

"Adrian…"

"You need to rest. The crew needs you."

She bowed her head. "You are right."

Chris's voice echoed in the room. "Commander."

"Yes?"

"The *Prometheus* crew is here. The meeting is about to begin."

"Thank you, Dr. Kent. We'll be there soon."

TITAN, CONFERENCE ROOM, DECK 2

Anastasia stepped into the conference room with Adrian. As she expected, she saw Mykel, Katia, and Evan sitting around the table. Chris stood near the large screen with Aceline and Isaac. Isaac looked uncertain and stood with his arms folded, leaning on the wall. Anastasia took a seat near Mykel, trying to keep her expectations low.

"Okay. Now that everyone is settled, let us talk about our mysterious asteroid," Chris said enthusiastically.

At least someone is in a cheery mood.

"We detected the asteroid over six days ago. Our scans showed it was similar to several asteroids in our system, except it was denser and had a hidden compartment. We couldn't scan its interior as heavy metallic deposits surround it. Given repairs were our priority. We left it alone. *Titan* was monitoring it, and when it arrived at the exit point, it sent out a brief signal and vanished."

"Where did the signal come from?" asked Anastasia.

"The asteroid generated it," said Chris.

Anastasia was stunned.

"How?" asked Mykel.

"We don't know," replied Chris. "I can confirm that this signal opened a portal, and the asteroid slipped through it."

The conference room became silent.

"Where does this portal lead to?" Mykel asked.

"No idea."

"Can *Titan* go through it?" Anastasia inquired.

"We need to open it first," replied Chris.

"This is all we have got?" Mykel said, clearly disappointed.

"For now, this is all we got from our preliminary scans. If we had known it could open and jump through a portal, we would have done something. Unfortunately, since the asteroid has disappeared, we have no way of getting more answers," Chris said.

CHAPTER 22: GHOST IN THE MACHINE

RAVEN

Emmeline could not believe her eyes. The hologram was a woman with deep blue eyes, short white hair, and a narrow, expressionless face. The eyes glared at her innocently, unable to interpret her reaction.

"How? How did you get on the computer?" she said.

"I am the prototype."

"The prototype," Emmeline muttered. "It's the AI..." she added, realizing her mistake. She was only focusing on the databases but forgot that the computer had its own internal core integrated with an AI. She should have wiped it clean before installing it.

"Precisely," replied AI. "This is not the *Intrepid*."

"No. It's not."

She had asked the computer not to give it access to the ship's mainframe. But it appeared that it didn't stop the AI from interacting. It could be an independent program.

"You are not..." AI paused. "You are not with the Imperial Command. This is a private ship. I belong to the *Intrepid*. You should return me to my ship."

Emmeline was dumbfounded. "You were...in a salvage yard...I...I got you because I needed a computer."

"I am created to serve the *Intrepid*."

"I know. But you are a prototype that did not meet the Imperial Command's requirements, and they decided to…" Emmeline hesitated, trying not to cause any pain. But she realized she was talking to a computer. It had no feelings.

"They decided to destroy me. Why?" concluded the AI.

"I don't know."

"Was I inadequate?"

"I'm unsure."

The AI became silent.

Emmeline waited. Then she asked, "What are you doing?"

"I have conducted a complete diagnostic and determined that I am not damaged."

"You were offline. Left to destroy. I needed a computer, and I connected the computer to the *Raven*…so that…it could help me," she said, not knowing if the AI understood.

"I was created to serve," said the AI. "I am detecting several databases recently added to my memory."

The AI tilted its head as if going through the database.

"Yes. I am creating a database…like I had on *Titan*."

"*Titan*. The military and science space station that guards the perimeter."

"Yes."

"It was your home."

"Yes…"

"Where is it now? Why aren't you on *Titan*? Can't you go back?"

This was too much. Emmeline rubbed her forehead. "Look…just…stay quiet, okay?"

"As you wish. I did not mean to upset you."

"I am not upset," said Emmeline, turning to the screen and starting to work.

"But your face is red. Your voice is breaking, and you are not looking me in the eye. Your facial and verbal expressions show you are upset. And yet, you deny it. Why?"

Emmeline sulked. She started checking through the databases. She began with the imaging database. Trying to find anything remotely close to the image on the plaque.

AURORA, BRIDGE, DECK 3

The work of the *Aurora* crew hardly impressed Lady Vermont. They were confused, frightened, and she didn't blame them. War was unpleasant, and their enemy was ruthless. They needed fearless leaders, experienced crews, and they were short of them.

Emmeline had escaped from their clutches. There was no trace of her. But they had other concerns at the moment. Her eyes settled on the broken perimeter. She watched as the Collector ships cleared the debris. They appeared like big bulldozers flying through space, swallowing the wreckage.

Once it entered the massive machine, it sorted the debris into salvageable and non-salvageable parts. After the cleanup, their next step was to rebuild the perimeter. She wished *Titan* was here. Its crew was well-trained for the task. For now, they will have to manage without them. There was no trace of the Orias, but she had a feeling they were waiting for an opportune moment.

"How long will it take to clear the debris?" she asked Desmond.

"Two weeks at least."

"Can't we speed up the process?"

"No."

"How long would it take for us to rebuild the perimeter and bring it online?"

"Six months at least."

Enraged, she cursed under her breath.

CHAPTER 23 POSEIDON'S WAKE

TITAN, BRIDGE, DECK 1

Leaving the *Prometheus* behind, *Titan* flew toward the coordinates where the asteroid had appeared for the first time. It was Dr. Chris Kent's theory that it might have appeared the same way it disappeared. However, none of the other senior officers agreed with him. Anastasia cared less about where it came from. She wanted to know its destination and if she could take her crew safely through the portal. Her motivation for this dangerous adventure was that she didn't want to waste time. It would take them over eight years to get back to Earth, and she knew they would not last that long.

Maybe the portal could be a good option to reach home earlier.

The bridge crew remained quiet as *Titan* flew past the event horizon. Its radiance fell on *Titan's* hull, illuminating it. The black hole was so vast it could swallow a dozen planets in one go. *Titan* was just a blip in the cosmos. They had sent three probes to study the event horizon. Soon, they would gather more information about Poseidon.

More data to catalog.

Deep down, Anastasia knew that if it were up to Chris, *Titan* would have been diving in the stream of photons around the singularity.

As they turned away from Poseidon, its radiance dipped, and *Titan's* lights brightened to adjust the illumination on the bridge. It was so silent and peaceful that Anastasia felt like she was in heaven. She felt one with the universe, with the gods.

"Commander, approaching the coordinates," announced Adrian.

"Let's have a look."

Titan's speed dropped and slowly came to a complete halt.

"Scan the area," she said, despite knowing that Chris would have already begun.

She waited for answers.

"No other ships in the vicinity," reported Edward.

Anastasia turned to the science station.

"Nothing," Chris reported, looking dejected.

"No residues or any kind of energy signatures?"

"No. They might have disintegrated."

She turned to Adrian. "Can we trace the asteroid's trajectory beyond this point?"

"I can make an estimate," he replied.

"Do it. Evan, inform the *Prometheus* that we are following the asteroid's trail."

"Affirmative," responded Evan.

"We are all set to go," said Adrian.

"Execute," said Anastasia.

Titan's engines roared, and it surged ahead at immense speed.

Titan followed the asteroid's trajectory until Anastasia had enough. They had been searching for over ten hours. Her crew was jaded, and she had lost her patience.

"Anything?" she demanded.

"No," replied Evan.

Leaning on the arm of her chair, Anastasia observed the viewer. It was packed with unblinking white spots. The singularity appeared like a bright yellow dot in the far-left corner.

Evan faced her. "I think we should head back."

Anastasia nodded. She had to conserve *Titan's* resources.

"Let's turn back."

Adrian announced, "Preparing to…"

A bleep sounded.

"Commander!" Chris shouted.

A bright flash of light blinded her momentarily. Out of nowhere, an asteroid appeared.

"Holy shit!" said Evan.

"This is unbelievable," said Adrian.

Anastasia blinked. "Is it the same one?" she asked.

"Scanning. No…" answered Chris. "This one is bigger. It's about eleven-point-seven kilometers long, twenty kilometers wide…it is made up of the same materials as the first one, but this one is denser."

"That's interesting."

"Adrian, can we move a bit closer?" said Chris.

Adrian eyed Anastasia.

"Engines? Weapons?" she asked, not taking her eye off the screen.

"Not that we can detect," answered Edward.

"Shields up, take us closer," she ordered.

Titan's engine powered up, and it glided forward.

"We are about five thousand kilometers away from the asteroid. Matching course and speed," said Adrian.

"This one also has a compartment," Chris said excitedly.

"Why am I not surprised?" she muttered.

"I'm heading to the Crystal Lab to do a deep scan," Chris stated and left the bridge.

"Adrian, where is it heading?" she asked.

Every sound on the bridge died out.

Adrian slowly twirled in his chair. "It's following the same trajectory as the first one."

CHAPTER 24: THE HEDIN

PROXIMA 8

They were stunned.

"I do not believe this," Micah remarked, marching toward the crashed ship.

"Be careful!" Byron warned.

"Most of it has turned to dust," said Micah, looking at his device.

Byron felt his pulse rise. First, the black portal. Then the mysterious signal followed by the alien structure, and now they had discovered a ship. He estimated the ship was about fifteen feet long and six feet wide. He stepped inside the old, broken, rusting craft, which looked like a passenger ship. Layers of red dust covered the interior. Skeletons of chairs sat in rows. Only the legs of the tables remained.

"Oh shucks," muttered Clio.

He turned toward her. "What?"

"This is the...*Hedin*. It's one of the four Earth ships that vanished about thirty years ago!"

"This is unreal. The Orias possibly took the crew of *Nightingale* because we found the remains of a crew member. No one knows what happened to the other three ships," Byron said.

"I tell you, this is bad," said Micah. "Do we have the passenger manifest in the database?"

Clio shrugged her shoulders. "I am unsure."

"Let's take a look," said Byron.

The floor of the ship bent under their weight. The broken windows, destroyed walls, and cracked doors told a story that terrified Byron beyond imagination. After so many years, he wasn't sure if his device could detect human remains. He wondered how they had died. Lack of oxygen? Starvation? He hoped they had a quick and painless death.

"Nothing. There are no signs of human remains," said Clio in a muffled voice.

"This is terrible," muttered Micah.

Byron entered the command center. *Hedin's* roof was ripped off, and they saw the cosmos just above their heads. The workstations belonged to the dark ages and were buried under years of dust. Instead of a triangular viewscreen, only a frame stood as a sign of its existence a long time ago. Byron observed the skeleton of the captain's chair in the middle of the command center.

"Can we get access to the ship's logs?" Byron asked.

Clio did a quick scan, and her pale face was all the answer he needed. But Micah was more optimistic. Clearing the dust with his hands, he found the operations section.

"We might get something here," he said and placed a power hub on the dusty surface.

A light glowed on the small circular object. The old operations dashboard groaned to life as if awakened from a deep sleep.

"This will not last long," Micah said, plugging his scanner into the console and beginning to download.

Byron peered in. A star chart appeared showing the path of the *Hedin*. The picture vanished, and the console died.

"Oh, crap!" Micah said.

"What happened?" Byron asked.

"It's fried."

"That sucks!" said Byron, "What did we get?"

They moved closer to Micah.

"I have got a few logs. Let me see if I can make sense of it. They left the perimeter unharmed. Traveled with no incident for two years. They charted and visited several moons and planets. Until a black cloud captured them."

Silence fell.

"Then what?" Byron asked.

"The helm lost control...one of the engines blew up...that is all I got."

They fell silent.

Byron glanced around. "Did any of them survive?"

"I don't know. This is all we got from the console," answered Micah.

They stepped out of the ship's port side and headed to the other section, which sat at a short distance. Byron grabbed the frame of the door and peered into the dark interior.

"Stay here," he said to the others.

"That is not a good idea," Clio argued.

"Stay here..."

He felt claustrophobic; the walls were narrow. It seemed like he was stepping into oblivion. The lights on his helmet were not enough. Trying to maintain his balance, he slowly walked over the tilted surface. Most of this section was the engine room. The engine had cracked open in the middle. The roof was fractured, and half of the section was buried under dust and rocks. Byron stopped. There was nothing here. He was about to turn when he spotted something buried under disintegrating metal on the floor. Fear paralyzed him.

"It cannot be," he muttered.

Slowly, he lifted the broken panel and saw a crushed human head. The rest of the body vanished under the mesh of metal and flakes of red dust. He hung his head and wished he had never left *Titan*.

Still not able to grasp the situation, he stepped out. A part of him wanted to get rid of his helmet and breathe normally. But the red mist, the rocky gray terrain with cracks and fissures of all sizes, was a brutal reminder that he was not on Earth or the *Titan*. He told his friends about the corpse.

"What happened to the rest of them?" asked Clio, looking around.

"They could be anywhere."

Leaving the craft in its resting place, the trio headed back to the structure. They still needed to know the signal's origin and find a way back home. They wandered around the strange structure. They found nothing new. Nothing that could help them.

"It's just a structure...abandoned and means nothing. Maybe we should head to Vega 9," Clio remarked.

"May—" Byron stopped mid-sentence. The ground below their feet vanished, and they plummeted into a void.

CHAPTER 25: CIRCUITS WITH SECRETS

RAVEN

At the end of the third day, Emmeline was tired and frustrated. This was taking more time than she had expected. The picture on the plaque still wasn't making any sense, and she couldn't find it in the database.

"This is unbelievable."

She remembered it had taken her over two months to solve the previous riddle.

I hope I can solve this one quickly.

She returned to her solitary quarters and looked out at the stars. They were so silent. Quiet. She may die out here, all alone. Perhaps it was for the best. She wouldn't cause any more trouble and wondered if someone would remember her after she died. Of course, her family would, but would they cry over her loss? After what had she done? Her stomach grumbled, and she cringed at the idea of food.

She hadn't eaten for the last forty-eight hours. Not only because she didn't like the food, but also because she couldn't afford to consume three meals a day. If she did, she would have to leave her hiding place. Credit wasn't the problem. She had enough of that. Getting rations without being detected by the Imperial Command was a risk she wasn't willing to take.

She stepped into the small kitchen and reached out for a small tin. The smell of coffee was intoxicating. She put one spoon in the funnel-like object and started the machine. In seconds, the aroma of fresh coffee dominated the ship. She strolled back toward the science room, not knowing what to expect. The computer must have finished running the algorithms. She faced the screen, and the AI appeared again.

"I can be of assistance," it said.

"No. Thanks."

"I've noticed that you have not linked me to the ship's mainframe."

"I've not granted you access. I don't intend to. You want to return to the *Intrepid*. I will return to you in a couple of days. Now. Deactivate."

"You do not trust me."

"You are an AI that was built for the *Intrepid*. I need a computer…not an AI…"

"I can run these algorithms faster…"

"I am aware."

"Why won't you let me help?"

"Deactivate," she ordered.

The figure vanished.

Guilt consumed her, as she longed to have a conversation. AI was not a living being, but it could interact. For the last several days, she had been on her own. The AI might be a pleasant company and help her interpret results. The problem was that if she connected it to the main grid of the *Raven*, it could also take over communication and alert the Imperial Command. It was too risky.

There was no way to control it.

She drank her coffee in peace as the computer ran the algorithms. Part of her wished to bring the AI online. Listen to its story. How did it end up at the wasteland, and why? She had heard truly little about the *Intrepid's* prototype. Suddenly, an idea came to her mind. She began searching for information about the prototype and found three files. She opened them and began reading.

"If you are curious about me, why not just ask?" said the AI.

Emmeline sulked. "Fine. Tell me everything about you."

"Six years ago, I was designed by Dr. Willis on the Discovery Colony. Then I was stationed at the colony to talk with passengers and crew to test the level of interactions and my programming ability to decipher human behavior. After that, they updated my computer program and tested me again. I served on passenger and cargo ships temporarily. It was again a test by my creators. I was deactivated for six months, and when I came online, I had superior memory, programming, vision, hearing, defense and offense abilities, and a vast database. I was then integrated into the *Intrepid's* central processor."

"Nice."

The AI didn't know the entire story, and Emmeline didn't want to tell it.

"I see. What can you do?"

"Everything. Fly, engage in battle, conduct scans..." boosted the AI.

"Can you repair a ship?" she interrupted.

"No."

"Can you clean the ship?"

"No."

"Can you feed data?"

"No."

"So, you can't do everything."

"I get your point."

Emmeline smiled and turned toward the reports.

"Are these reports written by the humans who tested me?"

"Yes, and stop eavesdropping," she said.

The AI fell silent.

She read quietly and discovered the prototype had impressed the Imperial Command. However, they had learned of several irregularities in the AI's functions. They believed it was flawed and needed an upgrade. She read the second report. This was from the captain, who was fascinated by the AI and thought it needed more work and testing. Emmeline knew that *Intrepid's* sister ship self-destructed, and the documentation was thin on that incident, or perhaps it was because it was classified.

Maybe they were afraid that the Intrepid might explode as well.

A beep echoed. It was the communication array, Utopis. She had received more transmissions. After it finished downloading, she grabbed the pad. With excitement, she read the messages. The repairs for the perimeter had started. They had assigned a fleet to defend the perimeter. A search had been launched to track her whereabouts. Emmeline bit her bottom lip. They wouldn't stop hunting for her.

"If I am not mistaken, those are classified messages. You are a civilian. You should not have access to them," said the AI.

Emmeline frowned.

"I cannot see the entire screen from this location, but you are tracking messages between several parties, including Imperial Command. Interesting. You forbid me from eavesdropping, but you do the same. Why are there different rules for humans and AIs?"

Emmeline regarded the AI. She had an idea why the Imperial Command had disassembled it. It was a pain in the ass.

CHAPTER 26: HARD DECISIONS

PROMETHEUS, MYKEL'S QUARTERS, DECK 3

Captain Mykel Lockhart woke up with a headache. The doctor had been hounding him to rest. Take a break. Finally, he had followed the doctor's advice. Although he had slept well, his head felt heavy. He lay back on the bed, crossed his legs, and relaxed.

The alarms blared.

He sat up. "What is happening?"

Jumping out of bed, he rushed out of his quarters. Katia's voice echoed in the passageway. "All hands report to your stations."

He stepped into the elevator and pushed the button several times. Huffing, he reached the bridge.

Katia stood up. "Good morning, Captain."

"Morning. What's going on?" he asked.

"Another asteroid has appeared. *Titan* is following it."

"What?"

Mykel contacted engineering. "Ingrid, is the core online?"

"We need two more days."

"Can we move if we want to?"

"Chief, I said two days means two days."

"Just in case there is an emergency."

"In that case, we can. But I cannot guarantee the safety of the ship."

"Fine," he replied and banged his fist on the chair's handle.

The alarms continued to blare over his head.

"Shut that thing down," he said to Patrick.

The bridge calmed down, and the throbbing around his temples reduced. He strolled near to the viewer. "Okay, what do we know?"

"*Titan* has completed its preliminary scans. If it's correct...the asteroid will take about seven days to reach the exit point," Katia replied.

"Like the first one," he remarked.

"Yes."

He gritted his teeth and loathed. His ship was crippled. *Prometheus* was still under repair. If *Titan* was attacked, there was nothing he could do. Patience had been his friend all these years, but now he was losing it.

TITAN, CONFERENCE ROOM, DECK 2

The asteroid had reappeared, and the crews of both ships came together to decide a course of action. Mykel entered the conference room. As everyone settled in their chairs, it dawned on Mykel that the crews of *Titan* and *Prometheus* were quite different. *Titan's* crew had lived in a sheltered environment. Away from harm or fear. Every day would have been almost the same with the assurance of their daily needs being met.

On the other hand, the *Prometheus crew* had been on a voyage in deep space. They'd had their triumphs, sorrows, and a fear mixed with excitement always hung in the air. Today, the atmosphere was different. It was full of anxiety, judgment, and dread.

He and Anastasia sat at one end next to each other. To his left were Katia, Nick, and Ingrid. To his right were Adrian, Evan, and Cyr. Chris sat opposite him. He swiveled back and forth in his chair. Mykel had expected Dr. Aceline Keston to show up, but when she did not, he wasn't surprised.

As Anastasia studied his proposed plan, he noted Katia eying Adrian, who avoided looking at her, and Nick and Evan were having a staring contest.

"You two know each other?" he asked, breaking the ice.

"Yeah," both said acidly.

"Good," said Mykel, feeling a lump in his throat.

"How have you been, Evan?" asked Nick

"Oh, I've been better," replied Evan.

Adrian turned to him, looking surprised. Katia crossed her arms and regarded the men.

Hoping the engineers of the two ships would be more friendly, Mykel eyed Cyr and Ingrid. No such luck. They sat with their arms crossed, not even looking at each other.

Oh, this is just wonderful.

Anastasia placed the pad on the table and casually sat back with her legs crossed. Mykel secretly wondered if she had realized the tension between their crew members. Their eyes locked.

Oh, she noticed it as well.

"Okay, it appears we have different opinions," Anastasia said, starting the meeting.

"This could be our only chance. We should study the asteroid," Chris said excitedly.

"Our priority is to find its destination and attempt to open the portal," stated Anastasia.

"But we do not know where it leads," protested Mykel. "We might end up further away from home or into enemy territory."

"Or it might lead us closer to home," argued Anastasia.

"It's dangerous."

"We have to take some risks," said Anastasia.

"I suggest we plot a course—" Mykel said, but Anastasia cut him off.

"And spend eight years in space!"

The room became silent.

Mykel felt his pulse rise. He wanted to lash out. But this was Anastasia, and a part of him agreed with her. The truth was, he was scared. They had been lucky so far and survived a catastrophe. What if their luck ran out? "I don't like taking the long way home, but this could be catastrophic," he said.

"I am not denying that it's dangerous, but we need to find out if it is possible."

Mykel was about to argue when Chris interrupted, "Don't we have a say in this?"

All heads turned to him.

"What do you suggest?" Mykel asked, clearly agitated.

"I've got a plan. We hitch a ride with the asteroid," offered Chris.

An unsettling silence spread throughout the conference room.

"What the heck are you saying?" said Ingrid.

Chris explained, "If we align our ships with the asteroid and expand our shields. When the portal opens, the pull should take us through with the asteroid."

"You make it sound too easy," remarked Evan sarcastically.

"It is not," Chris said.

"A small mistake could rip us apart," commented Katia.

"It's a risk," said Chris.

"You detected a signal before the portal opened. What if we replicate that signal?" said Mykel.

"I don't think we can. The asteroid generates it," replied Chris.

"How?"

"Unknown. That is why we need to study it."

"Any other options?" asked Anastasia.

"No," replied Chris.

"This is a bad idea," said Mykel.

"Mykel...we should give this a shot," said Anastasia.

"It's too risky," he said.

"We have taken risks before," commented Katia.

"Yes. But this situation is unique," argued Mykel.

Everyone looked distressed.

"What do you think, Adrian?" Anastasia asked.

He shrugged his shoulders, "I'm unsure...it's all so uncertain."

Everyone felt a weight on their shoulders. Any decision they made would define everyone's fate. They could prevail or perish.

"You know what? We can always vote," Evan mocked.

All heads turned toward him.

"Really? That's what you got?" said Katia.

"At least I had an idea," replied Evan.

"Actually, it's not a bad idea," Chris said thoughtfully.

"It's a stupid idea," argued Nick.

Mykel and Anastasia exchanged worried glances.

Evan leaned forward. "We live in a democracy, right? Let us see what the people have to say. And this time, let's actually listen."

A chill ran down Mykel's spine. Nick and Evan had some unfinished business, and he was concerned that might intervene in their mission to return home. Whatever it was, it sounded personal, and for the time being, he let it slide.

TITAN, CONFERENCE ROOM, DECK 2

Somehow, Evan's suggestion led to a deeper discussion. Given the situation, all senior officers deemed it necessary to involve the crew in the decision. The commanders of the ships explained the situation to their crews and asked them to vote within an hour.

Mykel felt better. He knew Anastasia's idea might still get more votes, but at least whatever they do will be a group decision. Well, more or less. The monitor behind him displayed the votes as a blue and a red bar. A beep echoed, and the voting began.

They leaned closer and chatted as their crews ignored or glared at each other. A bell sounded, and Mykel's idea of getting home the long way appeared to be gaining popularity. Anastasia eyed him.

"If I grow old and wary in space, I am going to blame you," she whispered.

He smiled. "We'll find a different way."

She said nothing. Her eyes, the sound of her voice, and her face brought Mykel immense joy. At first, they discussed trivial matters and then turned toward repairs.

"I'm glad we have each other. I have no one else I can talk with to such an extent," he said

Her face softened. "I'm very pleased and glad you are here."

Another bell sounded, and more votes poured in.

In the next ten minutes, the idea of hitching a ride on the asteroid was gaining popularity.

"Okay. Has everyone voted?" asked Mykel.

Katia checked and said, "The *Prometheus* crew has finished voting."

"Evan, is everyone done?" Anastasia asked.

"All but one," Evan said with a smile. "The crews of both ships agree to hitch a ride with the asteroid."

Mykel felt like this was going to be a disaster.

At that moment, the doors to the conference room opened, and Dr. Isaac Finch stepped in. Mykel thought the exobiologist looked unwell.

"Commander," he said, looking at Anastasia, "pardon my intrusion."

"You are not intruding, Isaac. How can I help? Are you well?"

"I am well, thanks. Just worried. I'm considering our options. I had never left Earth until a few weeks ago. Now I am…so far away from home. I'm confused. If we make this jump, what is the guarantee that we will be safe?"

Mykel looked at Anastasia.

She tried to smile. "There is none. It might take us closer or farther away from home if we jump. It's risky, but most of us believe it might be worth it."

"And if we decide to fly home without using the portal?" asked Isaac.

Before Anastasia could reply, Evan said, "We will run out of fuel and food in two years or die before that. One by one, all of us will perish. Perhaps an alien exobiologist might find our remains, or another alien race might find us, kill us, and have us for breakfast."

Mykel held his head. Sometimes he wondered if Anastasia should be stricter with her crew. But *Prometheus's* crew was no different.

"Thank you, Lieutenant," Anastasia commented in a skeptical tone. "Isaac…"

A bell interrupted her.

The last vote was added to the two colorful bars on the screen behind them. Mykel turned. The blue bar was much higher than the red one. Ana had won.

TITAN, ANASTASIA'S OFFICE, DECK 1

In her office, Anastasia studied their plans. She was not thrilled about it either but strongly believed they had to give it a shot. It was apparent Mykel disagreed with her. It wasn't the first time, and it wouldn't be the last. She had thought he would change after being in deep space for years. It appeared that hesitation in taking risks remained ingrained.

After finishing her work, Anastasia didn't want to sleep. She meandered through the empty corridors of *Titan*. She soon found her way to the Midnight Orchid. The venue was quiet, and the plants that adorned the large hall sat under dim blue light. Glad to be alone, she took a seat and admired the cosmos.

She wondered if she should have a drink but decided against it. A shadow fell over her, and she looked up to find Mykel.

"Morning."

"Are you also burning the midnight candle?" she asked

Without answering, he relaxed beside her. "Yes. I just can't sleep. By the way, *Prometheus* will be ready in a day."

"Good."

"It would be better if we combine our efforts. I'm worried that the opening of the portal may not be wide enough."

"I have given it a thought. But we won't know until we give it a shot," replied Anastasia.

"And a probe wouldn't work?"

"No. It will stop transmitting the minute the asteroid passes through the portal," she said.

They watched in singularity, each trying to ponder their situation.

"Anastasia, there might be a possibility that only one ship can go through. If *Titan* can cross…"

Her face hardened. "No!"

"Ana…"

"Absolutely not! I am not leaving you or the *Prometheus* behind. Either both the ships get through or none."

"But if you have the chance…"

"No!"

Argon's dead face flashed in front of her eyes. Delta's screams rang in her mind. The image of Emmeline behind bars, labeled a traitor by her own people, would haunt her for the rest of her life. She had let it happen. It was on her. She did not wish to lose *Titan* or Mykel. It was not an option. They had to stay together.

Mykel was sensible enough to remain silent. Although she was infuriated, she wanted him to stay. He reached out and held her hand. A couple of days ago, she would have reacted differently. Now she welcomed it.

"We leave this place together," she said firmly.

Poseidon's radiance fell over them.

"Whatever you say," he said, leaning forward, getting closer to her. Anastasia's hand slid over his neck, and they kissed. Their lips parted for a second, but she wasn't done yet. Nor was he. He pulled her near, and she could feel he had wanted this for a long time. The truth was, so did she.

CHAPTER 27: DISTANT MEMORIES

HAIDES CASTLE

The queen was not excited about Aithon's plan. She would do what she had always done. Listen, use him, and then have her way in the end. She deserved it all. It was her birthright, even if it meant getting rid of all the obstacles from her path. No one could stand in her way. Everyone either had to obey her or die.

She relaxed on the throne in the massive hall. The rectangular pools of purple liquid remained still. Inside the shimmering circular band above the throne, the smoke of diverse colors moved counterclockwise. The sky was silent, with no traces of Orias ships or flying beasts. The sturdy walls of the castle were dark, and she welcomed the peace.

Taking a moment, she eyed her hands and then touched her thighs.

This form is intriguing

It ignited her curiosity. The sensations were thrilling. She didn't recall feeling this alive. She had spent most of her life formless, like a ghost. Remembering her encounter with the humans, she felt exhilarated, especially with Anastasia.

It was good to meet a formidable enemy. Someone who is a challenge and didn't run like a coward.

A laugh echoed; a memory emerged. It belonged to a time when the stars were different in the open sky. Shadows of small creatures danced around the hall, music played in the background, a silver mist fell from the sky, and the aroma of beautiful scents lingered in the air. Laughter filled the room. Bright light from the curved windows fell on the shiny ground, and the doors threw open into a world full of harmony, love, and peace. Surrounded by green and purple trees, the castle glittered under the sun. It was a long-forgotten memory. She recollected it, but had she lived it? She didn't know. Before passing away, her species could transfer memories from one to another. It was a choice. This memory could be from her sister or brother. She didn't know. Her father had deceived her and didn't part with his wisdom or love. Instead, he had exiled her.

A voice called, and the vision vanished.

"My queen?" said Aithon.

Her face turned solemn.

"Speak," she said.

A light flashed, and images of the perimeter appeared to his left.

"I have searched their realm."

A star map of a small solar system emerged.

"Their realm has eight planets, with several dwarf planets and asteroids. It expands to over sixty posts inside and outside of their solar system. The number of people on these posts is limited, and most of them are based on asteroids or planets with minimal resources or protection. They have built three heavily armed stations and have multiple ships."

"It's a minor insignificant realm."

"It's small, and we need to find one human amongst millions."

"True."

"The first piece should lead her to the second. We should capture her before she finds it," said the queen.

"Precisely. Also, she has the plaque. It is invaluable to us. We need it," said Aithon.

"I agree."

They fell silent. It was not her way, but she needed to conserve her energy for future encounters. Humans were insignificant. Once she had the piece, she could eliminate or ignore them. She had no recollection of communications between humans and her predecessors. She rose and walked down the stone passageway. Her eyes settled on a dark figure half-buried in the wall. Her long hair fell around her rounded hips, and her face had delicate features, with eyes that still revealed hope. Her mouth remained partially open as if trying to speak. The queen huffed. She was glad it was quiet. Finally, she couldn't talk anymore. She didn't want to hear what her mother had to say a millennium ago. Why would she care now? She sensed Aithon beside her.

"Prepare four ships," she ordered.

He bowed and left her alone.

RAVEN

Emmeline debated whether to connect the AI to the *Raven's* main framework. She was worried about the consequences. She was not a computer engineer and did not have the capability of manipulating AI programming.

It's best I don't take the risk.

One by one, she checked the algorithms she and Aceline had used to decipher the first figure. None of them were working. She was on her own, and she was struggling to think clearly.

The plaque was alive again, and it was telling a different story this time. Its border brightened. For a minute, it seemed as if she was looking at a window that opened into the heavens. Dark in the middle, bright on all four sides. The light died out, and a symbol of the sun glowed in the center. A dotted curved line appeared one dot at a time. It formed an elliptical shape. Once both the edges met, a small glow gleamed, and then the plaque became dark.

"I wonder what this means?" she muttered.

Another dotted line appeared from the right corner of the plaque and formed a similar elliptical pattern. When the endpoints met, she saw another glow, and the plaque dimmed again. The plaque continued until it reached the seventh pattern. Once again, the plaque became dark. She bit her lip, waiting for it to reveal more. Nothing happened. She tapped it, and once more, the border radiated, and she watched the elliptical patterns appear and disappear. All of them looked the same.

She banged her head. "Oh, this is useless."

Sitting on the floor, she studied the meteoroid and her notes. She didn't know if the meteoroid had any significance. Referring to her notes on the pad, she knew it was of unknown origin. Although it was found with the *Nemesis*, its secret remained unknown. Alexander Hendrix, her ancestor, who was working on the *Nemesis*, thought it was unrelated. Her analyses showed it was unremarkable.

But then why did he keep it?

Emmeline struggled day and night. Hidden from the sight of her enemies, she remained in the dark, attempting to solve this mystery. What was going to happen next? Even if she solved this puzzle, how would she get to the second piece? Where would it lead her? There were just too many questions.

The alien artifact in her hand appeared worthless. The piece was about five centimeters long and curved. It had no striations or drawings. The computer had failed to identify its contents, nor could it tell her the artifact's age. She placed the piece on the floor and played the musical tune Aceline had found to unlock the plaque.

Nothing happened.

"Okay, that didn't work," she muttered. She plucked the piece and closed her fingers on it.

"There has to be a way," she muttered.

She felt a pinch.

"Ow!" she cried out, dropping the piece to her feet.

She looked at her palm; it had punctured her skin.

"That can't be right," she said, lifting the piece. Her blood smeared a section. She flipped it over. There was no sharp end.

"What the hell?"

The blood smeared a section of the piece. Like magic, it absorbed the blood. She gasped, dropped it, and moved away. She watched in horror as variations of striations appeared on it as if an invisible hand was carving on its surface. It didn't move. Nor did it glow or make any noise. Then the patterns stopped emerging. She waited in anticipation.

"Okay, that was weird," she muttered, glancing at her palm.

At first, she thought the piece might have unlocked the puzzle on the plaque. She checked, but that was not the case. She put the plaque aside and picked up the piece to study the patterns. Emmeline walked to the computer, working on new algorithms to solve the puzzle. She searched the databases for the patterns on the piece. They were far too common. She shook her head and let it go.

Alone with her thoughts, she went inside the cockpit and collapsed into the chair. The monitor connected to the processor in the science room was on. Her mind began wandering. At first, she remembered her home. It was the most beautiful place she had ever known. Her mother adored the garden full of hybrid flowers, and she smiled at the memory of her father working in the study. Her mind then wandered from *Titan* to Argon. His smile, his soft voice, and beautiful eyes. Blood trickled to the floor, and with a thud, she saw him fall. Emmeline's heart raced.

A surge of anger that she had been repressing emerged. She visualized and rejoiced in watching the queen suffer, burn in agony.

"I'll destroy her," she muttered.

The queen had ruined her life, her world. She would not spare her and burn every Orias to the ground, bringing a reign of fire to her world.

"Ahem, you are angry," observed the AI.

Emmeline sighed. "I am fine, thanks."

"I detected an elevated pulse, heavy breathing, and you were talking to yourself."

"I said I am fine."

"May I ask the reason for your emotions?"

"No."

"Why not?"

"Just...stay quiet."

"You are not very fond of me."

She ignored it and checked the computers' progress on the algorithms.

"You didn't answer my question."

"Let's say I prefer *Titan's* computers," she replied.

She rubbed her neck, thinking she might have to create and run another set of algorithms. Old techniques may not work this time.

"*Titan's* computers are last generation. They are slow, inefficient, and hardly interactive."

She frowned at the AI. "They have a unique quality."

"What?"

"They shut up when you tell them to!"

CHAPTER 28: THE SPECTER

PROXIMA 8

Screaming, Byron fell hard on his back. Panting, struggling to get back on his feet, he looked around for his friends. Loud clashes resonated.

"Clio? Micah?" he called.

Moans echoed. Byron carefully got to his feet and checked her suit. It wasn't damaged. He walked with a limp.

"Clio! Micah! Where are you?" he asked.

The *Titan* Squadron was lost and alone. The signal they had followed led them to an old crash site and an alien structure. Byron glanced up; he could see the stars. He blinked, but the image did not change.

"Byron?" called Micah.

He focused on finding his friends. "Here…"

The trio found each other.

"Are you two all right?"

"Yes. What happened?" Micah asked.

"We fell," Clio replied.

"I figured. What the hell is this place?" said Micah.

Byron smacked his helmet, and lights came to life. The illumination wasn't enough, but it would have to do. The trio walked in different directions.

"It's like an enormous hall. About ten-by-ten meters," deduced Byron.

"Do you see anything?" Micah said.

"This way. There is a tunnel," Clio said.

Byron and Micah followed her. The trio moved through the gloomy hall and stopped when they saw a sculpture atop an ancient-looking rock.

Micah whistled. "That's cool…"

The sculpture was made of whitish fluid flowing upward, shimmering in the dimness.

Byron stepped closer to examine it. "This is unusual. I can't get any reading. I think it's disrupting my scanner."

Clio tested his theory. "Agreed. As if it's there…and then…it's not."

Byron sulked. "Let's see if there are any doors and figure a way out of here."

They marched in different directions. The surfaces of the hall looked as if they were created from the moon's rocks. Despite no signs of water or life, Byron's device showed that the air was breathable.

That's odd.

The levels of oxygen, nitrogen, and carbon dioxide were lower. The air pressure was comparable to higher altitudes on Earth. It reminded him of when he went hiking in the Alps. He smiled, remembering the snow, fresh, chilled air, and his father.

I wish I could go back.

Byron focused on his current situation.

"Hey, guys, the air is breathable," Micah said.

"I know. Do not remove your helmets," warned Byron.

"Agreed," said Clio.

He walked along the long, uneven wall. It was so silent he could hear his pulse.

"Here," Micah called.

Finally, something.

They converged at the far end of the hall, which looked slightly different.

"This could be a door. My scans show there is a corridor behind this wall," Micah said.

"Where does it lead?" Byron asked, checking his device.

"No idea."

They spread around and looked for a way to open the door. The wall refused to reveal its secrets. Byron walked in circles, thinking of a way to get out. Were they supposed to get out? Would they find a way home? He did not know. Perhaps time would tell. Even if they opened this door, how would they get back to *Titan*? *Hiden* was not salvageable. Their crafts did not have enough power to get through the Kuiper belt. They needed a bigger, better ship.

Byron halted when he noticed something. The statue had changed its color. When they had arrived, the fluid was misty, whitish. Now it was purple.

That's interesting. Why did it change color?

He stepped closer to it and scanned again. To his surprise, the reading made sense. The statue was made from carbon, silicates, water, ice, and an energy force.

What is this?

A whoosh resonated. He spun. The door opened.

"How did you do that?" he asked Micah.

"I didn't!" he replied.

Byron thought it was better not to ask any more questions. They rushed down the dark, curved, rocky passageway. He examined their surroundings. It was cold, silent, and daunting. Byron wished Micah would say something or Clio could make a comment. But they remained quiet. The silence was killing him. They might be the only humans alive for thousands of miles. His heart was racing, and sweat gathered on his skin. The suits were comfortable, but still, they were constricting. He took a heavy breath and tried to remain calm.

They came to an abrupt halt when the corridor ended, and another door that looked like a wall blocked their path.

"Now what?" Micah asked.

Byron was already at work. His device beeped several times, and the readings made no sense.

"My scanner is not working," he admitted.

With a loud thump, the rock moved to the side.

"How is this happening?" Clio asked.

"I don't know," replied Byron.

They stepped through the door and froze. Breath left him, and he gaped at a charred figure on the floor.

"Holy crap!" Micah cried out.

A loud humming resonated as if something had awakened and rumbled through the walls. Byron pulled out his disruptor and spun. Beyond the dim yellow glow emitted by his helmet lights, all he saw was darkness.

CHAPTER 29: DANGEROUS ENDEAVORS

PROMETHEUS, BRIDGE, DECK 1

Mykel paced while the ship's crew rushed around preparing for their mission. He bit his lips, remembering the kiss the night before. He sensed as if her scent stayed with him. Blood rushed to his face. It was brief, but enough to leave a mark on his mind and change everything. No one needed to tell him what it was. He already knew. Brushing his thoughts aside, he focused on the task ahead.

Hopefully, they can leave this section of space. Their attempt to piggyback their way into the portal of the asteroid seemed like a promising idea. But in reality, he was worried and saw several loopholes in the plan.

"Captain, we are ready," said Katia.

Mykel dropped in the captain's chair and watched the viewscreen split into four sections. In the upper-left corner of the screen, he saw the asteroid. It kept moving at its usual pace. The lower-left section gave him the birds-eye view of the Crystal Lab. The science team was busy doing final calculations. In the upper-right corner, he saw Ingrid prepping the engineering crew. He was thankful to her; she had brought the ship's core online as promised. In the lower-right corner, he saw the bridge of *Titan*. Everyone was on their post, ready for action.

The alarms blared, and the image changed. Now all he saw was the asteroid.

"*Titan* is ready," said Anastasia on the intercom.

He looked at Katia, who nodded. "We are good to go."

Mykel reached out to engineering. "Ingrid, are we ready?"

"Chief, let's go. I have put additional shields around the core and engineering."

"Excellent," he replied.

Now all he could do was hope for the best.

The ships flew closer to the interstellar object. While the *Prometheus* positioned itself above the asteroid, *Titan* hovered below it. They moved toward the exit point.

Prometheus's floor vibrated.

"Get the probe ready!" Mykel shouted.

The bridge trembled. A tremor passed under his feet, and his heart leaped to his throat.

"Okay," said Katia, "if our calculations are correct, the gateway should open in…five, four, three, two…one."

A bright yellow flashed, and a glittering ring appeared. Mykel closes his eyes momentarily. The portal shimmered like millions of colorful gems. They sat in awe. Mykel leaned forward, trying to see beyond the radiance. All he saw was blackness.

"Dispatching probe," announced Katia

A flare left *Prometheus* and vanished into the portal. As they neared the portal, the ship vibrated, which he expected. But then it jolted unexpectedly, almost throwing him out of his chair.

"What was that?" he muttered.

Lightning struck the ship. It vibrated.

"Shields at eighty percent and holding," announced Katia.

Out of nowhere, an immense ball of energy appeared.

Mykel's eyes widened. It hit the ship. *Prometheus* shuddered, and the tremors increased. The engine's humming intensified, and the lights dimmed on the bridge.

"Captain, our shields are weakening... *Titan* is compensating," said Katia.

"Increase power to the shields," he ordered.

Stability returned, and the ships stayed with the asteroid for a moment.

Another massive bolt of energy struck both ships, releasing a rage of uncontrollable shuddering. All the lights went out, and alarms echoed.

Bang!

A panel caught fire.

"Take care of that!" he shouted, shielding his eyes with his hand.

"We better move fast. I can't keep this up!" yelled Ingrid on the intercom.

"Nick, push it..."

"Sir, the portal is not expanding! It's too small!" yelled Katia.

The shaking intensified, escalating the *Prometheus* to a deadly fate. Mykel knew something was wrong. Very wrong.

"Can we increase speed?" he asked Nick.

Mykel froze. If Nick answered him, he didn't hear.

Giant sparks of lightning appeared from the edges of the portal and struck the ship. *Prometheus* dipped. The energy surges attacked the hull of the ship, weakening its shields. The asteroid slipped into the portal. From within the darkness emerged a bolt of fire.

"Nick, turn! Turn!"

Like bombs, multiple panels around the ship erupted into flames, and fire and gases filled the corridors. The bridge shuddered vigorously, and Mykel was pushed off his chair.

The emergency lights blinked on, and Mykel sat up, feeling dizzy. The surrounding sounds were muffled at first, but then they became clear.

"Oh no, not again," he muttered.

He turned and saw Seiko sitting on the floor, looking dazed. Their eyes met.

"Captain," Seiko said.

"Lieutenant," he replied.

The men got on their feet.

"What happened?" Mykel asked

"Our shields weren't stable enough. Also, something stopped us from getting closer to the portal and jumping with the asteroid."

"Like a security system," remarked Seiko.

He glanced at the viewer. "So, we didn't make it."

"No."

"Damn! Report," he said, walking with Katia to her workstation.

Katia began going through damage reports. "Fires on decks three, five, and six have been sustained. Sensors and power are working at seventy percent capacity. Environmental and gravity systems were not affected."

"So, we were lucky," Mykel remarked, feeling utterly disappointed.

He opened a channel. "Engineering, how is everything down there?"

"Alive. Can we try not to blow ourselves up!?" Ingrid replied in a high-pitched voice.

He smiled.

"What about the probe?"

"It transmitted data before the portal closed," said Seiko.

"And?"

"We need time to process it."

Mykel grunted.

"Captain, *Titan* is hailing," said Patrick, dusting his clothes.

"Put it through."

Anastasia's frustrated face appeared in the viewer. "*Titan* has sustained minimal damage, and there was a fire on deck three. How is the *Prometheus*?"

Mykel looked at the burned wall. "We'll survive," he remarked.

All eyes shifted toward him.

"What happened?" he asked, placing his hands on his waist.

"Our shields collapsed. It couldn't hold, and we were thrown out since we did not have the same polarity as the asteroid. Also, the asteroid emitted a signature signal. A frequency, to be exact. It worked like a key and opened the portal. We need that key if we want to get through."

"Ah! Did the Crystal Lab get anything?"

"Dr. Kent, report," said Anastasia.

The screen split in two, and Chris appeared, waving his hand in front of his face and coughing.

"What's going on?" Mykel asked, looking past Chris.

Smoke engulfed the lab. The fumes cleared for a moment, and he saw Aceline on the floor. She slowly sat up, holding her head. The medical team rushed in.

"Chris! Aceline!" called out Anastasia in a worried tone.

Chris ran his hands through his hair. He looked dazed. Isaac came to stand on his side. "Any other bright ideas!?" he yelled.

CHAPTER 30: FINDING CLUES

RAVEN

Emmeline sat on the floor, trying to concentrate. The AI tried its best to remain quiet, but it failed miserably. It was like a curious child who had been locked away for years and then sent out into the world. It had so many questions and wanted Emmeline to answer everything. She did not blame it. It was the forgotten prototype. Created to replace computers on ships like *Prometheus*. It never saw the day of light.

The algorithms did not work. And now she was preparing a new set. Perhaps integrating images from different databases would give her solutions. Emmeline couldn't understand. It was such a simple picture—was it so hard to solve? She scratched her hands. The minor wound in her left palm was healing.

"How could it have pinched me?" she wondered out loud, glancing at the piece lying in the middle of the mess on the floor.

She was so engrossed in her work that she had forgotten that her dinner tray was still on the floor beside her.

"I know you have asked me to remain silent," said the AI. "But it has been twelve hours. You have not eaten, slept, or consumed any liquids. That could be hazardous to your body. If you do not eat, your sugar levels will..."

"Stop."

"Fine. I'll stop. See, I can listen."

Emmeline rolled her eyes, then shut them. She was tired, hungry, and frustrated. Finding the second piece was challenging. Without decoding the picture on the plaque, she could not go further. Thoughtlessly, she gulped down the food and drank some water.

"Ahem. I can help," said the AI.

Emmeline disregarded it. She was too tired and slept.

Blood filled the floor, screams echoed, and a pair of icy hands grabbed her throat. She saw Argon's face. It was all scratched, bleeding, and with his last breath, he said, "Run."

Emmeline sat up on the bed, screaming. Panting hard, she grabbed the pillow. Taking deep breaths, she tried to calm down.

It is just a dream. Another nightmare.

"Emmeline?" called AI. "Emmeline?"

Wiping her face with a cloth, she cursed under her breath. She hated her life. Emmeline dragged her feet to the science room.

"Uh, there you are. I know you asked me not to speak. But I heard a scream."

"It's okay. It was me."

"Good morning, or I should say, afternoon."

"Afternoon."

"I think there is an important thing I should mention."

Emmeline frowned.

"There is an Imperial Command patrol ship nearby."

Emmeline's drowsiness vanished. She rushed to the cockpit and found out the AI was right.

How did it know?

Emmeline marched to the science room. "How did you know? You are not connected to the ship."

"I do not have access to the mainframe of the computer, but I can see."

Emmeline turned to look outside the rectangular window. She squinted and saw a tiny moving object at a distance.

"Have they detected us?" Emmeline asked.

"I cannot tell," replied the AI

Emmeline returned to the cockpit and quickly turned off all the equipment. *Raven* was beyond the scanning range. With nothing to do, she returned to the science room and sat down to watch the ship. A part of her wanted them to find her, end her misery. If she were caught, this nightmare would be over.

What was she going to gain by running? What would be the point? It would not bring Delta or Argon back. Nothing would ever be the same again. The queen's face appeared in front of her eyes, and she wanted to strangle that woman to death.

The patrol ship slowly drifted away. Emmeline turned to the screen and found that her latest algorithm had not worked. She rose to her feet and walked away without saying a word to the AI.

In the cooking area, she flung open the cabinet underneath the bench and grabbed one of the sealed packed containers. With a heavy heart, she ate. If she were to survive on her own, she would need supplies. On *Titan*, she did not need to think about these things.

This is harder than I thought.

Once she finished her meal, she prepared a hot drink. Taking a sip of her coffee, she thought about her day. Another frustrating endeavor of searching for a way to unlock the next puzzle on the plaque. It would not be a straightforward task.

For hours, she sat and created another algorithm. Every minute, her determination grew. She knew she could do this. Power was everything, and it could fix everything.

RAVEN

Minutes turned to hours and hours to days. Emmeline did not give up. The drive to get the piece and avenge Argon kept her going. She did not know what had happened to *Titan*. Whatever it was, it was all the queen's fault. Emmeline's body ached, and she closed her eyes. She drank another glass of water and kept working.

Emmeline did not remember when she fell asleep. When she woke up, her back was stiff, her eyes were swollen, and her throat was dry. When she got to her feet, a cramp ran down her leg. She yelped. Placing her hand on her hip, she limped like an old woman.

The AI watched her from a distance with a subtle smile on its face. Emmeline walked into her quarters. When Emmeline reappeared a few minutes later, she was wearing a new set of clothes and wasn't limping anymore.

"Morning."

"Morning," Emmeline replied.

That was their conversation, and the AI quieted. Emmeline was glad. The AI had learned to listen, and she appreciated it. It had begun to grow on her, and she enjoyed having it around. Still, she had reservations and didn't want to give it complete access to *Raven*.

Drinking coffee, Emmeline walked around the *Raven* with the pad in her hands. If she was to solve this new mystery, she needed more information. She could happily consume all the knowledge in the universe. Always learning, finding new things, discovering the unknown was her passion. That was why she had come to *Titan*.

When she checked the pantry, only one day's rations were left. She sighed.

I think I am close. I cannot go running around for food. I need to get this done.

RAVEN

Three days passed, but Emmeline did not notice. She sulked and banged the console. The algorithms had not worked. After she calmed down, she watched the dotted lines on the plaque, wondering what they meant.

For the next two hours, she created a computer simulation that matched the plaque's design and the pattern.

"Computer, search this pattern in all databases."

The computer began working. She expected the AI to say something, but it watched curiously.

"Too many possibilities. Define parameters."

Emmeline rolled her eyes. "Okay. Search for similar patterns in all archeological databases."

"Searching."

Emmeline tried to distract herself and went for a walk. When she returned, it had completed its search and failed. Frustrated, she ran the pattern through linguistic, anthropological, and historical databases to ensure no one else had found and reported similar patterns on Earth or elsewhere.

The computer searched through thousands of records. Nothing matched the pattern on the plaque. Of course, dotted lines were common, but Emmeline felt these were something more.

"Computer search the astronomical database."

"Affirmative."

The astronomical database included many patterns, and the computer tried to match the image of the plaque with several star charts, constellations, solar systems, and star clusters.

The computer beeped, completing one task after another. She walked to her cabin and collapsed onto her bed. She snuggled the blanket and slept.

Memories appeared as dreams. The scent of jasmine dominated the fresh air. Voices, friendly and full of love, surrounded her. A warm bed covered with plush toys. A hand touched her face, and a voice called.

"Wake up, my darling."

Emmeline opened her eyes, and she was nine again. Arthur lifted her from her bed and carried her to the family room. She was still feeling sleepy.

"What is it, dear?" asked her father.

"I don't want to go to school."

"That's unusual. I thought you liked school."

"But I don't feel like it…"

A jiggling noise echoed, and she looked up. The roof sparkled. Dad had brought something new. It spun in an anticlockwise fashion. It was made up of multiple rings around a silver globe. The rings were flat and balanced several balls that moved in various directions.

"What's that, Dad?"

Arthur smiled. "That's for you to find out."

Emmeline snapped out of her dream and sat up. Bringing her knees together, she sobbed silently. She missed her family.

The computer was still running the algorithms. She had designed it to consider all possibilities, which took time. Emmeline remained patient and thought of ways to kill time.

She began making Argon's quarters her home. Since she would be here for a while, personalizing it made sense. One by one, she unpacked the bags. She stored Argon's clothes in one cabin and then put hers in another.

She regarded the box of credit chips. She had used a few and knew she would need them during her journey.

Photographs from *Titan* filled the bottom of the bag. Emmeline's dry lips curved into a smile as she flipped through the photographs of Delta, Argon, Byron, Clio, and Micah.

I've been lucky.

She stopped at the last photograph of her with Argon. Her heart swelled with sorrow. She touched Argon's face with her fingertip, wishing to see him one last time. Something shimmered in the light, and it drew her attention toward the background. Multiple rings formed three golden globes. She put the photograph down and glared into the void.

"Oh, could that be possible?" she muttered and rushed to the science room.

The computer was still running simulations.

"Stop," she said to the computer.

The AI appeared, but she gave it no attention.

"Show pattern one."

Emmeline had stored each elliptical pattern and given them a number from one to seven. The computer displayed the dotted lines. When the two ends of the lines met, a small glowing circle appeared.

"Change the dotted line to a smooth one."

The computer obeyed.

She eyed the pattern.

"What are you thinking?" asked the AI.

"This could be a system," Emmeline replied.

"A solar system?"

"Yes. The dotted lines could be orbits around a sun," she muttered. "Computer, display pattern two and apply similar changes."

The computer obliged. One by one, the computer updated all the patterns.

"Display all patterns," she ordered. The images appeared on the screen, and she folded her arms. "Merge all patterns with the smallest at the center."

As if by magic, all the patterns came together.

"Put an image of a sun in the middle."

An image appeared.

"Computer," she said, leaning forward, "calculate the distance between the orbits and the number of planets and use this information to identify similar systems in the database."

"Searching."

"There are too many possibilities," remarked the AI. "And this solar system might not be discovered yet."

She nodded. "I know. I know. But at least we are making some progress."

"Agreed."

She waited as the computer searched.

"Five hundred and fifty-two near possibilities found."

Emmeline paced the floor, rubbing her neck with her hand. She returned to the chair.

"Computer, save search."

"Saved."

"Show only pattern one."

The pattern appeared on the screen.

"Show the original stimulation."

The simulation displayed.

"Match starting and ending speeds for patterns one and two."

"Matching," it said, "Pattern one ends zero-point-two seconds earlier than pattern two."

"So, it's faster."

"It appears so," AI said.

"Compare speeds for all patterns," Emmeline ordered.

"Comparing," responded the computer, "Each pattern is slower as it progresses outward."

"Just like in a solar system, the further the planet from the sun, the slower its speed," said Emmeline.

"Agreed," said the AI.

"Let's consider that these are all planets. Computer, from the search, keep solar systems with only seven planets and remove the rest."

"Applied filter."

"Remove systems with asteroid fields or moons."

"Done."

"Calculate their average orbital speed and apply it to the simulation."

"But that wouldn't be accurate," said the AI.

The computer ran the simulation.

There was no change. The plaque didn't reveal its secret.

Emmeline ran her hands through her hair.

"I am missing something."

She turned to the plaque. Its corners shined, displaying several stars as if parts of a nebula, and one after another, the dotted lines appeared.

"This might be a long shot, but try to calculate the overall size of the solar system."

"Computing. Completed."

"Let's assume it revolves around the celestial orbit."

"Assumption added."

"Now, considering the sun as a midpoint, calculate the coordinates where the dotted lines meet and complete the orbit."

The list of coordinates emerged. The computer searched, but the results were disappointing. They were vague numbers.

Pressing her lips together, she said, "What about the axial tilt of these planets? Is there a way we could estimate that?"

"A planet's tilt can be affected by several factors, including an impact of a large celestial object or climate change. Also, it is unknown if the planets rotate clockwise or anticlockwise. The outcome will not be accurate," said the AI.

"Well, I am speculating. Let us see what happens. Computer, using solar systems you found in the database, compute hypothetical tilt for all these planets and apply to the simulation. Then try to find a match."

"Computing," said the robotic voice.

Emmeline sat and watched as the planets moved in different directions.

CHAPTER 31: ENTOMBED

PROXIMA 8

Byron trembled with fear as the voice died out. The rumbling stopped. He held the disruptor tightly in his trembling hands.

"What was that?" asked Clio in a deep voice.

"I don't know," Byron replied.

"My scanner detected nothing," Clio said.

He knew that. But he sensed it. It was here.

"I do not believe this," muttered Micah.

Byron came to kneel beside him.

Micah finished scanning the charred figure on the ground.

"What have you got?"

"He's human."

Byron shut his eyes in frustration.

"He could be one of the survivors of the crash," Micah said.

"Why do you think they crashed? Maybe they were brought here. Just like us," Clio said.

Byron nodded in agreement. "How long has he been dead?"

The device beeped several times as Micah searched for answers. When he finished, he slowly stood up to face his friends.

"What?" Clio asked.

"These are rough estimates, and I do not have a medical scanner. It is a male, around forty years old. The degeneration in the bone and muscle shows he has been dead for over ten years."

"The ship crashed over twenty-eight years ago," Clio mumbled.

"He survived the crash," Byron concluded, standing up slowly, "And he was down here alive for eighteen years."

"If he survived, there might be others," suggested Micah.

"Let's check this entire place," said Byron.

Byron cautiously walked down the dark corridor. The short beams of light emitting from their helmets were not enough. Cautiously, he walked around the curve, ready with his disrupter. His skin crawled with goosebumps, and adrenaline rushed through his body. The unkind blackness surrounded him, and he felt as if something was going to swallow them alive. He sensed both Clio and Micah behind him.

They came to a stop, and Byron glared at the wall. It opened with a thud. Another door, another invitation. To what? What waited for them? Death. Despair. Torture. All he saw was a void, and the darkness was hard to read. There was no other way but forward. He calculated each step. It was here. Something was lurking in the unknown. Suddenly, he was pushed forward and fell on his face. A wall appeared between him and his friends.

"Byron!" yelled Clio.

Byron struggled to his feet. The lights on his helmet flickered and died out. Horror-struck him.

"Micah! Clio!" he called, reaching for the wall.

He pushed it. It did not budge. His fingers searched the wall like a blind man looking for a switch. He couldn't find one. Mist gathered on the screen of his helmet. He turned and saw the statue. Was it following them? Or were they walking in circles? What did it want?

"Who are you?" he asked.

Silence.

"What do you want from us?" he demanded.

No answer came.

It remained still, and the color of the misty statue was now gray.

"We don't mean you any harm. Why have you brought us here?"

It seemed as if he was speaking to stark brick walls.

"We will try to find a way in!" shouted Micah from the other side.

Byron lowered his disrupter. He knew it would not be effective against the entity. A force grabbed him and slammed him against the roof. He cried out as his helmet got knocked out of his head.

"No! No!" he screamed, gasping for air.

But to his surprise, he could breathe. He recalled they had detected breathable air.

"Do not be afraid," a deep voice echoed in his head.

Byron opened his eyes.

"Release me, I mean you no harm," he said.

"You think you can harm me?"

"No. But you are hurting me."

The grip on his neck did not loosen.

"Why...why did you bring us here?"

"Because I can."

"We are a peaceful race. We won't harm you or —"

"Stop," it said.

Byron lost his voice. He could not speak. His throat turned dry, and he struggled to utter a word. Suddenly, the invisible entity released him, setting him down on the ground. Byron stood, unsure if he should move. He rubbed his neck.

The breath of fresh air was welcoming. It was humid, thin, and warm.

Sensing the surrounding, his gravity boots turned off.

There is gravity here. How?

He waited for it to say something. It did not.

"Hi," he mumbled.

There was no response.

"What are you?" he asked.

"You're afraid," said the voice.

"I am. You brought us here against our will."

It didn't answer.

"What is this place?"

Without warning, a force grabbed his neck.

He winced. "Let me go."

It pushed him against the wall, and he felt as if an object was being forced into his skull.

"Stop asking questions!" yelled the voice.

Byron cried out in pain as he sensed thousands of icicles piercing his skull.

CHAPTER 32: BREAKING AND ENTERING

TITAN, ANASTASIA'S OFFICE, DECK 1

Anastasia watched the stars and did not like what she saw. They were different. Too different. She closed her eyes. Sleeping in her office was a bad idea. However, she did not want to be in her quarters, nor did she want to face her crew. She felt she had failed everyone, her crew, Mykel, and her daughters. Their first attempt to escape from this part of space had failed.

Since their last meeting at the Midnight Orchid, Mykel hadn't had the chance to come to *Titan*. It was complicated. She missed him and didn't want him around. His presence was a distraction, and she was sure he felt the same.

Why can't I be logical about this?

But algorithms and logic couldn't predict love, and it was easily resurrected. The feelings she thought were gone had returned with a vengeance. Every moment with him was priceless. The kiss was amazing, even better than she remembered. When it ended, they remained speechless. After Mykel had left, she had wondered if he expected to be invited to her quarters. She didn't know, and the truth was she didn't want to find out. She shivered. They were both commanders of ships lost in an unknown region of space. What if one of them was lost or died? How would it affect the other?

"It's better not to get attached," she said to herself.

A voice popped into her mind. *Too late!*

A beep woke her, and she sat up. Anastasia did not know when she had fallen asleep. Shutting the alarm, she stretched her legs and then her arms. She had slept but didn't feel rested. She marched out of the office.

TITAN, ENGINEERING, DECK 5

As soon as the door opened, Anastasia was stunned. She checked the time; it was 0500 hours, yet it appeared no one had slept. Engineering was well lit, like a stage for a concert, and it was crowded. The enormous drill was the center of attention, and the crew was preparing it for the mission. Cyr was standing on top of it, scanning its hefty blades. She felt proud but feared that if their plan did not work, it would devastate crew morale. They needed a win. Knowing they were busy, Anastasia left without a word.

TITAN, DOCKING BAY, DECK 10

With her hands clamped behind, Anastasia entered the large hall and observed the *Aeolus*. It was an old ship with fourth-generation engines. The gray oval spacecraft was around ten feet long. Its four engines were fitted in a hefty circular structure attached to the rare end. The crew had managed to upgrade it as much as possible to meet their needs. The vessel looked ugly because of the thick slab of steel attached to its roof.

But beauty or shape was not a priority. Stability and strength were. Sparks flew as Adrian and two other crew members stood on ladders and fused the metals.

TITAN, CRYSTAL LAB, DECK 2

Anastasia walked into the Crystal Lab. The science team, Chris, Isaac, and Aceline were deep in discussion, with images of the asteroid displayed on the large monitor.

"Good morning," she said, drawing their attention.

"Commander," replied Chris. He ran his hand along his graying hair. The dark circles under his eyes were growing. His skin was pale, and she was sure he had not slept for a while.

"Progress report," Anastasia asked.

"We will finish on time," said Aceline.

"Good. Chris, you must take some rest."

He was about to argue when she raised her right hand.

"Dr. Kent. We need every member of this team at their best. If you are exhausted, you will jeopardize the mission. I won't have it. Finish your work and get some rest."

He hung his head. "I wish I had more help, and Emmeline is not here,"

She felt his loss. "We have to manage. Do your best."

"You are right. You are right. I just wanted to make sure everything was all right. This is a tremendous risk. I needed to make sure every calculation was correct. There is no room for error," Chris explained.

"I admire your diligence. But we have only twelve hours. Get some rest. That's an order."

TITAN, MIDNIGHT ORCHID, DECK 3

Most of the crew, except the senior officers and those involved in preparing for the mission, were assembled at the Midnight Orchid. She thought this was a better location than a conference or a meeting room. Her crew was rattled and scared. They needed to know she was there for them.

For the next two hours, she spoke with her crew and discussed their plan at length. Everyone understood their jobs. Yet, uncertainty hung in the air.

After the discussion, Anastasia felt good, and she sensed as if the atmosphere had lit up. It was not only for them; it was for her as well. She believed she needed to connect with her crew. They were alone, away from their home. They needed each other.

TITAN, DOCKING BAY, DECK 10

At the end of the day, when Anastasia returned to her quarters, she was exhausted. She drank another cup of coffee and spent half an hour stretching. When she was done, she showered and got dressed. Within minutes, she was back in the hangar. Her heart swelled with pride. She had come at the perfect moment. An overhead crane carried the hefty drill. Then it was lowered to the drill top of *Aeolus*. A loud thud echoed, and the drill perched on top of the craft. The crew got to work, and she watched as they sealed the drill's base above the *Aeolus*.

Adrian came to stand beside her. "We should be done soon."

"Good."

"Cyr and Ingrid have cross-checked all the calculations and ran several simulations. They were all successful."

"We cannot fail," she insisted.

Adrian looked at her. There was a sparkle in his eyes that she had never noticed before.

"This will work."

"Good," Anastasia replied, looking at *Aeolus*.

Clapping his hands, Adrian announced, "All right, let's get her ready to fly in half an hour!"

The deck began clearing, and Anastasia rushed to the bridge.

TITAN, BRIDGE, DECK 1

Anastasia took her seat. Evan was manning his station. The scientists were not on the bridge. She presumed they were in the Crystal lab. Edward, the tactical officer, peered into the screens as if trying to find a mistake in their plans.

"All right," Adrian announced over the comm, "I am good to go."

"Begin the test," said Anastasia and observed the viewer as the engines fired up. *Aeolus* lifted and left the hangar. The bridge crew watched as Adrian tried out several flight patterns.

"How's she doing?" Anastasia asked.

"All systems are working within normal parameters. She is a bit hard to maneuver, but it looks like she could do the job."

"What about the drill?"

"Testing," replied Adrian. After a brief silence, his voice echoed, "It's stable and works fine. We should prepare a casing. Just in case."

Anastasia nodded. "Good idea. Return to *Titan*."

"Acknowledged."

PROMETHEUS, BRIDGE, DECK 1

If their second plan were to succeed, *Prometheus* would have to play its part. Mykel had to make sure they were ready. The ship slowly glided away from *Titan's* location, conducting long-range scans.

Mykel sat on his chair, his headaches long gone, and he had slept very well for the last two nights. Doubts filled his mind as he wondered if the doctor had slipped him a sleeping drug. It was unlikely. The ship's doctor would not do that; he was just too tired. They all were. The crew was frustrated when their first attempt failed miserably. Ingrid was all over the engineering crew, sharing her disappointment. Mykel had to intervene and explain that it was not the end of the world. Sometimes he thought Ingrid pushed too hard.

"Captain, approaching the asteroid cluster," reported Nick from the helm.

Mykel swung back and forth in his chair, "Let us see what we can do…shall we? Edna, start the test."

Edna Lamer had taken Lyle York's post as the tactical officer on the bridge. Lyle was still in a coma. There was nothing the doctors could do. Neuro scans revealed her low neural activity. She was almost dead but not there yet. Peter suggested pulling the plug. Mykel couldn't do it.

Edna had served on the bridge only twice and tried to give a reassuring smile as her chubby face reddened. He didn't feel confident, but he was happy to give her the benefit of the doubt. Katia wanted to take over weapons, but he needed her at her post.

"I have chosen a target," said Edna.

"Good…begin," said Mykel.

"I have made the adjustments to the phasers, and I think it will work. We don't need to test," said Edna.

"It's always good to be prepared. Ready whenever you are," Mykel said, turning to the screen.

"The target approximately matches the size and make of the asteroid," Edna reported, "Firing in three, two, and one."

Prometheus fired, obliterating the asteroid.

Everyone except Mykel gazed at Edna.

Mykel swung his chair toward the tactical station. "Right, let us try that again."

Edna swallowed hard. "Adjusting firepower and narrowing the beam. I think this should work."

All eyes turned to the viewer.

Prometheus fired and blew the asteroid into several pieces. Mykel did not look away from the screen.

The communicator chimed, and Ingrid said, "This is engineering. Can we stop blowing stuff up?"

Nick and Seiko exchange glances.

"We shall try our best," Mykel replied and closed the channel, "Edna...again."

"Adjusting..." she replied in a muffled voice, "and fire."

Mykel controlled his amusement as the third asteroid exploded.

The communicator chimed again, "Edna, if you don't stop, we will run out of asteroids!" said Ingrid.

"At least I can count the pieces this one broke into," remarked Katia.

Without another word, Mykel slowly got up and walked to the tactical station. Katia joined him.

He examined Edna's calculations for the next fifteen minutes, and Katia did a few computer simulations.

When they were ready, a narrow beam left *Prometheus*. Like a knife, it cut through a section of the asteroid. Mykel checked the calculation. He was already missing Lyle, and he was worried about having an inexperienced officer on the bridge.

"That's a good start," he said with patience. "Now let's see if we can refine it,"

He returned to his chair as the crew began working.

And I thought this was the easy part.

TITAN, BRIDGE, DECK 1

The next ten hours were strenuous. No matter how much Anastasia tried not to worry, it did not work. She leaned back in her chair and waited. The entire bridge crew was silent. Their last attempt had been seven days ago. After the fires were out, Chris needed two days to fix the Crystal Lab. During this time, they had come up with another plan.

The Earth ships flew past the wake of the Poseidon and stopped. They waited. The silence was daunting, and

Anastasia wished someone would say something. She would have welcomed a distraction. Something to take her mind off until they could act.

The door to the bridge opened, and Isaac walked in. Anastasia was surprised. He should be in Crystal Lab with Aceline.

"Dr. Finch, what are you here?"

"It's not every day we hijack an asteroid. This one should go in the history books!"

She raised her eyebrows.

"Commander...here it comes," announced Evan from the helm.

A bright light flashed, and as expected, another asteroid appeared.

"Engineering, be ready."

"Yes, Commander," replied Cyr storm.

"Science team, are you ready?"

"Affirmative," replied Chris

"Aceline, Chris will need some primary analysis on the asteroid."

"I am on it," responded Aceline.

Anastasia got to her feet and eyed the interstellar object. "Adrian, you are in command of the mission. If we lose communication, do everything in your power to get back to *Titan*. Do you understand?"

"Yes, Commander," Adrian said.

"The *Prometheus* is making its move," Evan announced.

The bridge crew watched as the Earth ship glided toward the asteroid.

"Opening a channel with the Crystal Lab and *Prometheus*," said Evan.

Faces of Aceline and Mykel appeared in a corner. Anastasia intertwined her fingers.

I hope this works.

"Fire," ordered Mykel.

A laser beam struck the asteroid. It did not destroy it but left a deep cavity.

The *Prometheus* waited.

"Scanning," said Aceline, "The hole is about seven meters in depth and twenty meters wide. Captain, we need more depth."

Prometheus fired again.

"Depth is now twenty meters," reported Aceline.

"Are we close enough?" asked Anastasia.

"Give me a moment," said Aceline as she worked on the console, "We need a few meters more."

"Are you sure?" Mykel asked. "We don't want to damage the asteroid."

"The structural integrity of the asteroid is stable. You can proceed, Captain," said Aceline.

The last shot by *Prometheus* deepened the opening.

Everyone waited.

"That was fantastic. It took off fifteen meters!" Aceline responded with a smile.

"The asteroid?" asked Anastasia.

"Several cracks around the opening, but its structure is stable. It has not changed its course, and its spin axis is stable," said Aceline.

"The compartment?"

"Intact," replied Aceline.

"Adrian, go!" said Anastasia.

A section of the hangar deck opened, and *Aeolus* lifted and flew out of *Titan*. It glided toward the asteroid, which moved at its usual pace, oblivious to everything around it.

"Engineering, now," ordered Anastasia.

A ring of detonators left *Titan*. As she watched it go toward the asteroid, she remembered the hours her crew had put in to develop it. It moved effortlessly through space. When it neared the crater, the ring expanded to adjust to the size of the opening. Its speed decreased and then attached itself around the crater.

"Commander, the detonators are in position," reported Edward.

It was a safeguard. If the opening collapsed, *Titan* would blow up that region of the asteroid to rescue the *Aeolus*. It was risky, but it was one of the best options.

She clamped her hands together to stop them from trembling and watched as the *Aeolus* vanished inside the asteroid.

"Commander, we have entered the asteroid," reported Adrian on the intercom.

"Acknowledged. Good luck."

Now the waiting game begins.

ASTEROID

Adrian's heart drummed louder and louder. He could sense Chris, who occupied the seat behind him. The astrophysicist was calm, which was a surprise to Adrian. Chris was the head of the astrophysics lab. Of course, he must have the basic training like everyone else. But Chris had never been on a deep space mission. Adrian looked over his shoulders and noted Chris appeared as if he was on *Titan*. Adrian felt envious. Chris was doing well, or maybe he is good at hiding it. On the other hand, Adrian was scared to death.

Adrian forced himself to focus. Aeolus glided into the dark cave. The ship's two enormous lights shone as it flew deeper into the asteroid. Debris floated lifelessly and smashed against the ship's shields. Adrian wanted to increase the speed, but he followed his guts and kept the ship steady. Beeping tones sounded in the cockpit, a clear sign that both Chris and Felix were monitoring their progress. One robot that had joined the small team hunkered motionless at the end. Adrian did not think they needed protection, but Anastasia had insisted.

Adrian grabbed the joystick firmly as the ship jolted. The bright lights of the ship flickered on the rough surface of the cave. His eyes rolled to the panel. They had made it. Adrian decreased the speed, and the engines quietened. The thrusters came online. The ship eased down on the uneven surface.

"We have landed. Releasing anchors," Adrian announced.

Four mechanical arms emerged from the ship and attached to the cave walls.

"Checking. The anchors are secured, and the ship is stable."

"So far, so good," said Chris.

"Commander, we have reached the end of the tunnel. We will begin the next step soon."

"Acknowledge. Keep us informed of your progress," Anastasia replied.

Adrian looped in his chair to face Chris.

"Okay, where do we begin?"

Chris remained silent for a moment, studying the data on his screen. "The compartment is about ten meters deep."

"Felix, do you think we should go further into the cave?" Adrian asked.

Felix's curly hair and small face made it unbelievable that he was a fully grown man. That was not the only thing. Adrian had seen him play games, gamble, get into fights, misbehave with his superiors, and miss his work shifts. So far, he wasn't Adrian's problem. Adrian handled crew shifts, duties, and well-being. Felix was a part of *Titan's* crew, but so far, they had assigned him on projects related to the Vesta in the asteroid belt. His demeanor bothered him. Perhaps he reminded him too much of Evan.

One Evan is more than enough.

"This is a good spot to begin. We must be careful and take our time to drill."

I wish we had more time.

"We've seven days until this asteroid reaches the jump point. As planned, we've to finish the drilling in three days," stated Adrian.

Felix nodded and got to work.

The casing built around the drill opened, and a hefty drill appeared.

"Initiating," announced Felix.

The blade rotated, and the drill moved forward. The ship vibrated as the drill hit the asteroid's surface and cut through the rock and ice.

ASTEROID

Adrian was startled as the debris spread around them. With nothing to do but wait, his thoughts turned toward their situation. He feared they might run out of time. Maybe they should have used *Prometheus* weapons to dig a bit deeper. But that could compromise the compartment.

After an hour, when the drilling stopped, Adrian was relieved and rubbed his temples. The ship had finally stopped shaking. The noise and the vibration were too much. He peered out of the front window. Dust and rocks filled the cave, affecting visibility.

"We need to clear some of that debris," said Adrian.

"Agreed. Initializing decluttering," Felix responded.

Two massive box-like structures emerged from the side of the ship. With a loud thud, the robotic cleaners began sucking in the remnants of the rubble. Adrian watched as the debris and dust cleared. He checked the panel and checked their progress. A beeping noise pulled him out of his thoughts, and he pushed the button. The machine stopped, and as a programmed, the rectangular box moved, and soon its mouth faced the opening of the cave. With full force, it threw the dust and rocks out into space.

The drilling began again, and Adrian felt bile rise to his mouth.

Another nine hours of endeavor got them deeper. The drill retracted, and Adrian was thankful for the silence. The last fifteen hours had been tough, and his fears grew. They might run out of time. The cockpit smelled foul, and cartons of food and drink were stacked in a corner. They had been here a little over twenty-four hours, and Adrian already felt a need to take a shower. They had been working nonstop, and it had taken its toll on the equipment and men. The drill reached its breaking point, heating quickly, and they had to stop several times. They were becoming restless and couldn't sleep because of the noise. The vibration made it hard to eat, and Adrian missed the privacy he had on *Titan*.

"I think we are nearly there," said Felix, wiping the sweat off his forehead.

Adrian felt a sense of relief. He had been waiting for a while to hear those words.

To make progress, they needed to push limits. Adrian was happy they had nearly finished drilling in a day.

"How much further?" asked Chris.

"About half a meter. I suggest we do not drill," said Felix.

Adrian was glad.

He left the compact command center and walked into the open living area with three beds, food and drink dispensers, and equipment boxes. He hated the setting. There was no privacy. Unfortunately, the ship was not made for luxury. Adrian and Chris suited up. The door of *Aeolus* opened with a thud. Adrian was the first to step out of the craft. The two small lights on his helmet made a minor difference since the ship's lights were bright and reflected on the walls of the cave. Some dust and small fragments of rock floated around them. He stood awkwardly on the rocky surface and gradually made his way in front of the ship. Chris and the armed robot followed him. While Chris seemed to be engrossed in taking readings, Adrian studied the cave. Who made it and why? Asteroids are usually leftover after the creation of a solar system, and the origins of many remain unknown. But this one had a compartment in it. Why? Most of all, how did it open the portal? He watched his step on the uneven ground and cautiously neared the opening.

The drilling had been successful. Smoke was still emitting from the opening. Adrian peered in. The yellow beams of light emitted by his helmet illuminated a few meters. Beyond it was a dark void. They would have to blow up the last bit to get into the compartment. He moved aside and adjusted the power of his weapon. The robot did the same. Chris took a step back. The two beams hit the rock. Adrian had thought the asteroid would shake. Nothing happened.

"Again," Adrian said.

They fired. Fragments of rocks and soot rose from the hole. They moved aside. Once it cleared, Adrian peeped in. This is the part he hated the most. The climb down the hole to reach the compartment.

Oh, this is going to be so much fun.

He waved toward the ship and then walked to its front. Adrian unlocked a rectangular section. Inside were three sturdy pulleys with carabiners. He grabbed one of them and attached it to his suit. He pulled it twice to make sure it was firm. The others did the same.

He took a deep breath and looked at Chris.

"Well, it's going to be a hell of a ride," Chris mocked.

Adrian chose not to say anything. He walked toward the opening. The tether's tension matched his movements, and the pulley adjusted accordingly.

Putting his legs in first, he crept down the hole. Immediately, he felt claustrophobic. It was dark, and his breath was the only thing he could hear. Slowly, he descended. When he was halfway down, he planted his feet on the walls and glanced up. He could see Chris and the robot at some distance. With a heavy sigh, he began moving again. Fear gripped him. Adrian grabbed the tether firmly. Sweat trickled on his forehead. As programmed, when it sensed his moments, the pulley lowered him. He saw something and pushed a button on the display of his suit to stop. Others did the same. In the dim light, he noticed a layer of rock blocking their path.

"I thought we had broken through," he said.

"Perhaps the scanner didn't pick it up," said Chris over the intercom. "It's a thin layer of rock. We can blast through."

Removing his disruptor, he fired. The debris sputtered everywhere. He waited for the particles to disperse. In the dim light, he saw an opening. He began moving downward, resting his foot on the uneven surfaces. Suddenly, the tunnel's wall became slippery, and he lost his footing.

"Ah!" he screamed.

The surrounding space expanded, and he hung in midair.

"Oh, my god!!" he cried out, reaching out to grab the tunnel's wall and gradually set his foot on the ground. The gravity boots activated, and he sighed with relief. Chris's screams echoed in his helmet.

Adrian stepped forward and caught him. Chris yelled, wiggling his hands and legs.

"Chris, I got you!"

Chris calmed down. His feet set on the ground, and the boots came to life.

"You, okay?"

"Yes. Yes…Thank you. I didn't anticipate that," Chris replied, looking at his feet.

"Nor did I."

They heard a whoosh. The robot dropped from the opening. It stood straight, surveyed the surroundings, and armed itself.

"Nice," muttered Adrian.

"That was nasty," Chris said, looking around and appearing as if he wanted to complain a bit more but was captivated by their surroundings. Adrian glared at the long, shadowy corridor.

"Adrian to *Titan*."

"Go ahead," responded Anastasia.

"Commander, we've entered the compartment."

Anastasia's voice was scrambled. "Excellent work. Adrian, be careful. Proceed as planned."

CHAPTER 33: PROJECTIONS

RAVEN

Emmeline's head spun. Over three hours had passed, and the computer was still running simulations. Finally, when it finished, she grumbled. It was all in vain. She wanted to get up and leave, but she had a feeling she was onto something.

"That didn't work," said the AI.

"Yeah."

"You don't seem frustrated."

"I am. You just don't know it," replied Emmeline, stretching her legs. "Let's think. We assume this is a solar system with no asteroids or natural satellites."

"Precisely," said the AI.

"What other factors can we look at?"

"Several. If we include a few factors like the size of the planets, temperature, atmosphere, gravitational force, orbital planes, and magnetic field, the possibilities are unmeasurable."

"But we can try," replied Emmeline. "Computer begin with sizes of the planets. Apply each characteristic of the solar system to the simulation and provide results."

"Affirmative," replied the machine.

The computer started working, and Emmeline decided to rest.

Proteus revolved around Neptune at its own pace. The dead moon was covered with millions of craters. Rocks had melded together to create various mountain ranges.

Darkness fell over its surface. The *Raven* sat in the crater, undisturbed. A thin layer of cosmic dust covered its hull. The ship was dark, except for the scanners left in surveillance mode.

When she awakened, the complete silence daunted her. Emmeline hadn't realized she had fallen asleep. She sat up, rubbed her eyes, and returned to the computer. It had been about two days, and the computer was still running algorithms. Maybe she was wrong, and this was a highly speculative strategy.

In addition, Emmeline was bored. On *Titan*, she had other things to do, and time passed swiftly. On the *Raven*, it was a different story. She returned to the living area and began going through her notes. She needed an answer soon. A sudden loud ring echoed, signaling the computer was done. She returned to check the results.

"That didn't work," announced the AI.

She crashed into the chair and knew she was missing something.

"Maybe we have not understood the figure," suggested the AI.

She nodded. "You could be..." She stopped as a realization dawned on her. "Computer, show original simulation."

The image appeared.

"Access and display the original image of the plaque from the folder MYTH."

The computer searched, and the rocky image of the plaque appeared.

Stone made plaque (front and back)

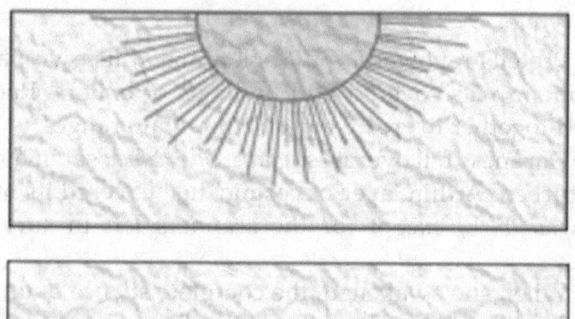

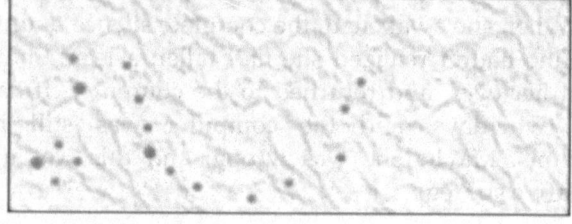

"Computer, complete the figure by duplicating the rays and make it a complete sun."

The image changed.

"Computer, access tune one from the database and standby."

"Tune?" asked the AI.

"So far, every puzzle has two steps. The musical tune had unlocked the first step."

"I see. You think the tune will solve the second puzzle?"

"Oh, can't be that easy," she replied and left the science room. Within a few minutes, she returned with the plaque and kept it on the console.

"When the tune played, it lost its rocky exterior and revealed a smooth tablet," she said, mostly talking to herself. "Meaning that it hears. Listens."

The AI glared at her.

"It might also sense, feel, see…"

"It's not a sentient being. It's an alien object of unknown origin," the AI pointed out.

"You are correct. But as Delta said, not everything is about science."

"Who is Delta?" asked the AI.

Emmeline looked at the AI but said nothing.

"Apologies. I did not mean to upset you."

It's more perceptive than any computer I have known.

"It's okay," she replied, "Computer, project the image of the sun on the plaque."

"Projecting."

A light emerged, and it superimposed an image of the sun on the plaque. The texture of the plaque changed.

"Computer, stop projecting and record the activities of the plaque."

The projection vanished, and Emmeline leaned closer. Purple and gray mist filled the plaque. It was like looking into a crystal ball. The mist dissipated, and she sat in awe. An image of a solar system materialized. But it was immensely different from the previous one. Out of the seven planets, three were blue, two were yellow, and the last two were ash-colored. She noted satellite moons orbiting two of the blue planets. A massive asteroid belt marked the outskirts of the solar system. A light appeared from a corner, and she watched as a comet passed through the system.

"A match found. Ninety percent of the characteristics match with the Satori System," said the computer.

Emmeline squared her shoulders and became alert.

"The image on the plaque matches the Satori System. Identified and cataloged by *Marion* over fifty years ago. It is a million years older than our solar system. Information on all the planets is available in the current database. It is located thirty-five light-years from our current position," said the AI.

Emmeline sunk in her chair and crossed her arms.

"If we leave now, *Raven* can get to that location in fifty days," said the AI.

"It's not a star map."

"But we have solved the puzzle. You wanted coordinates. We have found a solar system that is a ninety percent match."

"It can't be that easy," muttered Emmeline.

"Easy?"

"What is the ten percent variation?" she asked.

"Well, the Satori System has two asteroid fields. One of them is close to the sun."

Emmeline rose to her feet. "What else?"

"The illustration on the plaque shows two moons. The *Marion* reported twenty-seven moons in that system."

Emmeline paced the floor. "Computer, project the picture of the Draco constellation exactly as found on the original plaque."

"That is not logical," said the AI.

"It's not," muttered Emmeline.

"Projecting," said the computer.

The plaque turned dark. She waited, and a golden mist sprinkled with silver filled the plaque.

"This object is interesting," remarked the AI.

"Tell me about it."

The mist vanished, and the image of the solar system emerged.

"The plaque has integrated the constellation into the display," announced the AI.

"The constellation won't be visible at that distance. But it's part of this puzzle," Emmeline said.

"The solar system has changed little," remarked the AI.

Emmeline disagreed. Now they had a closer look. The sun remained in a corner, and all the planets lined up with the two asteroid fields. The Draco constellation sat in a corner.

"Ninety-eight percent match. This is the Satori System," said the AI, "but I think you do not want to go there."

Emmeline wasn't listening to her.

The comet appeared from the left-hand corner, dived downward, flew close to the fifth planet, and then vanished.

"Computer, replay all the activities of the plaque in the last ten minutes."

She watched in silence.

"Computer, has the Satori System changed in the past five decades?"

"Negative."

"Does the system fall in a comet's path?"

"No comet has been reported in the Satori System."

"So, the constellation and the comet are anomalies," said the AI.

"On that, we agree, but what does it mean?" she mumbled. "How is it all linked? Computer, play the tune."

The sound resonated in the room. The image on the plaque didn't change.

"First, it was about the tune...now, it's about projections."

"What do we project next?" asked the AI.

"Well, the image in front of us looks complete," said Emmeline.

"Affirmative. What did the plaque do after the tune?"

"Well, it presented a puzzle which turned out..." She paused.

"What?"

"I assumed they were names given by the aliens to the stars in the Draco constellation, and it worked."

The computer found and displayed the names:

"NepththysLahmuEnkiAstarteUrukGoniLibraeCrcuisS eptuYawHaniAmumNaniApepErkWalhNimo"

"These cannot be identified without reference points," remarked the AI.

"I know. I gather that we need to solve two puzzles before the plaque reveals the star map. We have solved one of them. Why is this so difficult?"

"Whoever created this didn't want the pieces to be found," remarked the AI.

Emmeline eyed it. "True. I wish I had never found it."

They became silent.

"Computer, save the current image on the plaque. Search photographic references begin with the archeological and astronomical databases."

"Affirmative. Searching."

The computer searched through millions of images. They flashed one after another, and Emmeline felt as if she was watching a historical movie. The computer had begun checking from the Paleolithic era. A time when man lived in the wild and hunted to eat and slept in caves. As she expected, none of them matched the Satori System. The cave drawings and stone carvings denoted water, fire, animals, and the sky with the sun. The computer was efficient and skipped Neolithic and Chalcolithic times. The images showed how mankind had progressed and used stone tools, building huts, and showed signs of early agriculture. Art was always a part of human life. Earlier, it was expressed on the walls of caves, and then he began making statues and pots. Hours passed as the computer separated images that might be useful. When it reached the Bronze Age, it slowed down. It flipped through several images of brass plates, coins, and art pieces to search for a match. It found very little.

Emmeline turned to the other screen. While on one side, the computer was running through the archeological database. On the second screen, it was checking the astrological database. Over here, it appeared to have made some progress. The computer paused at the image of a petroglyph belonging to 1600 AD. She leaned forward and read the notes. Scientists speculated the rock carving was describing a supernova. The computer ignored it and moved on. It slowed down again, and the year was approximately 500 BC. Early diagrams and images of her solar system appeared.

She smiled at the intelligence of her ancestors, who built models and theories with crude instruments. It was intriguing. The computers selected a few images, saved them, and then moved on. Technological advancements increased man's understanding of the world and the universe as time passed.

The computer had to work hard, and the list of pictures was getting longer.

Bored, she looked at the archeological database. The Bronze and Iron Ages were more interesting. Weapons made of metal became popular, and images like the Satori System became rare. It found a few coins with images of the sun and planet and others with a crescent moon. The computer continued its hunt, and Emmeline dozed off in the chair.

A strain on her neck woke her up. Emmeline saw the computer was still working. She walked to her quarters and slept.

She blinked her eyes open and found herself surrounded by darkness. A foul odor bothered her nostrils. Shivering, she curled her arms around herself. A hissing sound dominated the darkness. She felt a lump in her throat. From darkness crept out long curved extensions. She moved away from them, and a shadow glided over her head. Hearing a sudden roar, she spun and shrieked. Two large yellow eyes glared at her. Emmeline fell and landed on her back. A roar echoed, and a black slimy tentacle grabbed her leg and pulled her into the void.

Emmeline woke up screaming.
"Emmeline are you alright?" asked the AI. She didn't answer and pulled the blanket close to her chest.
"Emmeline?"
"I am fine."
The AI didn't respond.
She remained still until her breathing returned to normal and her heart wasn't racing anymore. The nightmare had left her terrified. Why was she having them now? She had never had nightmares before.
She put her fears aside and made a cup of coffee. Before heading to the science room, she checked the scanners. No

other ship was in the vicinity, and there were no more communications from Utopis. She returned to the computer and saw that it had finished.

"Display results," she said.

The computer said: "Identified and downloaded ten thousand and fifty-one images."

"Good. Now project each image on the plaque. Wait for five seconds. If you do not detect a change in the plaque...project the next image. Understood?"

"Understood."

The computer continued. Emmeline thought she should leave, but she couldn't. She dreaded the thought of missing an image. The computer was, after all, a machine. She watched as it diligently projected pictures as the plaque remained still.

The day passed slowly, and Emmeline walked around the room to stretch her legs.

"Computer, status?"

"Fifty percent search complete."

She sulked.

Getting a few blankets from her quarters, she lay on the cold floor. She was tired, but she didn't want to sleep. She was afraid of the dreams. To distract herself, she read notes on her pad.

The computer beeped, and Emmeline sat up. She couldn't believe she had slept for over ten hours. She stretched and was about to leave when the computer beeped twice.

"Detecting activity. Detecting activity. Attention required," announced the computer.

The plaque came to life. It glowed and sparkled like a jewel. Then it became black, and a star chart appeared, displaying a set of coordinates.

"Yes! Yes!" Emmeline jumped.

"It worked?" said the AI.

"Yes."

"That is interesting," remarked the AI.

Curiously, she peered into the monitor to find out which image had unlocked the plaque. She observed the image of an ancient-looking clay plaque with a pinkish hue. The smooth stone was broken in a corner, and it was about thirteen inches wide and ten inches high. Seven circles in uneven planes had been craved around the sun. A thin band of tiny dots surrounded the sun and the solar system. A circle with a long tail was carved in the upper left corner.

"Computer, identify source."

"The image of the rock plaque was first taken and added to the database by the *Prometheus*. It was found on the planet Proserpina, which was destroyed by a comet approximately hundred years ago."

Emmeline was stunned.

"The plaque is assumed to be at least a million years old. It did not match the art, culture, or history of Proserpina and was believed to be of unidentified origin. Dr. Aceline Keston recently added a special note. According to her analysis, there is a possibility that the comet that destroyed all civilization on Proserpina was identical to the Nemesis."

"That's quite a coincidence," said the AI.

"It's no coincidence," she muttered.

The AI studied her face.

The plaque chimed. The computer read the star chart.

"System identified and coordinates found," the computer announced.

Emmeline picked up the plaque. She didn't need the computer to identify the solar system.

"You have got to be kidding me!" she cried out.

CHAPTER 34: FRIENDS AND ENEMIES

RAVEN

Emmeline walked up and down in the cockpit. The AI tried to remain quiet but failed because her actions raised its curiosity. It kept asking her about the encrypted message she had sent. Emmeline refused to share any information with the AI.

"It will be fine," she told herself.

She felt a cramp in her stomach and knew it was time. There was little choice. She had enough untraceable credits, and now she needed supplies.

Turning on the engines, she sat on the chair. Argon had done well, and she had survived for a month because of him. Now it was time to take care of herself. If she wanted to find the next piece and complete her mission, she had to take full responsibility for her actions and take control.

Dust flew in every direction as the *Raven* rose from its hiding place. Leaving Proteus, the craft flew around Neptune. Emmeline's stomach twitched with anxiety. All the dreadful possibilities haunted her. The idea of spending the rest of her days behind bars or on the run was daunting. But she didn't have a choice.

Do not get caught. Just play it cool. You will be fine. The Imperial Command is busy fixing the perimeter, and the Orias have left the system for now. I can do this.

The *Raven* flew toward its destination.

An hour passed. The *Raven* was on automatic surveillance, monitoring the movements of the Imperial Command ships. Most of them were guarding the perimeter, and others were out of range. There was no trace of *Prometheus* or *Titan*. Emmeline hoped they were safe and sound. The *Raven* dropped speed as it approached the asteroid field. Long-forgotten rocky fragments of the solar system hazardously flew in every direction. The craft entered the asteroid field. Several tiny rocks hit the shields of the ship, and *Raven* vibrated. Emmeline quickly stabilized the shields, and the vibrations stopped. The craft flew past the field and waited at the rendezvous coordinates.

At a distance, she could see blinking red lights. Despite the danger, the activities at the mining colony Vesta hadn't been reduced. Emmeline lowered her eyes and remembered the day Delta had left *Titan* to drop a drill to Vesta. Emmeline wished Delta had remained on the Vesta Colony or gone to Earth. Perhaps she would have never unlocked the puzzle or discovered the rogue planet.

There is no point in thinking about this now.

Fifteen minutes passed in agony. What if he didn't show up? What if he alerted the authorities? She pressed her lips firmly together. She had to trust Gael Stoll. There was no other alternative. Gael and Emmeline had become friends on Earth a few months before she moved to *Titan*. At that time, she didn't know if they would accept her application at the Crystal Lab. Argon was not in her life, and Delta was busy flying passengers through the system.

Emmeline remembered her cozy home. The soft blankets, the clean, fresh air, the beach a few paces away. She felt her mother's touch and heard her voice.

Oh, I miss her so much!

Like any parent, her mother was unhappy to send her only daughter away at such an early age. Despite how she felt, her mother was her champion. Arthur was vocal about his feelings and didn't want Emmeline to leave. He constantly reminded her not to pursue the mystery of the mythical device. She thought her father was her worst enemy. But her view about him had changed. No one needed to tell her. Arthur had helped Argon plan her escape.

I was so wrong about him.

Emmeline knew Gael was fond of her. It was written all over his face, but she had to be extra careful around him. He was a kindhearted, kindred spirit who enjoyed the little things in life, and his greatest ambition was to fly a transport craft. It suited him.

Guilt consumed Emmeline. Since she moved to *Titan*, she had hardly been in touch with him. There was another reason. She did not want Gael to find out about Argon. A beep distracted her. She quickly checked the identity of the craft and relaxed. He was here.

The small transport ship was not much to look at. The hefty craft appeared like a big rectangular box docked with the *Raven*. Emmeline waited for the airlock to open. She had turned the AI off and locked the science room. Emmeline did not want him to know anything more than what was needed. Her heart drummed in her chest. What if he told someone? What if he informed her father? She forced herself to think positively.

Just get this over with. Do not let him hang around for long.

But this was Gael, and as far as she knew, he loved to hang around and has all the time in the world. She reached out for her pocket and checked the chips. Gael was her friend, but this was a business transition. Taking the supplies without paying him would be unfair. The airlock opened, and someone she had never expected to see again showed up on her doorstep.

Gael looked older and had gained weight. He wore black clothing, and his hair was long and rumpled. Emmeline was shocked. As far as she remembered, Gael used to wear trendy, colorful clothes. Today, he looked as if he had stepped out of a funeral.

"Hey, Emmeline...wow...you look the same."

Emmeline smiled. "Hi. How are you?"

They embraced. She felt better hugging her friend. Seeing a human being after such a long time was comforting.

When they parted, Gael's face turned grim. "I heard the news."

Emmeline said nothing.

"I am sorry," he said.

She didn't smile.

What was he sorry for? Why do people say that? Why? Nothing can be done. It was all her fault. She should be the one who should be apologizing.

"Don't say that."

Gael looked around. "Nice ship."

Emmeline faked a smile.

"Is it yours?"

Emmeline controlled her tears. "It belonged...to a friend."

Gael raised his eyebrows. "And he just gave it to you."

"No. It's borrowed. How are you?"

Gael eyed her. "I am fine."

"How is the business?"

"Yeah, let's just get to that, and I think I should get out of here."

So, the talkative, free-spirited Gael is gone. Everyone changes.

"Agreed," she said.

"Well, and I am married now."

Emmeline nodded and wondered why he had to tell her that. Gael was two years older than her, and she was glad he had found someone. "Congrats. That's wonderful."

Gael's eyes dropped.

"I am helping you because we are old friends..."

"You don't have to explain. This is just a transition. You are a seller. I am a buyer. That is all."

"What if?"

"By the time they find out...I will be gone," said Emmeline, assuring him.

"Well...If they find out, I cannot protect you, and I'll have to give them your location."

"I understand. I don't want you to get in trouble. I will pay you, and I'll leave. As I said, this is just business," Emmeline explained, feeling her heart tearing apart.

Gael swallowed hard, and guilt filled his face. He turned and disappeared into the ship.

Emmeline was sweating, and her heart raced. She knew something was off. Gael was different. Maybe he was not her friend anymore. Maybe she should have chosen another trader. She almost jumped when she heard a loud clang. A shadow appeared, which turned into barrels. Emmeline relaxed and watched as Gael pushed the six barrels of fuel and a big box on a trolley.

"Where do you want them?"

"Leave them here," she said, giving him the chip.

He arched his eyebrows. "You want me gone."

"The longer you stay here, the more danger you could be in."

"Where will you go? You are alone. Emmeline...you can come and stay with us. Hide in my house."

And he is back. Why can't you stay cold?

"Gael, I can't stay," she said.

Opening the box, she picked up one of the firearms and checked the power cell. The lightweight steel gray weapon was about ten inches long. Its grip was comfortable, and its barrel was board.

"I hope you don't need that," he said.

She eyed him. "It's for protection."

"From the Imperial Command?" he asked worriedly.

She put the weapon back in the box. "Something far worse."

The color drained from his face. "Emmeline, come with me."

She looked him in the eye. "No. It will put you and your family in danger. You'll always be my good friend, and that is why I need you to leave," she said, sensing her heart break.

"Emmeline…"

"You need to go," she said, handing him over the chip loaded with enough credits.

Gael's face turned grim as he accepted it. "I thought you would come to me when you needed help."

"I did. Now, you must leave."

Gael slowly nodded. They hugged, and without another word, he stepped into his ship and the airlock shut behind him.

After the ship disembarked, Emmeline rushed to the cockpit and started the engines. She wiped her tears away as she watched Gael's ship fly past the rocks, which spread over miles. All her friends were lost. The few she had left, she had to make sure she didn't hurt them.

No one else needs to suffer.

Increasing *Raven's* speed, she plotted a course toward her next destination. It was going to be a long ride, and she had to stay hydrated. She drank some water and walked to the barrels for fuel. She scanned the container to check the quantity.

I should have done this immediately.

Gael had distracted her, and her emotions clouded her judgment.

I should've been firmer with him. He was here for too long.

HORUS

Two hours later, she found herself at the Horus, a small trading post farther away from the perimeter. It sat in orbit around an exoplanet that could not hold any life. The trading post was a hub for space travelers to get supplies and a pit stop for ships on a long voyage. She already had all the fuel and weapons she needed. Now she needed something that would keep her alive. Food.

Emmeline had used the Utopis communication array to download a list of "flagged" ships. *Raven* was not on it. She was surprised. Adrenaline rushed through her body, and her brain reminded her of the danger. She recalled the episode on Vega 1.

That was too close for comfort. I do not want to go through that again.

Knowing the coordinates of the portal and probable location of the second piece was good, but where would the portal take her? She didn't know and needed to be prepared.

The colony had seven oval decks, with lights glittering on each one. Several small ships entered and departed the station. As the *Raven* approached, Emmeline heard a broadcast.

"All visitors and colonists beware. We are at war with a hostile species called Orias. Horus might be at risk. The Imperial Committee is now in session and is considering shutting down the colony and moving all colonists to safety. If you wish to return to Earth, you are free to do so. Further information will be transmitted soon."

Raven entered the hangar deck and landed in between two large vessels. She walked into her quarters and once more used the mask. This time, she used a new face. Ocean blue eyes and snow-white hair with ginger skin. She looked at herself in the mirror and gasped.

"Just one more time," she told herself.

Taking a deep breath, she hoped her plan would work. She had already placed the order, but she needed to pick up the supplies. Trying to look as confident as possible, she stepped out of the craft.

The air was foul, and people too busy in their own worlds crowded the space station. Horus was a colony dominated by traders, and the Imperial Command had less influence here. A union of private companies who wanted to expand business to every part of the system had created it. Over the years, Horus became invaluable to private ships and a major food supplier to space stations like *Titan*. Emmeline tried to remain as calm as possible.

Taking the elevator, she went to level four. Emmeline knew where she had to go. It was just a few meters. She did not see any guards or patrols, which was good. Entering the shop, she approached the woman behind the counter.

"You have an order for me," she said.

"Consignment number?"

She handed over a chip. Without another word, the shopkeeper placed it on a round, glowing platform. The lights turned green. Emmeline expected her to say something, pass a comment, or raise her eyebrows. However, to her delight, the lady did not care.

"Pay now."

Emmeline handed over another chip.

Again, the shopkeeper checked the credits and said, "Wait here."

She disappeared behind the rows of boxes filled with supplies stacked on top of each other. Emmeline turned, and she could see several people walking up and down the passageway. None of them paid any attention to her. She hoped it stayed that way. The shopkeeper appeared with her package, which was on a small trolly.

"Here you go. Rations for six months."

Emmeline checked the boxes. "Thank you," she replied and left.

Like most people in the crowd, Emmeline pushed the trolley, and it was tough walking in a straight line. She had to maneuver several times to avoid bumping into people. Her eyes rolled toward the surveillance cameras, and she hoped no one was watching. Although she was happy that she had food and it was of better quality than before, eating the same thing for the next six months was not appealing. She paused when she saw a shop with fresh food. Emmeline knew it was made from synthetic materials developed in a food lab, but it did not matter. Anything was better than eating food that tasted like cotton. Acting quickly, she entered the shop, bought some fresh products, and rushed back to the *Raven*.

Securing the supplies, Emmeline turned on the engine and left Horus. She released a long breath and pondered about what she could eat. Her thoughts were interrupted when the console buzzed. Terror struck her when two Imperial Command ships approached the Horus Colony.

CHAPTER 35: UNREAL

ASTEROID

A drian was bewildered. During his career on *Titan*, he had been stationed near the perimeter. It was a job that involved no adventure and almost no risk. Drilling into an asteroid to find out what made it tick was something he thought he would never do.

Ah, God help us.

His gravity boots felt heavier, and his breath was strained. Adrian knew there would be no one on the asteroid. But still, it was foreign. Unknown. Dangerous. Their equipment was not built to detect all kinds of life forms. Something could lurk in the darkness.

The ground was solid, uneven, and full of broken rock fragments. His throat clutched as he took the first step and then the next. With the robot in the lead, the three figures slowly made their way down the passage. It was a lonely, mysterious walkway. He wondered how someone could create a compartment within an asteroid. It was incredible.

The interior fascinated and terrified Adrian. It was an irregular interstellar object created from piles of rubble, converging to produce a complex mixture of metals infused with carbon and silicon compounds. For a moment, he felt like he was in an underground cave on Earth. The stony asteroid was big, and he could not say it was the usual rock flying through space. Most of the asteroids were formed from the rubble during the formation of the solar systems. The tectonic findings from *Titan's* deep scans had revealed an intriguing history.

Technically, S class asteroids have a lower density and are porous, but this one had a high density. The rock layers were infused around two hundred years ago, which could have happened during its creation. However, that did not explain the compartment and the fact that it was protected by a three-meter-thick layer of rock rich in metal that blocked their scans. No wonder they needed to drill.

"This is very interesting," said Chris, looking up and down.

Adrian's device showed it was minus forty degrees. The interior was a vacuum. There was no tremor, no sound, and no life. There was no engine, at least none that he could detect. They expected the temperatures to drop as the asteroid moved away from Poseidon. That didn't worry him. His suit regulated body heat and protected them from radiation.

The two men followed the robot.

"Adrian, how are you doing?" asked Chris.

"I'm fine. Why do you ask?"

"Nothing. Just checking."

The robot stopped and turned. "Stay here."

"What's wrong?" Adrian asked.

"There is a door…it could be rigged."

Adrian looked ahead. It did not look like a door, more like a hatch made of the same material as the surrounding walls. The robot rotated the circular handle and pulled the door outwards. As if it had been closed for centuries, the robot had to use immense strength, and when it opened, dust flew in every direction. They walked through the door to enter the chamber.

"Amazing," muttered Chris, looking around.

Adrian nodded, feeling a mix of fear and excitement. The chamber they entered was double the size of *Titan's* bridge. It had no comfortable chairs, ceiling lights, high-tech equipment, windows, or a smooth carpet. He felt like he was in a dark, cold cave in a mountain with a small circular window that opened into space.

Adrian's attention was drawn toward the broad panel, which formed a part of the wall. A large rock sat in front of it. Chris took a seat and began examining the panel. Adrian noticed the wall behind him. It was like a painting. Made of the gray rock, it appeared as if a liquid flowed down from both sides. At the bottom were huge waves crashing against each other. The top half was plain, with several hexagonal shapes spread over the surface. Adrian scanned the wall. The data told him it was a part of the asteroid, just more rock. But he didn't believe it. Under the yellow glow of his helmet lights, he saw another tunnel.

Adrian spoke into the intercom, "Commander, we have entered the compartment."

"Good. Remember, you have only six days. We need to work fast."

"Understood."

Chris had already made himself at home. He closed the scanner and pushed a button. The panel came to life.

"There is power," said Adrian.

"Yes. But where is it coming from?"

The panel made noises, and lights blinked all over.

Chris began clearing the dust.

"I will check out that tunnel,"

"Okay," replied Chris.

Adrian said to the robot, "Stay with Dr. Kent."

"Affirmative," it replied.

Armed, Adrian walked ahead and left the chamber through another uneven opening. This passage was smaller, and he had to bend and move slowly. The ground was made up of large, disproportionate pieces of rock.

"You pick the best places in the system, don't you?" he muttered to himself.

After several minutes, he found another small chamber. He was astounded. Under his helmet's dim lights, he observed an inverted funnel that emerged from the roof and vanished into the ground. The wall was smoother, as if polished by a machine. There were no lights, sounds, or radiation. The temperature was similar to that of the asteroid. His heart pounded, and the air inside his helmet seemed warmer. *Titan's* sensors would have never picked up this section. It was too deep. The chamber was crude but marvelous. He imagined all the ways it could have been created. Perhaps they dug inside the asteroid, built the compartment, and then used the rock to seal it. With years, the rock became fixed and looked no different from the other.

"But why built it?" he wondered aloud.

It could be a weapon. The thought did not bring any peace to Adrian's mind. Maybe it was a ship, but it had no doors, quarters, or an engine. All they had found was a panel in a chamber, which could be a control panel.

He bent over, and the scanner beeped several times. He kneeled.

"What's down there?" he said, looking at the readings.

The device showed that there was an object buried under the rock.

"It could be an engine," he muttered.

He got on his feet and tried to stretch as much as possible to reach the roof. Adrian's device was not powerful enough. But it did the job. When it stopped beeping, Adrian read the data. He was taken aback. Whatever was up there was in liquid form.

Was it a tank? Maybe a fuel tank.

He bit his lips and wondered if they should blast through.

Making a note of his findings, he saw another small passageway. He wondered if the builders were short and skinny. A species that could crawl or walk-through compact spaces. He took the small passageway, bringing him back to the main corridor. Adrian returned to the front compartment and found Chris. Multiple screens were now active. Adrian noticed one rectangular screen with rounded corners was filled with figures and symbols.

"Okay. What do we have here?" he asked.

"This makes it tick," Chris replied.

"A computer?"

"You could call it that."

"Do we have the frequency?" Adrian asked.

Chris frowned. "Not yet. We need to decipher these figures and then locate the frequency that opens the portal."

Adrian raised his eyebrows. "We have only six days."

Chris eyed him. "Yes. I know. To find the frequency, we need to understand the language. Also, we need to know how the frequency is generated and where to find it."

Adrian scowled.

PROMETHEUS, GYM, DECK 6

It was late at night, and his crew had gone to bed. But Mykel couldn't sleep, no matter how hard he tried. At first, he thought he should go to *Titan* for a swim. He decided against it. With nothing else to do, he ended up at the gym.

It was a gray rectangular hall with equipment attached to the wall. The crew had the options of running to lift weight or doing high-impact exercises with a holographic instructor. Mykel hadn't turned to any of the equipment. With a loud grunt threw a punch. The punching bag swung. Sweat dripped down, soaking his shirt. Every muscle in his arm ached, but he enjoyed it. He punched harder, not stopping until he was breathless. Walking away from the punching bag, he glanced out into space. The asteroid glided at a casual pace. He stood by the window, catching his breath. They had successfully entered the hidden compartment, and their next task was to get the frequency. He hated waiting and feeling helpless.

"This better work," he muttered.

Pounding against the wall, he turned to the bag and hit it hard.

CHAPTER 36: DARK TERRITORY

TITAN, BRIDGE, DECK 1

Anastasia watched the asteroid from a distance. *Titan* and *Prometheus* flew along with the interstellar object at a slow pace. She could neither rest nor sleep. She couldn't focus, and even the melodic sounds of the piano didn't calm her nerves. The crew had been on the asteroid for over forty-eight hours. Adrian and Chris had entered the chamber. Their last message said they were attempting to decipher codes to unlock the console.

Anastasia left the bridge and walked at a slow pace. She did not know where she was going. There was nothing to do at the bridge, and her crew was efficient and did not need her for now. The unsettling feeling didn't leave her, and she was hoping a stroll around *Titan* would help. Two crew members walked past her. They nodded. She smiled and nodded back. To her, their smiles appeared cold and forced. She knew she had made a terrible mistake following the queen into the rift. It was her fault they had to chase phantom asteroids to return home. On the other hand, if she hadn't fired, maybe they would have been prisoners of war.

Anastasia found herself at the Midnight Orchid. It was a pleasant atmosphere. Groups of people sat around a table sharing a meal. Since the separation from the outer section, there was no bartender. To lift spirits, the crew selected a time after shifts and came together for drinks. Today, Edward was on bartender duty. She hadn't realized that the tactical officer could be such a professional. He attempted to add colors to the drink and make each of his customers laugh.

He grinned as she approached the bar. "Commander, I'm glad you came."

"I am glad too."

"Your usual drink?"

"Yes, thank you."

As Edward prepared the drink, she glanced around and saw Katia with Phoebe. They sat close, eating from the same plate. She wondered how Katia handled her relationship with Phoebe. To make their marriage work, Anastasia and Martin had been on several missions. Instead of bringing them closer, it drove them apart and brought misery to her family.

Katia and Phoebe kissed, and she smiled to herself. She turned her attention to her elsewhere and wondered why she had married Martin. Was it love? Was it lust? What had drawn her toward him? If love was a thing that faded with time, she should have forgotten about Mykel a long time ago.

"There you are," said Edward.

She sipped the drink. It tasted fantastic.

"This is marvelous. Thank you."

"You have a good drink, and now all you need is good company," he remarked, looking past her.

She turned and saw Mykel.

"Hi," he said, appearing stunned to see her.

"Hey," she replied and turned toward Edward.

He smirked and said, "Captain, what would you like?"

After Edward served another drink, Mykel and Anastasia settled near the window with the view of Poseidon. Anastasia wondered if this was a set-up. "So, what brings you here?"

"Well, after work, I thought a swim and a drink would do me good."

"Good idea," she replied.

Anastasia looked at her drink, trying to think extremely hard about a topic.

"Are we going to talk about that night?" Mykel asked.

Blood rushed to her face, and she glimpsed at other people. "Do we have to talk about it now?"

"If not now, when?" he asked calmly.

She studied him. He didn't look agitated or push her for an answer. Instead, he waited.

That is new.

"Unless it meant nothing," he muttered.

"Don't say that."

"You know me. I don't like gray areas."

She sipped her drink, hoping to buy time. She already knew the answer but resisted the urge to tell the truth. "I think our involvement will complicate things."

He tilted his head, and a smile dangled on his face. "Tell me when it was simple?"

Anastasia was flabbergasted. She expected him to frown, curse under his breath, and leave.

When did he become so wise? So, patient with me?

He leaned forward. "Just think about it, okay? Are you hungry? I am starving."

No. Don't change the topic. I want to know what is going on in your head. What happened to you?

She dismissed her thoughts and said, "That would be great."

They had dinner, and Anastasia felt guilty for enjoying herself while her crew was on the asteroid. Although she could see that he wasn't happy to leave her all alone, Mykel was tired and had to return to his ship. Left alone with her thoughts, she admired her surroundings. Her eyes settled on Poseidon. She wished she could stay and study it for several months. But the Orias would tear her world apart and turn it into dust. She couldn't let that happen. They had to fight and rebuild the perimeter, bringing peace to her world. She had to look for Emmeline. Either get her back to safety or free her from the clutches of the Imperial Command. She had to decide her relationship with Mykel. Then she could think about exploration.

Maybe I won't see Poseidon again in my lifetime.

Anastasia sensed someone around her and turned to find Selina sitting opposite her.

What was she doing here? It was late. She shouldn't be out of bed.

She noticed a few heads turned toward the nine-year-old who had lost her only brother.

"Hello, Selina," she said, ignoring the stares.

The girl nodded and curiously looked at Poseidon.

Anastasia sipped her drink as Edward served Selina some ice cream.

"There you go," he said.

"Thank you," Selina replied.

For several minutes, they sat in silence, and Anastasia noticed that the ice cream was melting.

"You should eat that."

Selina ate silently. She paused and glanced over her shoulder, catching the eye of a few spectators.

"Why do they look at me like that?" Selina asked her.

"They just want to know you are okay."

"No. They don't care. They stare at me because I am the traitor's sister."

Anastasia's face turned stone. "No."

Their eyes met.

"According to the records, Argon freed Emmeline and helped her escape. He planned to run away with her," Selina replied sadly.

Anastasia lowered her gaze. "It is true, and Argon did what he thought was best. But it doesn't matter now. We have to figure out how to get back home."

Selina said nothing and fixed her gaze on the event horizon. Sadness filled her features. At that moment, Anastasia realized Selina had not only lost her brother, but all her friends had left. She was the only child aboard. Her mother had buried herself with work and was probably spending more time at the lab than with her daughter.

The world was indeed a cruel place.

"What have you been up to?" she asked.

"Nothing," Selina replied, still peering at Poseidon. "It's so beautiful. Mom tells me it will kill us if we go near it."

"She is right."

They became silent, each wanting to stay with their own thoughts. Anastasia referred to her pad, but there were no updates from Adrian. She was worried. What if they did not get the frequency in time? What if they failed?

"We'll jump with the asteroid, right?" Selina asked.

She is quite perceptive.

"Yes, we will."

"I voted yes. I believe we should find new ways to get home."

"I am grateful for your support," Anastasia replied with a smile, but her face fell as she continued to observe Poseidon.

"We'll make it."

Anastasia chuckled.

"I am serious. I know we will make it," said Selina.

"Oh, I am sorry. Thank you so much for your vote of confidence."

"I am not confident or smart. I just know."

"And may I ask, how do you know?" Anastasia asked playfully.

Selina's eyes turned toward Poseidon. Her expression turned blank, her eyes fixating as if she saw something Anastasia did not.

"Selina?" Anastasia asked.

"What do you see?"

"What do you mean?"

"What do you see when you look at Poseidon?" asked Selina.

Anastasia smirked. "Hmm, an enormous black hole surrounded by millions of stars."

Selina beamed and clapped.

"Your turn," said Anastasia.

Selina smiled. "I see a darkness that swallowed the sun, but it still found a way to shine."

"Wow! That's a fantastic way of putting it."

"Thank you. What do you think is on the other side?" asked Selina.

"You mean the other side of the portal? We know little. *Prometheus* is still analyzing the data from the probe."

"It was open for a while. You must have seen something."

Anastasia was too busy trying to keep *Titan* intact. She forced herself and said, "Darkness."

Selina studied Anastasia's confused look.

"We'll find out when we make the jump," Anastasia said.

"What do you wish for?" asked Selina mischievously.

Anastasia shut her eyes. "I wish to go back home. You?"

Selina shut her eyes. "More chocolate ice cream."

Both laughed.

"I like this game," said Selina. "Okay. Let's see. What do you see on the other side of that portal?"

Anastasia closed her eyes and let her imagination fly. "Stars, several systems with plenty of planets and moons." She opened her eyes and added, "It would be fascinating to see a binary star system."

Selina smiled wholeheartedly.

"What about you?"

Smiling, the little girl shut her eyes. Anastasia waited. The smile faded from Selina's face, and her features became constricted.

"Selina?" Anastasia said softly.

She did not respond.

Anastasia reached out to touch her hand.

Selina jumped.

"I am sorry. I didn't mean to frighten you."

"I'm fine. I-I am fine," Selina said, avoiding eye contact and gulped down the ice cream.

"What happened? Tell me."

Their eyes met. Selina's face was full of horror.

"I said nothing happened," she said. Rising to her feet, she ran out.

Anastasia was uncomfortable leaving Selina alone and followed her to cargo bay one. The lights were on, and she tried to find the girl among clusters of barrels stacked over one another.

"Selina…where are you?"

It was silent. She peered behind a barrel and found Selina sitting on a blanket with some toys and a basket.

Anastasia beamed. "There you are."

The girl's head bowed, and she didn't look her in the eye. "Please do not tell anyone about this place."

"I won't," Anastasia replied, sitting on the floor facing Selina. "This is nice and quiet. But it's a bit cold and barren. Why not play in your room?"

Selina shrugged her shoulders. "I don't know. I like it here. Please don't tell Mom."

"I won't tell anyone."

"Promise?"

"Promise. Now you have to tell me what upset you."

Selina shook her head.

"Why not?"

"If I do, you wouldn't want to be my friend."

Anastasia took Selina's hands into her own.

"I'm sure that won't happen."

Selina studied her face as if making sure she was not lying.

"Tell me."

"You promise?"

"Yes."

Selina dropped her eyes for a moment and said, "On the other side, I saw fire, death, and carcasses. And...and a monster in the dark."

Anastasia's blood turned cold.

CHAPTER 37: MEMORIES

PROXIMA 8

Byron felt his head burst from the inside. He sat up, trying to breathe normally. Darkness surrounded him, and he yearned for something to alleviate the throbbing pain. He mourned and wanted to weep at his fate of being kidnapped and tortured by an invisible force. He thought about his life before Orias and wished nothing but to return home. His hands trembled as he touched his head. There was no injury, but it hurt. A lot.

Illumination filled the room, and he shut his eyes. He had become accustomed to the dimness that the sudden exposure nearly drove him blind.

"You are fragile," said the voice.

He did not answer. Desperate for water and something to relieve his pain, he forced himself to get on his feet. Putting his weight on the wall, he limped. His eyes ached, so he kept them shut and searched the walls, using his hands to feel for any hint of a door. There had to be one. He needed to escape. Where were his friends? He didn't want to be alone.

"You cannot leave until I allow it."

"You have got what you wanted!" he yelled.

"Not precisely. The information your inferior mind provided is inadequate."

Byron's mind was blurred, and he did not know how to respond. Confused and tired, he leaned on the wall and tried to catch his breath. The illumination in the room dimmed, and several images appeared on the roof. Byron narrowed his eyes and tried to focus.

"What the hell?" he muttered when he saw pictures of Argon and Micah drinking at the bar before the war. The roof went dark momentarily, and he saw pictures of his families in his quarters on *Titan*. Images of his ship, the hangar deck of the space station, and perimeter gates flashed one after another.

They were his memories. It had taken them all.

"You have no right!" he yelled.

"This is all I could retrieve. It's rather useless."

Byron gaped at the statue in disbelief. "What do you want?"

"I thought you were intelligent. I want information."

"About what?"

It did not answer.

Byron strained his eyes, trying to find a way out, but he was losing hope.

"The craft you fly, it's more advanced than your predecessor's," said the voice.

Byron recalled the human remains in the dark corridor. He could be a crewmember of the *Hedin*. This is what it did. It kidnapped people from different systems and brought them here. For information.

"I need it."

Byron closed his eyes. His head spun, and he lost his balance.

"Bring the SFR to me."

Byron tried to understand what it was saying. SFR. What the hell was it? Then he remembered. The space flight recorder. Why did it need it? But he was worn out and collapsed.

Byron heard voices and opened his eyes. Clio's kind face emerged. At first, he could not focus, but soon his vision cleared.

"Hi," she said.

"Hey," he said, trying to sound normal.

The continuous beeping of the device irritated Byron.

"You are hurt," Micah said, finishing the scan.

"It's here. It's here."

"We know. We heard you scream, but we couldn't open the door," Clio answered.

Byron wanted to tell them to leave, but he knew it was not a choice. They were prisoners, and he had to figure out how to get out. He had to save them.

A loud grunt echoed.

The trio huddled together. They waited in silence. Byron felt Clio's hand grip his arm. An image appeared on the roof. It was his spacecraft.

"Bring me the SFR."

"What the hell do you want with that?" asked Micah.

Byron sensed a throbbing ache in his head and yelled in agony. His body convulsed, shaking vigorously.

"No. No. Stop it! Stop it!" Clio shouted.

Byron twisted and slumped on the frigid ground. Pain rippled through his body.

"I'll get it! I'll get it! Stop! Just don't hurt him!" yelled Micah.

The affliction ended, and Byron could breathe again. Every muscle in his body was on fire. His breathing was strained, and he felt he would pass out any time.

The door opened.

"Go. Now. Hurry back," it ordered.

"I'll get the damn thing only if you promise not to hurt him anymore," Micah said.

"If you don't do what I tell you, he will die, and then I will start with the girl," it said.

Byron rounded his fist and wanted to tell him to go to hell.

Micah looked at Byron. Their eyes locked.

"I'll be back. Hold on," Micah said.

With Clio's help, Byron sat up. He was still in agony.

"You'll be all right. Micah will be back soon," Clio said, staying on his side.

Their eyes met, and he said, "And then what? Will it set us free or kill us?"

Clio's face turned to stone. "What should we do?" she asked.

"Did you find anything out there?" Byron asked.

"There is no way out. It controls everything."

"What is this place?"

"It might be an underground facility," she answered.

"Like a space station."

"That is what we think."

"How big is it?"

"So far, we have found several passageways, and all of them are linked to this hall."

"How far are we from the moon's surface?"

"We don't know."

Byron became quiet.

"What does it want?" Clio asked, her eyes roaming the dim room. The figure remained silent as the images continued to flash above them.

"Information."

"About what?"

Byron shrugged. He was confused. The entity had extracted most of his memories, and now it was after the SFR. Why? Something dawned on him. The last ship crashed thirty years ago, and now it has captured more humans during a battle. Was it possible his captor was looking for the Orias? The roof kept showing the images, one after another. It was still going through the information.

Suddenly, the slideshow paused, and Byron recognized the image immediately. It was *Titan*. Then they saw another photo, which was a close-up view of *Titan*. Several images of the interior and exterior of the space station appeared. Byron gulped and exchanged worried glances with Clio.

CHAPTER 38: DAMAGES

RAVEN

E mmeline froze in horror. The Imperial Command ships were on her tail. The communication buzzed, and the voice of the ship's commander ordered her to surrender.

She whimpered.

"Emmeline! Emmeline! Focus," said the AI.

"I...I can't believe this..."

"Why are you surprised? You should have expected them to find you one day."

The AI was right. She couldn't hide forever.

"Emmeline Augury, if you do not shut down your engines and surrender, we will fire," said an authoritative male voice.

Emmeline's hands were shaking. She pierced her lips and pushed herself to think. It didn't matter how they had tracked her down. It could have been Gael, or they might have been monitoring Horus or other outposts. She punched in the coordinates, and the *Raven* gained speed, racing ahead. The distance between the two ships increased, and she felt now she could think.

"What are you going to do?" asked the AI

The voice on the communicator shouted, "Emmeline, surrender! There is no escape! Turn yourself over now! Give up!"

Emmeline ignored the voice. There had to be a way. Then she remembered. She rushed to the science room and began working frantically.

"What are you doing? Fly the ship," said the AI.

She ignored it and typed on the keyboard. She pushed the execute button several times.

"That should have done it!" Emmeline said.

She rushed back to the pilot's seat, altering the ship's course.

"I can help," said the AI.

"No."

"Why?"

"I don't know you!" she shouted.

"People you knew might have betrayed you. Perhaps it's time you made new friends."

Emmeline glanced over her shoulder. "How..."

"I can help fly the ship."

Laser beams hit the starboard section. The *Raven* jolted.

"They are firing at us..." Emmeline said.

"Emmeline..." AI said.

Emmeline grunted and hurried to the science room.

Boom.

Raven shook. She almost lost her balance and grabbed the chair for support.

"I don't believe this!" she muttered.

She opened the program that connected the AI to *Raven's* mainframe. A window popped up, and the computer asked, "Do you wish to grant control to the AI?"

She was unsure. The AI was still unfamiliar. She was uncertain if she could fully trust it. It could sabotage the ship, take control, and kill her. There were too many possibilities.

Boom!

The *Raven* shuddered. An alarm went off.

"Yes," she said.

The program started running.

By the time she left, the computer had announced, "Connection complete."

Returning to the pilot's seat, she said, "Prove yourself."

"Aye. Aye. I have control. Flying pattern one," announced the AI.

Suddenly the *Raven* turned, dodging the phaser fire.

"Emmeline Augury...surrender now!"

"Oh, yes! I have got it," she said, punching the keys hurriedly.

A smile spread over her face.

"They are gaining on us. Plotting a new course," announced the AI.

The ships fired. *Raven* dipped and shuddered. Suddenly, it became quiet. Emmeline checked the scanners; the Imperial Command ships had changed their course and headed toward the perimeter.

"Yes! It worked. It worked!" she said, throwing her hands in the air.

"What did you do?" asked AI

"Get us out of here...now!" she said.

Raven powered up and flew in the opposite direction. Taking a deep breath, Emmeline sat back.

"I am efficient, but all my maneuvers would not have saved us. What did you do?"

She smiled. "I gave them something bigger to worry about."

The AI waited.

"I planted a fake transmission in Utopis communication array that the Orias were back at the perimeter. The last time I was there, I had left a hidden receiver called the trojan under the control panel. I sent a signal and activated it. Once it was activated, I sent a fake transmission which might have been sent to all ships."

"Impressive."

She turned toward the screen and thought about disconnecting the AI from the *Raven*. She could only use it when necessary.

"You are considering disconnecting me again."

"I am on the run. You might send information to the Imperial Command. They built you. They are your creators."

"That is true. But I am loyal to the craft I am connected to and its captain. Since Argon Keston is not here, and you are the commander, I will take orders from you. Moreover, my primary function is to serve aboard a ship. I was built for the *Intrepid*, but I am of no use on a derelict. I would like to be useful."

She smiled. Emmeline was no commander. She knew nothing about leadership and didn't seek anyone's loyalties. All she wanted was to get the pieces and destroy the queen.

She leaned forward. "Let's see if we can work with each other."

ASTEROID

The temperature inside the asteroid was dropping, and Adrian could sense Chris's annoyance. Two days had passed, and they had made little progress. The sleep-deprived and tired men were waiting for a break. Adrian stretched his back and couldn't wait to remove his suit. The little sleep he had on the *Aeolus* was not enough, and the food was cold and tasteless. He moved close to the astrophysicist. The computer was running thousands of algorithms. He observed a large triangular object on the panel.

"What is that?" Adrian asked Chris.

"I am one person with a small computer. I am transmitting the data to *Titan's* computer. They are faster. Aceline and Isaac can run a separate set of algorithms and find the information we need."

Adrian nodded. "What about the language?"

"So far, the computer has deciphered their alphabets. But I must tell you. This asteroid has been to several places.

Right now, I believe I have found about five hundred flight logs."

"Wow," Adrian said.

Chris smiled, giving him a pad. "You are a pilot. Maybe you can figure out the star systems while I find the frequency."

"Great," said Adrian, feeling excited. He had something to do. Something to keep him busy.

With the pad in his hand, Adrian walked to the opening. He was jaded and wanted this mission to be over. Since there was no apparent danger, the robot had powered down and was in surveillance mode. He walked past it and came to stand below the opening.

"Felix, how are you doing?" he asked, speaking into the comm. He looked up. From here, he could see nothing but darkness.

"Yeah, I am good. A bit bored, though."

"Aren't we all? Is the opening stable?"

"Yes, it is. We had some debris, but it's fine."

"Stay put," Adrian said.

He walked up and down the corridor. Stretching his legs felt good. His intercom sounded.

"Hey, how are you?" said Evan.

Adrian smiled. "I'm fine, you?"

"It's a bit quiet up here...when are you coming back?" said Evan, teasing.

"When my work is done. How is everyone holding up?"

"They are fine. Waiting. I saw pictures of the asteroid. It looks fascinating."

"It is," Adrian said, trying not to dwell on the fact that he had to share space with two other grown men. The living space had the faint scent of sweat and garbage. His attempts to keep it clean had failed.

"Try to get back soon," said Evan.

"I will."

The intercom became silent, and he opened the first star chart on the pad.

TITAN, CRYSTAL LAB, DECK 2

Anastasia rubbed her hands together as she stepped into the lab. Chris had transmitted a lot of data to *Titan* in hopes they could help him unlock the panel and find the key to open the portal.

Aceline Keston stood near the console, staring at the figures that made little sense to Anastasia. It was an alien language. Aceline was running it through the language databases. Isaac was on her side, observing.

As if sensing someone was behind them, they turned. "Yes, Commander," said Isaac.

"Any progress?" she asked, glancing at Aceline, who turned back to focus on her work.

"It's a lot to deal with. But our first step is to unlock the panel. Once we have done that, then we can focus on getting the frequency."

"How long will it take?"

"I can't say."

"We will work as fast as we can," Aceline commented, glancing over her shoulder.

"Great, continue your work. Please let me know if you have something," said Anastasia and left.

TITAN, ANASTASIA'S OFFICE, DECK 1

The waiting game was getting on Anastasia's nerves. They had sent several transmissions to Imperial Command, yet there was no response. She again went through the list of the people who had disappeared. She didn't know if they were dead or alive. Her eyes stopped at Emmeline's name. Regret filled her veins.

I should have done better.

The communicator buzzed, and Mykel's face appeared on the screen.

"Hey, there is my favorite person," he mocked, breaking the ice.

"Oh really? How many do you have?"

"Only one, I promise."

"Ha! I don't believe you."

They had a good laugh. She did not know why, but she wanted him back here. On *Titan* with her. She tried not to think about it.

"How's the crew on the asteroid?" he asked.

"Without proper sleep or rest…not good. They tell me they are fine."

"It has been four days."

"I know. We should have got the frequency by now."

"What is your backup plan?"

"On day seven, if we still do not have the frequency, we pull them out before the portal opens."

Their eyes locked.

"They can do it. They will get the frequency on time," Mykel said.

She was surprised and relieved. "Well, that's encouraging."

Mykel changed the subject. "We've finished analyzing the data collected by the probe."

Anastasia clasped her fingers together. "And what did you find?"

His face turned grim. "Before we lost contact, the probe transmitted the coordinates of the exit point and sent through images of the surrounding region. According to our calculations, the portal opens five thousand light-years closer to home. If we make a successful jump, we will save at least two years of our journey back home."

Anastasia threw her fists in the air. "Yes! That's the best news I have heard all week!"

Mykel did not smile. Anastasia felt a twist in her gut.

"The probe detected something else."

"What?"

Mykel shared an image with her. She narrowed her eyes and noted a dark globe surrounded by a dull yellowish glow. She assumed it was near the sun. Anastasia recalled Selina's words. Fire. Death. Despair and a monster in the dark.

"What is it?" she asked, hoping to get answers.

"We don't know."

"A spaceship?"

"That remains to be seen. The object has a radius of thirty thousand kilometers. I estimate its half the size of Jupiter. The probe didn't detect engines or weapons signatures. It's not a planet or a moon."

Anastasia let the news soak in.

"I feel we are walking into a trap," he said.

She remained silent and wondered if Selina was right. She didn't speak of a globe or a craft on the other side.

"Or it might be nothing. I'm just speculating. I think we should be careful," Mykel stated.

"Or it could be full of dead people and haunted by a monster!" she blurted.

"What!?" Mykel asked, stunned.

CHAPTER 39: COLD AND DARK

PROXIMA 8

Byron Thames wished he could erase all his memories so that this entity could not track *Titan* or find his friends. He heard footsteps, and soon Micah appeared.

"Place it on the rock," the entity instructed.

"Fine. Fine. Just do not hurt anyone else. Okay!" said Micah.

Micah placed the SFR on the rock and came to kneel beside him. "How are you doing?"

Byron nodded. "I am fine."

He observed the bulky square box. It compressed files and kept copies of flight plans, star charts, and other valuable information. It wasn't easy extracting data from it, but he was sure it would be a simple task for the specter.

"We must get out of here...how did you leave?" Clio asked.

"Would you believe it? I found a staircase just around the corner."

At another time, Byron would have laughed. "I am sure it's gone now. We need to leave," he said, struggling to get on his feet.

"How?" Clio asked, helping him stand up.

"You will go nowhere," said Spector.

They froze.

"We have given you what you wanted," Micah said.

"I will see how useful it is," it said.

The trio stood glued together. Several images flashed, showing the life of the craft. Its creation. The first time it left the hangar. Its first pilot. All the navigation logs. Its path around Saturn and the perimeter. Several numbers flashed. It was too much, and Byron lost track. Then the images slowed, revealing pictures of the first battle with the Orias ships. Byron remembered that day. He had fought with valor with his best friend, Argon. It continued studying the data on the Orias ships one by one.

The information was too much for the human mind to digest, but it seemed easy for this being.

"What do you know about the Orias?" Byron asked.

Several other images appeared, and the trio watched in amazement.

"They have traveled far to find something," it said.

Byron observed the images of the Orias ships at various locations.

"How long have you been tracking them?" he asked.

"I see everything," it said.

"How long have you been here?" asked Micah.

Several seconds passed before it replied, "I have forgotten."

"So, you just sit here while they destroy civilization," Clio remarked.

Her anger was met with silence.

"Too many blanks...too many puzzles," the voice said as if talking to itself.

They exchanged confused glances.

CHAPTER 40: A LONG WAY FROM HOME

RAVEN

Emmeline rechecked her calculations for the third time. She examined the plaque, which was pointing to her next destination. The next portal was in the heart of her world. She gritted her teeth. Going back there was like going back through hell. She wanted to run away. It reminded her of Argon, Delta, and everyone on *Titan*. All her friends were gone, and the AI was right. She needed to make new ones. Emmeline punched in the coordinates. She looked at the stars beyond her reach, and with a subtle smile, she pushed the button. The engines came to life, and the *Raven* turned and headed toward its realm.

TITAN, ANASTASIA'S QUARTERS, DECK 4

The last three days were agonizing, and Anastasia had to remind herself it was worth it. *Titan's* crew was working round the clock with Chris, and finally, they believed they had found the key to unlock the control panel. She wished they had more time to study this asteroid. To find out who built it and for what purpose? Why did it appear at one point and vanish at another? The data they had gathered would keep their scientist busy for decades. Right now, getting home was her only intention.

I got them here. I must get them back.

She peered out of the window and watched the *Prometheus*. Every soul on that ship felt the same way she did. But they weren't responsible for their situation. She was. She saw the blast clear as day. Her mind switched to a pleasant memory, and she remembered the kiss. Blood rushed to her face.

Oh, stop it.

It was no use. Mykel never left her thoughts, even when she was working, and she lied to herself that she wasn't thinking of him. He was always there, and he was making it harder. Especially when he wanted her to leave him behind just in case *Prometheus* didn't make it.

What a ridiculous idea!

She walked to her desk and tried to focus on her chores. All departments reported everything was in order. There was nothing to do but wait. She rose to her feet and stepped out of her quarters.

ASTEROID

Adrian tried hard to control his frustration and felt they had made limited progress. He finished checking the star charts. They were not in their databases. This asteroid had been to the regions of space they hadn't found yet.

Leaving Chris in the control room, he entered the tunnel to step into the small chamber at the back. He observed the funnel.

The robot joined him. "I am ready," it said.

Adrian nodded as he pulled out the disrupter. Carefully, he cut through the rock on the roof. The dust and rock hung in the air. He stopped to allow the robot to clear the space with a vacuum.

After several attempts, Adrian saw a narrow hole. Grabbing his small bag, he retrieved a tube and connected it to a ten-by-ten pad. He handed it over to the robot, who stretched and inserted one of its ends into the rock. Adrian waited for the pad to activate. The camera began transmitting the feed. He saw nothing extraordinary, just more rock.

"We need to dig further," he told the robot.

It tugged out the tube, adjusted the firepower of the disruptor, and fired. After a few shots, the robot reinserted the tube.

Adrian watched the feed. The tube traveled upward. In the murkiness, he noticed the wall curving.

"Okay, this is a good spot. Get the probe."

The robot left and soon returned with a box. The probe looked like a two-by-two cylinder. It pulled out the antennae and activated it. They waited for it to connect to the pad.

"We are good to go," Adrian said. He felt restless in his suit again. That meant returning to the ship, changing, and eating. He didn't want to do any of that. He dreaded crawling through the hole. The robot inserted the probe. Once inside, it came to life, flew a short distance, and attached itself to the curving wall.

"Okay. That's great," he muttered.

Adrian waited. The data started pouring in. It was unremarkable. Of course, the asteroid was made up of nickel, iron, clay, and silicon. He gasped and peered in.

"Wow," he muttered.

Just above him was a tank of a one-kilometer radius. The probe continued transmitting. The data showed the tank was full of unidentified material. Adrian squinted. The data showed it was liquid, thick, and viscous. He needed a sample to confirm if this was fuel.

Once he had discovered what was above them, it was now time to find out what was below their feet. The robot fired, cutting through the rock. It required patience, and one mistake could cost them. Adrian waited in anticipation. He turned the vacuum on and cleared the rubble and dust. The rock was hard to break. It was more tedious than he expected. After two hours, they had success.

The robot inserted the tube, and the camera came online.

"Holy moly," Adrian said.

The enormous hall stretched as far as he could see.

"Let's send the camera further."

Like a black snake gliding through the air, the tube flew above the vast, dark room. Two substantial, long cylinders were stationed in the heart of the dome-shaped room. Adrian noted that their pointed ends were aiming at a semicircular tunnel.

What the hell is this?

He wondered if they could enter the underground compartment. Anastasia would never approve. She sounded worried and kept reminding him they had less than forty-eight hours.

Maybe after we cross the portal, I can look at this.

His comm buzzed. Adrian winced.

"Adrian, come up here," said Chris.

"Coming," he replied and turned to the robot. "Send another probe and attach it to that vast structure. Download all data and then pack up."

"Affirmative."

Squeezing through the narrow corridor, Adrian wished to be back on *Titan*. He needed a shower, a good sleep, and better food.

"We have translated its navigation logs."

Adrian was a bit disappointed. He thought they would have the frequency by now. "Okay."

"Imagine a comet. Year after year, it follows a specific orbit. So does this asteroid. It follows a specific path and jumps from sector to sector using specific jump points."

"That's interesting."

"Aceline matched its navigation logs with our current and past star maps."

"And?"

"It has been to a lot of places. So far, we have identified ten systems that this asteroid and Imperial Command have visited."

"Really?"

"Yes. For instance, if we got this right, last year alone, this asteroid has visited the Zion, Tetra, and Spire systems."

"Wait, Zion is close to Oort's cloud,"

"Exactly, about ten light-years away."

"Okay. So, if we stick with this asteroid, it can get us to that system," Adrian said, excited.

"Yes. Aceline is going to discuss it with Anastasia. Also, there is a possibility that we might find a jump point closer to home."

Adrian was happy. Their hard work was paying off. Chris got up and stretched his legs. It was hard to move around in a spacesuit.

"This is fantastic! Okay, it has been to several systems. Tell me, what has it done? What has it seen? Has it recorded anything? Images or collected data?"

"Nope. Nothing at all. It travels through several systems just like its brothers and sisters."

Adrian was shocked. "Brothers and sisters? There are more of them?"

"Yes. We have already met two in the last two weeks. According to the information I have collected, there are about fifty such asteroids. Keep in mind, this information may not be updated, and there might be more of them."

Adrian straightened his back. "So, these asteroids are floating around space, going in and out of portals at their will."

"Not at their will...someone has programmed them."

"Programmed?"

"Do you see this panel?"

Adrian peered in and saw several figures moving circularly.

"Interesting. Can they be reprogrammed?"

"I think we can. I have asked Aceline, and she is working with two programmers on *Titan*," Chris said, and then muttered, "Of course, they are no match for Emmeline,"

Adrian smiled.

Yes, Emmeline would have been a fine addition to this team.

But she wasn't there. They were unaware of her whereabouts. Emmeline was in trouble, lost, and probably alone, and he wished he could help. He had failed Delta, and he had presumed helping Emmeline would remedy his guilt. He didn't get the chance.

Dismissing his thoughts, he said, "Who made this?"

"Ah. Good question. I think a machine created this craft or asteroid. Whatever you want to call it. We do not know who created the machine?"

"Makes sense. We have robots that create ships."

"Certainly, and this…species capture asteroids, creates compartments inside them, and then dispatches them into space."

"It has to be a powerful machine or robot."

"Agreed. I hope we never find it," Chris said.

Adrian eyed him. "Why?"

Chris shrugged his shoulders. "Don't you think the Orias are enough?"

"Excellent point. But traveling through these systems would need a lot of power and fuel."

"Yes. I think the two hidden sections could be its source of power."

"I agree. But why create it?" he wondered, looking around.

"I do not know. I have unlocked this panel. It monitors engineering, navigation, and communication. Right now, I am focusing on navigation. I've to find the frequency that opens the portal."

"Then what?"

"In theory, just like this asteroid. If we transmit the same frequency, the portal should enlarge and enable us to jump with the asteroid."

Adrian felt an invisible burden on his shoulder. "In theory?"

Chris looked at him. "Don't worry. It has worked well so far."

"How long until you find this frequency?"

"Give me a few more hours. We are trying to understand this language. Aceline should have something for me soon."

Adrian nodded.

Titan, Keston Quarters, Deck 4

Aceline had been working day and night. She wanted Dr. Kent to find the frequency so that they could find a way home. The asteroid intrigued her, and it had come at the perfect moment. It was a wonderful distraction. She had indulged herself in solving this new mystery. The pain of losing her son didn't leave her, and she didn't expect it to leave. It lingered in her chest, and the only thing that brought a smile to her face was Selina. She felt for her daughter. She was the only child, alone with no one to play with. There was no school, and Selina spent her entire day in the lab or with the bridge crew. She had noticed that Selina was becoming friendly with Anastasia.

That is a good and a bad thing.

A commander's job was risky. She wondered how it would affect Selina if something happened to Anastasia. She tried to stay positive.

At least she is making friends!

She sneaked into her daughter's room and watched her sleep. She recalled their conversation. Aceline wanted to know why Selina had left the pod. Her response had astonished her.

Argon called me.

That was an interesting response. She tried to find out more. Selina claimed she had heard her brother, which was odd. Aceline knew her children were not telepathic. Then how? Instincts? Guts? They did say that twins felt each other's pain, remorse, and happiness. But Argon and Selina were not twins. She recalled Selina's last medical checkup. It showed she was a healthy child with no genetic markers for diseases. She didn't have any allergies or trauma. In general, Selina was a happy child.

Most of the time.

She smiled. The Orias attack was traumatic, and Selina didn't want to leave *Titan*. Maybe she made up a story or believed something that didn't happen. For now, Aceline had to accept that.

TITAN, CRYSTAL LAB, DECK 2

Anastasia saw Aceline and Isaac were busy working on the console. The tower of mugs and empty food ration cartons were spread over the table and workstations. Two assistants were working feverishly in a corner. She walked over to the doctors and waited.

"Ah…Commander," said Isaac.

Aceline turned, and their eyes locked. "Commander," she said.

"Doctor," Anastasia replied. She had a sudden urge to tell her how sorry she was about Argon. But she felt it would be a painful reminder to Aceline.

"So, tell me it was worth breaking into that asteroid," Anastasia said, lightening the mood.

"It was worth it. We've found a gold mine."

Anastasia smiled. "Goldmine?"

"A historical goldmine. This asteroid is over one-point-three billion years old. It has gone through this region of space one hundred thirty-three thousand times. It takes around six hundred Earth days to complete one rotation."

"Wow…" she said.

They turned toward the screen, and she showed Anastasia a star map. "And these are all the regions it travels to?"

"Are there more asteroids like these?"

"Yes. Chris has found over fifty, but we might find more."

"What's their purpose?"

"Unknown," Aceline replied, "I have gone through the logs. I cannot find why they are traveling through these portals."

"And they do not have specific targets?"

"Not that we know of."

Anastasia bit her lip and observed the star maps. She was intrigued and terrified as several questions ran across her mind.

"Okay, let's talk about opening the portal."

"Yes, we have located the frequencies that open the portal."

Anastasia smiled, "That's great!"

But Aceline did not look excited. "I have good news and bad news."

Anastasia gulped. "Tell me."

"The good news is we have the frequency. The bad news is that it changes."

"Changes?"

"It's a randomized number that is generated every time the asteroid nears a jump point."

Anastasia held her head. "Oh, no. No! This is not good! I was thinking of getting the crew back to *Titan* before the jump. Now they will have to stay on the asteroid until we cross!"

Anastasia noticed Aceline was smiling.

"Yes. But I wouldn't look at it that way. In my opinion, even after the jump, we shouldn't abandon the asteroid."

"We might have hijacked it and deciphered the codes to get the frequency, but we can't control it."

Aceline smirked. "Maybe we can."

CHAPTER 41: GATEWAYS

HAIDES CASTLE

The queen and Aithon walked to the middle of the big circular hall behind the castle. Twelve columns were connected by substantial spherical stones at least a hundred inches wide.

"My queen, let me."

"No. I should try."

"You need to recover."

"I am fine."

Uttering those words brought back painful memories. Her life had been full of agony, betrayal, and remorse. Condemned to darkness for several centuries, she hated her family for being so unfair. Her parents, grandparents, and sister had enjoyed their people's powers, luxury, and loyalty. They had luxurious lifestyles. One by one, they ruled and prospered, creating their extraordinary legacies. She sulked. Her father thought she wasn't good enough.

She compelled herself to stop thinking.

They closed their eyes, and soon their humanoid bodies turned into mist. The red and the white mist hovered in midair. At first, their pace was slow, then it increased.

Faster.

Energy flowed in every direction.

The twelve stones began glowing. The queen's energy and power intensified. She felt exhilarated. It had been ages since she felt alive, a part of the universe. She was everywhere and nowhere. The stones glimmered. Rays of lights emerged from them and merged into the heart of the hall. Several white fragments spun clockwise, merged, and she reappeared. The queen blinked her eyes open to the exhilarating sight. Millions of planets, stars, and nebulas moved around her in slow motion. Goosebumps lined her skin. A sun went supernova, and she watched as two planets in its path vanished.

"Are you ready, my queen?" Aithon asked.

A rush of vitality ran through her. "Yes!"

A group of four Orias ships flew over the hall and came to a standstill.

"Show us the way," said Aithon.

The queen focused and raised her hands. The stars, nebulas, galaxies rose above the ground, and the sky above her transformed into a map.

Oh, if only I could get the mythical device and reach every realm. Sustain my power and rule. That was what I was made for.

The stones turned into circular doorways. She began searching. With a thud, eight of the twelve doorways closed. Salvaging the rest of her energy, she concentrated. Thunder roared, and clouds formed over the castle. Only one door remained, and the other three closed with a bang.

"Yes. Yes," she whispered.

The door expanded, becoming bigger. She concentrated. Pushed herself and gave it all. The door stretched. The queen felt a dip in her power. Her species were mighty, but her ancestors had the device. It enabled them to push their limits.

Focus.

She sensed every star, every planet in the realm. A dark opening appeared, and she passed through it. She felt steam and heat. She opened her eyes and saw layers of lava encircling her. She floated through the molten rock, unaffected by the extreme heat. A part of her admired the chaos.

Nothing could survive here.

Moving upward, she drifted across miles of rocks formed millions of years ago. Pressurized steam arose from the large cracks. She left the crust of the planet. Black smoke broke through the surface, mixing with the hazy reddish atmosphere. She casually flew above, passing through the thin atmosphere. She sensed the dust storm raging from the south pole and wondered if the artificial structures on the surface could withstand the storm.

She left the lifeless red planet. Hovering in space, she noted several small structures on the planet's surface.

They know how to survive.

She let herself connect to her surroundings, and far beyond her vision, she became aware of life. When her eyes opened, she saw an amazing blue planet. Full of water, fresh air, several continents, and billions of souls. A memory flashed, and she saw her planet. It was the perfect mix of blue and green. It was full of beauty and wonder. Her father had diligently taken care of it. Shaking her head, she disregarded her memories. They were taking up her energy. She turned her attention to the blue planet, but the girl wasn't on it.

Her vitality dipped. She ignored it and clapped her hands. Billions of planets and stars surrounded her.

Where are you? Where are you hiding?

Fear grasped her as she felt her limits.

What if I can't find her? I have come a long way.

But then a surge rushed through her. Aithon. She felt his presence. His energy combined with hers. With a sense of renewed pride, she continued her search. The stars danced to her tune. The sun's rays were bright, and she felt its warmth. It turned colder when she glided in the opposite direction.

Where are you?

A swarm of floating rocks surrounded her. She tilted her head in awe, watching them fly upward. It was wonderful.

Here, she felt it.

"I feel it too," said Aithon.

She did not need to ask for help. Aithon knew what was required of him. Gathering her energy, she concentrated. The four Orias ships standing over the castle dematerialized. She snapped out of her vision and fell to her knees. She sensed her existence fading. She did not like weakness and even more so showing it. Resentment consumed her.

It's not fair!

CHAPTER 42: THE KISS GOODBYE

PROXIMA 8

The voice remained silent. The entity kept going through one image after another. Byron had lost track of time. Clio and Micah remained on his side.

"What is it doing?" Micah asked.

"It's going through all our confidential files. It's creepy," Clio pointed out.

Byron felt lightheaded and could hardly keep his eyes open. His body was numb. He laid his head back and stared at the hall.

"Is there a way out?" he asked Micah.

"Not that I can find."

His eyes rolled upward, catching sight of several star charts. He appreciated the limitations of his ship's database.

At least it wouldn't get everything.

From what he gathered, the entity knew about their solar system, *Titan*, the perimeter, their planet, some details on Imperial Command's colonies and fleet.

How would this affect them? Their future. What is this thing going to do? What was it? Why did it bring them here?

Tired of waiting, Byron pushed himself to stand up.

"You shouldn't be standing," she said, getting on her feet.

Byron disregarded her comment and walked with a limp around the hall. Micah followed him.

"Hey, man, you shouldn't be walking."

Byron didn't listen. He wanted to leave, go home.

The images quit flashing, and the hall became bright. Byron blinked several times, his eyes adjusted to the illumination. He was stunned. The hall looked different. The floor was rocky and uneven, and the walls were dark silver.

"What's happening?"

The ground shook.

"What are you doing?" Byron demanded.

The voice didn't answer.

As the ground trembled, the trio grabbed the walls. One by one, the wall sections began disappearing into the ground.

"What's happening?" Micah asked.

"I don't know," Byron answered.

The tremors increased. He grabbed Clio's arm and pulled her away. They moved to the center of the hall and stood by the sculpture, which remained silent. The tremors stopped. The vanishing of walls had left a four feet wide opening in the floor. Byron stepped forward.

"No!" Clio said, pulling his hand.

"Stay here."

He stepped closer to the square edge and glared at the void. He squinted but couldn't see what was ahead. Should they jump over the gap and rush to the other side? He turned and saw Micah. He was standing with his back toward Byron, looking at the other side.

"Anything?" he asked.

"Nope."

They were standing on a platform surrounded by darkness. The only source of illumination was the faint blue light emitted by the sculpture. A loud horn blared, and a tremor passed under their feet. With a deafening groan, pillars sprouted from the void.

"Oh my god!" Clio cried out, losing her balance. Micah caught her.

"What are you doing?" demanded Byron.

No answer came.

On the moon's surface, large cracks formed. An enormous cloud of dust hit the atmosphere, and from a distance, it appeared as if a bomb had exploded. Rocks broke into fragments as the tall structures moved, forming a pyramid-like shape and then became still.

"What is going on?" demanded Byron. "You have no right to keep us here. Let us go!"

The Spector didn't respond.

Dim blue lights surrounded them, and fear gripped Byron's heart. Between each pillar were multiple strings that glowed in the darkness. The strings formed a hexagon around the platform with the sculpture.

"What is this?" asked Clio.

"God knows," muttered Byron.

Smooth ringing echoed. He feverishly glanced for a door, wanting to get out. Thunder roared, and an engine revved.

TITAN, BRIDGE, DECK 1

It was time, and they used the same arrangement. *Titan* flew below the asteroid, and *Prometheus* glided above it. The viewscreen split in two, and Mykel's face appeared.

"We are ready."

"Acknowledged," replied Anastasia

"Did Adrian get the frequency?"

"Not yet."

Mykel's features constricted. "Okay."

She had told him about Selina's vision. He didn't believe her, but she did. Their different views didn't matter. It was best to deal with one thing at a time.

"Commander," said Evan from the pilot's chair, "we will reach the coordinates in one minute."

Anastasia's mouth went dry, and Mykel's eyes remained locked with hers. She opened a channel and said, "We are nearing the exit point. All hands standby."

The alarm sounded.

ASTEROID

Adrian glanced at the timer and said into the intercom, "Felix, is the ship ready to leave?"

"Yes. We are clear for take-off."

Adrian turned to the robot. "Get back to the ship and begin launch procedures."

Nodding, the robot grabbed the floating tether and, with a whoosh, vanished into the dark hole. Adrian looked at the two tethers. It was their only way out, and he wanted to leave now. But they needed the frequency. He rushed to the control center and found Chris hovering over the console.

"Have we got the frequency yet?"

"Not yet!"

He looked out through the narrow window, searching for the portal to appear anytime.

"Thirty seconds to exit point," announced Evan on the intercom.

"Something is happening!" Chris said, alarmed.

The wall behind them came to life, showing waterfalls on both ends and a storm raging at the bottom. It shimmered, and the hexagonal shapes turned dark, blew up like small explosions, and split into various points. The points connected and turned into a star map.

"That star maps look similar to the ones that we downloaded from the control panel," said Chris.

Adrian turned to Chris. "The frequency?"

"Wait for it."

The communicator buzzed.

"Yes, Commander," said Adrian

"Did you get it?" Anastasia demanded.

Rows of figures began appearing on the navigational monitor.

"There are too many. Which one?" Adrian cried out.

Chris studied them for a moment. "These are previous ones."

The figures stopped running.

"That one!" Chris said excitedly and downloaded the frequency on his pad.

Adrian wished Chris would hurry.

"Ten seconds to exit point," said Evan on the intercom.

Adrian looked out; the portal had not appeared yet.

"Transmitting the frequencies," Chris replied.

Adrian wanted to run to the exit, but he had to wait to make Titan had the frequencies.

"We have them!" Evan announced.

"Yes!" Chris shouted getting on his feet.

Bright light blazed, and the portal opened. The ring blazed, and he stood in awe glaring at the opening into the unknown.

"Expanding force fields," said Evan.

The whitish shield fell over the three crafts.

"Here we go!" shouted Chris with pure exhilaration.

Adrian was drawn out of his thoughts, "We must get out of here."

Chris nodded. The asteroid shook, and the men stopped dead on their feet. They turned and peered out of the opening.

"The portal is expanding," announced Evan.

The three objects glided toward the gateway.

The asteroid shuddered. Adrian tried to maintain his balance.

"Is it working?" asked Chris into the intercom, almost shouting. "*Titan*, did it work?"

Adrian waited in anticipation.

"Yes! Get out of there! Now!" shouted Anastasia on the comm.

Adrian was mesmerized. He watched as the portal grew bigger, glittering like a large ring in deep space. Its glow fell over the ships and the asteroid.

"We have to leave," said Chris.

But Adrian was looking beyond the opening. "What is that?" he asked.

Chris followed his gaze. "I-I don't know..."

Beyond the portal, Adrian saw a massive, dark globe.

"Is it a ship?" asked Chris.

"I..." Adrian's voice trailed off.

Bright lights crept through millions of small cracks on its surface. Its center opened, and a ball of fire emerged from the heart of the globe.

Adrian pulled Chris. "Get out...get out now!"

RAVEN

Emmeline sensed danger, but that was expected when one entered a lion's den. She felt the temperature in the cockpit rise, and blood flooded her cheeks. Her hands trembled. Collaborating with the AI had made her tasks easier. As she flew toward the perimeter, she saw debris floating in both directions. The *Raven* glided through the wreckage. At a distance, large crafts were swallowing the debris. *Raven's* sensors spotted an Imperial Command ship, the *Aurora*, but Emmeline did not change course.

"How are we doing?" Emmeline asked the AI.

"So far, I have detected only one ship near the perimeter."

"Stay alert," she ordered.

The *Raven* moved toward the coordinates, and the thin rings of Neptune glided upward. She studied the plaque and confirmed her coordinates thrice. She had expected more action. Perhaps more Imperial Command ships, but it was all too quiet. Uneasiness filled her as she sensed something watching her. Waiting for her.

The bell rang. She gasped.

"Emmeline Augury," a female voice said on the communicator. "This is Lady Vermont."

Emmeline exhaled.

"We need to talk," the woman said.

"The time to talk is gone," Emmeline muttered angrily. She turned to AI. How long till the *Aurora* is in range?"

"Less than five minutes," replied the AI.

"That's all the time I need," Emmeline said, getting up and returning to the console with the plaque. She placed it on the dashboard. She entered the coordinates, and the ship turned toward the sun.

"Oh god, please let this work," she said.

An alarm blared.

"Proximity alert. Proximity alert," said the computer.

"What the hell?" Emmeline asked, checking the monitors.

Four Orias ships materialized. Two crafts pursued the *Raven*, and the others headed for the *Aurora*. Two beams hit the *Raven*. It rocked violently.

Emmeline covered her mouth in horror. "What? No. No. This cannot be possible. How did they find me?"

"You are asking me questions I cannot answer," replied the AI.

She disregarded the comment. "Get ready to fire."

"*Raven* is no match for the Orias."

"I know. Power up the phasers. Now!"

A whoosh echoed.

"The phasers are ready."

She waited for the plaque to come to life. The sun was shining. It was in its path. Why wasn't it working? It should have glowed. Floated or rotated like before.

"Come on!" she cried.

As the Orias ship neared Earth, its spikes turned bright red. A blaze hit the *Raven*. The craft shook.

Emmeline lunged forward.

"Returning fire," replied the AI.

Raven phasers barely scratched the Orias ship's hull.

"Come on, work!" Emeline screamed, tapping the plaque.

"Emmeline, hold on. The *Aurora* is just a few minutes away," said Lady Vermont on the intercom.

Another hit sent the *Raven* off course, almost throwing Emmeline off her seat. The plaque remained silent. She didn't understand. The portal should have opened.

"Emmeline, we are unable..." AI spoke, but she did not let it finish.

Jumping on her feet, she dashed to the backpack and got the first piece. She did not know what to do. There was no instruction manual. She grabbed the piece in her hands and said, "Just do something..."

As if it heard her, obeyed her. The plaque came to life.

"Oh, thank goodness!" she cried out.

The Orias fired. The beam struck the *Raven*. It slightly tilted. Emmeline gripped the console and quickly stabilized the ship.

The Orias ships could destroy the Raven *in seconds. What are they waiting for?*

Realization dawned on her. "They want me alive," she muttered to herself. "No. No. I cannot let that happen!"

The lights went out, and *Raven* lost power.

"Get the power back!"

"Working on it," said the AI.

The plaque was glowing. It rose above the console, and as if it was connected with it, the piece changed color from golden to silver. The plaque began rotating.

"Is it supposed to do that?" AI asked.

"Yes, get the power back!"

Leaving a trail of smoke, the *Raven* flew past Saturn's rings. The Orias ships pursued.

"Emmeline, I am detecting six Imperial Command ships, including the *Aurora*," said the AI.

She did not care.

The lights flickered back on.

"Go!" she ordered.

The glow of the plaque spread. She wished *Raven* was in a better condition and moved away from the console.

"Keep flying," she told the AI.

The glow expanded over the console.

"Emmeline, we cannot take more hits. Our shield is at twenty percent, the engines are failing, and our phasers are ineffective."

"Just a few more minutes."

The glow moved over the console and then penetrated the ship's walls.

"Emmeline, something is happening."

"I kn…" her voice faded.

The AI was right. Her eyes became fixed on the console. It was changing. Turning shiny and brand new. The old, cracked walls of the ship sealed, and the exterior was now in pristine, polished condition. The ship was altering.

"No. No. Open the damn portal! We need to go!"

A blast occurred. The shock wave hit the *Raven*.

"What was that?"

"The *Aurora* blew up an Orias ship," AI replied.

Two Orias ships flew past the *Raven* and turned, blocking its path.

"Oh, no, this is not good. This is not good!"

"We need options," asked the AI.

"Evasive maneuvers?"

"That may not be useful…," said the AI.

The glow from the plaque spread to the science room, and AI fell silent.

Emmeline spun. The AI had vanished.

"Where are you? What is going on?" Emmeline cried out, holding her head. She tried to take control of the ship.

Raven quivered.

Emmeline was confused. What was she to do? She was trapped. She pushed the buttons. The ship did not respond. The glow extended to every part of the ship, and suddenly, everything turned dark.

"No! No! Not now!" she shouted in despair, trying to control the ship. The engines shut down. Shields fell, and the consoles froze. The *Raven* was dead.

The Orias ship's tails glowed. Tears filled her eyes. There was no escape. She would never finish her journey. She had failed on her first attempt.

Suddenly, the cockpit illuminated. The equipment and consoles came back to life. A voice filled the cockpit.

"Fire," said the AI.

Two massive balls of fire left the *Raven* and hit one of the Orias ships, shattering it into pieces.

Emmeline faced the AI. "How did you do that?"

"It was not me,"

Emmeline observed the ship's schematics. It had a thicker bulkhead, powerful phasers, two torpedo launchers with shields at maximum.

"How is that possible?" Her jaw dropped once she observed the piece. "Oh, my god."

The plaque glittered like a rectangular plate adorned with millions of diamonds and lifted above the dashboard.

"Whoa!" said Emmeline.

A light beam passed through the viewscreen into space, and the portal opened.

"Interesting. We have full power," remarked the AI.

"Go! Go!" shouted Emmeline.

The *Raven* raced toward the portal. The Orias ship followed. A blaze hit the *Raven*. It jolted.

"Just fly…" she told herself, increasing pace.

Raven dashed toward the gleaming gateway.

"Emmeline. No, do not go! Wait! We can help you!" said Lady Vermont on the intercom.

Emmeline turned off the communicator. She had made her choice.

The last Orias ship got closer, with the *Aurora* on its tail.

"The Orias ship is closing," said AI.

"We cannot let it follow us!"

The Orias ship prepared to fire when the *Aurora* attacked. It shattered into millions of pieces. The *Raven* shuttered and plunged into the portal. Waves of light moved circularly. The bright light almost blinded her. She felt like she was in a tunnel with millions of stars surrounding the ship.

"Amazing…," said the AI.

An alarm sounded.

"Emmeline, the portal is closing!"

"Oh, no!" Emmeline cried out, "We need more power."

"We do not have it," said the AI.

She could see the stars vanishing. "Faster…faster."

But the *Raven* was doing its best. The opening was becoming smaller. The engines raved. She might have to blast her way through. Emmeline prepared to fire. Suddenly, a blaze of light hit the ship. She covered her eyes. In a flash, the *Raven* returned to normal space.

"We are clear," said the AI.

Emmeline placed a hand over her chest, feeling an immense wave of relief.

"All systems working at optimal levels," said the AI.

She relaxed.

"What happened to the ship? How did it transform?" asked the AI.

Emmeline gaped at the piece and the plaque. It could alter the material. How? Its abilities remained a mystery, and they had begun to terrify her. The modifications to the *Raven* were welcome, but what else could it do? Why did it do it? Did it sense that she needed it? These were questions she could ask later. Right now, she needed to locate the second piece.

"Where are we?" she asked.

"Interesting."

"What?"

"I have long-range scanners…"

"The *Raven* isn't equipped with long-ranged scanners…"

"Now it is."

She put her thoughts aside and began searching for the signal. Like before, the piece should send out a signal revealing its location. It should be here. The data from the long-range scan started pouring in, and she froze. She blinked several times, trying to interpret what it meant.

"That can't be possible…"

"It is…"

"It cannot be!"

A beep sounded. An unfamiliar craft flying sluggishly with no engine appeared on the viewer.

"It's a ship," she said, raising shields and preparing to fire."

"It cannot harm us."

"Why not?"

The image enlarged. She knew what it was; she had read about it in history books.

"It cannot harm us because it was built around four hundred years ago."

Emmeline's jaw dropped, and she stared at the ancient craft.

To Be Continued

End of Book 2

THE ADVENTURE CONTINUES IN

REALM BOOK 3

ICARUS

COMING IN 2022

Author's Note

Enjoyed Poseidon? Please leave a review and share your thoughts about the book. I would really appreciate it, and thank you in advance!

To find The Realm Series by H.G. Ahedi scan

Author's website: <u>harbeerahedi.com</u>

Acknowledgments

A special thanks to these people for making this book possible.

I would like to thank Shwetha D'Souza for her beautiful insight. Rebecca, my cover designer, is a fine lady who gives power to my imagination. I would like to thank Liz, who helped me edit and develop this book. I would like to thank all my friends on Twitter for their support. Most of all, I would like to thank my family for believing in my dreams and helping me in this journey.

OTHER BOOKS BY H.G. AHEDI

When Roumoult Cranston drives to Newburgh, a hired assassin awaits him. While trying to unearth this mystery, he discovers a darkness within himself and could be hanged for murder.
Black Moon is a mystery thriller with a supernatural twist.

When three men commit suicides without reason, the hunt for answers become a frantic race against time.
If you are interested in gripping crime thrillers, you should read Haunted.

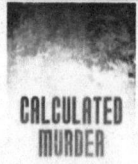

If you love scandals, secrets affairs with explosive consequences then you should read, Calculated Murder

A soldier trying to survive, a scientist trying to save his world and a dark force that will define them both. Transcendence is a historical sci-fi novella that will keep you at the edge of your seat